FROM FINLAND
WITH LOVE

Also by J. S. Volpe

Anomaly Hunters
I. INTO THE WOODS
III. THE THING IN THE ALLEY

The Chronicles of Eridia
THE SINGULAR SIX
BLOOD TIES*
SCOUNDRELS' JIG
TILL THE MOUNTAINS TURN TO DUST

Rare Finds
DARK SECRETS*
CHAIN OF DESIRE*

* ebook only

FROM FINLAND WITH LOVE

Anomaly Hunters, Book 2

J. S. Volpe

Peridor Press

ISBN: 061578867X
ISBN-13: 978-0615788678

Cover image:
carlo dapino/Shutterstock.com

AH-2

FROM FINLAND
WITH LOVE

Chapter 1

"Okay, here's a question for you," Calvin Beckerman said. He took a quick sip of his jumbo coffee, then sat forward with a grin. "If you had to choose between sharing a true, undying love with someone for the rest of your life but never having sex ever again, or being able to have guilt-free, risk-free sex with whoever you wanted whenever you wanted but never being in love again, which would you choose?"

Frowning slightly, Cynthia Crow drank the last few drops of her own coffee (a small; it was late afternoon, and she didn't want the caffeine keeping her up half the night), then chucked the cup into a trashcan a few feet away from the picnic table they sat at. They were in the plaza outside the Ames University Student Center. It was a sunny mid-September day, and overall the plaza was pretty crowded. Students lounged at picnic tables, lined the bench that ringed the fountain in the middle of the plaza, or just sat on the sun-warmed pavement. The west end of the plaza where Calvin and Cynthia sat, however, was more sparsely populated at the moment thanks to its being in the shadow of the seven-storey University Library on the plaza's south side.

"That's an interesting question," Cynthia said. "Where'd you hear that?"

"I just made it up, actually," he said. "I was thinking about something my Evolutionary Psychology prof said in class today. So what's your answer?"

"Love, of course." Her "like, duh" tone made it clear she didn't see how anyone could answer any other way. Noticing his raised eyebrows, she said, "Let me guess: You'd choose the sex."

"Well, yeah." His "like, duh" tone made it clear he didn't see how anyone could answer any other way.

She tutted. "That's ridiculous. I mean, what, you'd throw away one of the most profound experiences a human being can have just to dip your wick?"

"Profound, my ass. Love is just hormones, a biochemical trick our brains play on us so we'll form mating pairs. The whole point of it is to get us to dip our wicks. Or get dipped into."

She cocked an eyebrow.

"Or, um…" He shrugged and gestured at her. "Sorry, I'm not really sure what the metaphor would be for lesbians."

"Thank God for that."

A flash of movement nearby caught their attention. The picnic table they sat at was right in front of the Marvin Osterberg Memorial Auditorium, aka the Moma, a squat boxy building that was connected to the west end of the Student Center and was used mainly for performances of student plays and for the Film Club's Midnight Movie Madness every Saturday. A chubby girl with glasses and a *Doctor Who* T-shirt was pulling open the Moma's front door. In her hand was a khaki messenger bag from the mouth of which bulged heaps of glossy hair of different colors—brown, blonde, black, white. Wigs, presumably. Unless she was toting around half a dozen severed heads.

The girl disappeared inside. The door thunked closed.

Cynthia turned back to Calvin. "Do you honestly believe all that crap about wick-dipping?"

"Of course."

She tutted again.

"Look at it this way," Calvin said: "Since we evolved into rational beings whose highly developed brains are our main mode of survival, we could no longer afford to be at the mercy of instinctive animal behavior like the rut, so evolution had to come up with more advanced, more abstract ways to get us to mate."

"Oh, give me a break! How can you even say that? After..." She paused and looked around to make sure no one was too close, then lowered her voice and said, "I mean, after everything we've experienced and everything we've seen in the Collection, how can you be so reductionistic? We know there's more to reality than just...just *chemicals.*"

The Collection in question was a vast assemblage of objects pertaining to anomalous phenomena. Calvin had inherited the Collection and the old, sprawling house that contained it from Cynthia's weird old neighbor Robert May, who had spent his life investigating things that mainstream science regarded as abnormal or impossible— everything from poltergeists to rains of frogs, from UFOs to abiogenic oil. After being briefly mentored by Mr. May right before his death and then experiencing some highly unusual phenomena themselves, Calvin and Cynthia had vowed to follow in his footsteps. That was two years ago. They had spent the bulk of their extracurricular time since then reading through the files Mr. May had kept on the nearly four thousand anomalies he had investigated and collected evidence of. Calvin and Cynthia were reading the files in chronological order and were only up to 1977. Sometimes it felt like they would never reach the end.

Calvin shrugged. "Sure, there's more to reality than

chemicals, but the chemicals are still there. They still do what they do. And one of the things they do is turn people into moon-eyed morons."

"You know what I think?" Cynthia said. "I think you're just kind of soured on the whole subject because your parents split up last spring."

"That has nothing to do with it," Calvin muttered.

The Moma's front door flew open, and the chubby girl stumbled out. Her face was warped with terror.

"Oh, God!" she cried. "Help! Someone help!"

Calvin and Cynthia shot to their feet and hurried over to her, as did a few other nearby students.

"What's wrong?" Calvin asked.

The girl took a few gulping breaths, then managed to say, "I—I went in to set things up for rehearsal, and—and—there's a dead guy in there. On the stage. Oh, God, there's blood everywhere."

"I'll call the cops," said a square-jawed, bristle-haired fellow in an Ames U sweatshirt. He whipped out his phone and started dialing.

As the others led the hysterical girl to the picnic table recently vacated by Calvin and Cynthia, Calvin glanced around to make sure everyone was focused on the girl, then nudged Cynthia's arm and said, "Come on."

"What?" she said. "Where?" But even as she asked the question, she saw that he was making a beeline straight for the Moma's front door. "What are you doing?" she whispered, hurrying after him.

"It's a mystery," he said. "Let's investigate." He opened the door and slipped inside.

"Yeah, it's a mystery for the cops," she said, darting in after him. "It's not anomalous or anything."

"You never know. It's worth a look."

"Curiosity killed the cat."

"Feh. They've got nine lives."

"All right. But we'd better be out of here before the cops come. As we well know, they don't look too kindly on outside investigators."

"Yeah, yeah."

They crossed the lobby to the wooden door that led to the auditorium proper. Calvin laid a hand on the knob and glanced at Cynthia.

"You ready?" he said.

"Not really. But let's hurry up and get it over with."

Calvin opened the door, and they stepped into the auditorium. Curving tiers of seats descended toward the stage. The stage curtains were up, and the stage was partially set up for a play. A backdrop painted to resemble a stone wall stood at the rear of the stage. Two black floor candelabra were stationed in front of it. In the middle of the stage was a high-backed wooden throne. A man sat slumped in the throne like a sleeping king, his chin on his chest, his arms hanging limp over the chair's sides. But this man definitely wasn't sleeping: Even from across the room Calvin and Cynthia could see blood splashed all over the chair's backrest. A faint stench of cordite hung in the air. The chubby girl's messenger bag lay on its side on the floor just inside the doorway. Wigs and props—a dagger, a crown, a bottle marked with a skull and crossbones—had spilled from the bag and lay strewn across the blue-gray carpet. The auditorium was as still and silent as a tomb. Which made sense, since that was pretty much exactly what it was at the moment.

"Whoever did this might still be here, you know," Cynthia whispered as they stepped over the props and descended the steps to the stage.

"The girl got in and out okay," Calvin said.

"She might have been lucky."

They stopped at the edge of the stage. The stage floor was level with their chests, and from their low vantage point, they could see up into the dead man's face. He was middle-aged, with receding gray-brown hair and a neatly trimmed beard. His face was frozen in an almost comical look of surprise. In the center of his forehead was a small red hole. He wore a white shirt, blue jeans, and brown leather cowboy boots. The front of his shirt and the crotch of his pants were dark and sodden with blood. It glistened in the bright work lights above the stage. Calvin and Cynthia could make out grayish blobs of brain matter clinging to the backrest amid the splashes of gore. The raw, coppery stink of blood blotted out all other smells. Both Calvin and Cynthia had seen a man with his brains blown out before, but they discovered now that it wasn't something that got easier to deal with through repetition.

"Oh, God," Cynthia muttered, cupping a hand over her nose and mouth. Her face had gone the color of cottage cheese. She glanced around the auditorium, partly to make sure the killer wasn't creeping up on them to increase his body count, but also so she wouldn't have to look at the grisly mess on the stage. "Let me repeat my earlier comment about hurrying up and getting this over with."

"Yeah," Calvin said. His face had gone as pale as hers, and his stomach was tightening in a way that made him wonder if he was about to get a second look at the cinnamon roll he had eaten half an hour ago. But then he frowned and peered more closely at the man in the throne. "Wait a minute. I know this guy. I've seen him around campus before. I think he works here. Maintenance or something." He climbed up onto the stage.

"Yeah, you're right," she said. She followed him onto the stage, her curiosity roused. "Now that you mention it, I recognize him, too."

They stopped a couple of feet from the fake throne and studied the body slumped there. Now that they were closer, they could see the exit wound in the back of the man's head. Jumbled brain matter gleamed in its depths. The hair around it was slick and matted with blood.

"I think it's safe to say he was killed here," Cynthia said.

"And not too long ago, from the look of it," Calvin said. "Apparently with a gun."

"One with a silencer, too. Otherwise we would've heard the shot."

"Not necessarily." Calvin nodded at the walls. "I think I heard somewhere that the auditorium is soundproof."

"Oh, lovely," she muttered, looking nervously around the room. "On stage, no one can hear you scream."

Calvin scanned the bare wooden floor around them. "No spent shells anywhere," he said. "No clues of any kind."

Turning his attention back to the body, he noticed a rectangular bulge in the breast pocket of the man's shirt. Excited, sure that he had found a clue, he got out a pen, then leaned over the body and used the tip of the pen to pull open the pocket to see what was inside. His excitement died when he found that it was only a pack of cigarettes.

"Hmp," he said, straightening up.

"We'd better think about getting going," Cynthia said. "The cops'll be here any minute. Besides, this doesn't look anomalous or paranormal or anything. It was probably just a lover's quarrel or a drug deal gone bad or something."

"Yeah," he said with a sigh. He started to turn away, then froze. "What's that?"

"What's what?"

Calvin crouched down next to the throne. The thumb and forefinger of the dead man's left hand were pinched together. Sticking out between them was a small triangular piece of paper.

Taking care not to touch the corpse's flesh, Calvin took the edge of the paper between his own thumb and forefinger and wiggled it free.

Looking at it more closely, he found that it wasn't paper after all. It was parchment. Two of its edges were smooth and the third rough. It was clearly a corner torn from a larger piece. On one side was a fragment of a painted pattern of intertwined flowering vines that looked like it might be a decorative border. The other side was painted solid black.

"That looks really old," Cynthia said. "Look how the paint's all faded and flaking."

"Yeah, and it feels really brittle." He frowned and raised the parchment for a closer look. "This looks familiar, too."

"What does?"

"The viny pattern. I think I've seen it before."

"Where?"

"I don't know. But I have a feeling it was in a context that was somehow related to strange phenomena."

"One of the files maybe?"

He shook his head. "I don't know. It could be. But it could just as well have been something I came across online or in a book or something." He handed her the parchment. "Hold this up so I can see it."

He got out his phone and used it to take a few photos of the parchment. When he was done, he took the parchment from Cynthia, then squatted down and carefully tucked it into the V formed by the body's pinched thumb and forefinger.

He stood up.

"There we go."

The paper dropped out of the V and landed in a small puddle of blood on the floor.

"Oh, that's just fucking great!" Cynthia said.

Calvin squatted again and reached out toward the paper, but then stopped when he realized there was no way to pick it up without touching the blood, too.

He looked up at Cynthia. "I don't suppose you have a pair of tweezers handy?"

"Why would I have tweezers handy?" she said.

"I don't know. Don't girls use tweezers for things?"

"Yes. But they don't normally carry them around."

"The ones with purses do."

She spread her arms. "Have you ever seen me carry a purse?"

"I'm just saying."

He stood back up. They stared at the paper in silence. It sat there atop the blood like a lily-pad on a pond.

"Well, it's not like the blood'll totally ruin it or anything, right?" Calvin said.

"Maybe, maybe not," Cynthia said. "But seeing as how you just fucked up a crime scene, I'd say the need to hurry up is now more pressing than ever."

"Agreed. Let's take a quick look backstage, then skedaddle."

Trying to move fast, yet also trying to be cautious in case the shooter was still around, they rounded the castle-wall backdrop and entered the cavernous backstage area. Here and there stood bits of scenery: more backdrops, plaster battlements, wooden tables and benches. No one was in sight, and nothing looked amiss. But something sure *sounded* amiss: Police sirens. Lots of them.

"Oh, shit," Cynthia said. "It sounds like they're in the parking lot already."

"Why the hell didn't we hear them before?" Calvin asked.

She jerked a thumb over her shoulder at the auditorium. "Soundproofing, remember?"

"Oh. Yeah. Crap."

They spotted a glowing exit sign on the rear wall. They started to race toward it, but then stopped when they saw that the double exit doors beneath the sign were chained and padlocked shut.

"Isn't it a violation of the fire code to lock the doors like that?" Cynthia asked.

"I don't know," Calvin said. "But we need to find another way out of here. If we try to go out the front door, we'll be spotted for sure. And I really don't want to have to explain what we were doing here."

"Isn't there a stairwell that connects the lobby with the second floor of the Student Center?"

"Yeah! I forgot about that!"

They sprinted across the stage, leaped off, and raced up the carpeted steps to the lobby door. There they paused and listened at the door a moment to make sure no one had already entered the lobby. They heard tires squeal not far away.

They burst through the door and hurried to another door at the east end of the lobby. A sign on the wall next to the door read, "Stairs." As they flung open the door, they heard the rapid clatter of running feet in the plaza outside. A deep voice barked an unintelligible command. Calvin and Cynthia raced up the stairs. The door to the stairwell clacked shut behind them.

They had just reached the landing at the top of the stairs when they heard the Moma's front door bang open. A cacophony of footfalls filled the lobby. Calvin quietly opened the plain wooden door at the top of the stairs, and he and Cynthia stepped through.

They were at the end of a long hallway on the second floor of the Student Center. To their left were closed doors that led to restrooms and conference rooms. To their right, a row of dark-red couches faced the tall plate-glass windows that overlooked the plaza below. At some of the more distant couches students sat chatting or reading or dozing. The nearer ones appeared to be empty.

Calvin and Cynthia strode down the corridor, staying well away from the windows so no one in the plaza would see them. Before they had gone twenty paces, a voice behind them said, "Hey, there!"

They spun around, their hearts jumping. A long, grinning head with spiked, black-dyed hair and thick-rimmed glasses rose up over the back of one of the couches they had presumed to be unoccupied. It was Brandon Taylor, a fellow sophomore and longtime acquaintance from Calvin and Cynthia's hometown of May, Ohio. He was officially a Graphic Design major, but he dabbled in practically every known art form, from sculpture to acting to poetry.

Brandon folded his arms atop the backrest of the couch, his black leather jacket creaking softly with the movement, and rested his chin on his crossed arms.

"So what's up, guys?" he asked.

"Oh, nothing," Calvin said, trying to sound blasé.

"Just passing through, really," Cynthia added with a forced smile. "What's up with you?"

"Eh, not much. Just sitting here skipping my drawing class. The prof is such a fascist." He held up a battered composition notebook. "I decided it'd behoove me better to work on some poetry instead."

"Ah," Cynthia said, barely suppressing a wince. She hoped this wasn't the prelude to one of his impromptu poetry recitals. Although Brandon was a talented artist in many respects, poetry was definitely not his forte. Thankfully he set down the notebook without opening it.

Calvin glanced at the door to the stairwell with a small frown.

"Say, how long have you been sitting here?" he asked Brandon.

"Oh, about an hour, give or take."

"Has anyone else come out of the stairwell?"

"No. No one. It's been totally dead down here. Well, except there was this one guy in cowboy boots who came clopping down the hallway like Gene Fucking Autry and interrupted me right in the middle of working on a really kickass metaphor. He was going *into* the Moma, though; not coming out."

"When was that?"

"Maybe twenty minutes ago." He cocked his head. "Why are you so interested in the traffic patterns down here?"

"Oh, um…" Calvin's mind raced in search of a plausible excuse. Brandon didn't know about their anomaly investigating. Hardly anyone did. And Calvin and Cynthia wanted to keep it that way. "We were, um…"

"We were supposed to meet someone," Cynthia said, coming to his rescue. "We thought they might have gotten the wrong door by mistake."

"Huh." Brandon eyed them dubiously, clearly not convinced.

A thump echoed up the stairwell.

"Well, we'd better get going," Cynthia said. "We've got a lot to do."

"Um, all right. Catch you later, then."

Leaving behind a clearly befuddled Brandon, Calvin and Cynthia hurried downstairs and headed out of the Student Center's southeast exit, which was on the opposite side of the plaza from the Moma. They had hoped to watch the police activity from there, but a slowly growing crowd of students and other curiosity seekers blocked the Moma from view.

Calvin and Cynthia crossed the plaza to the library and took the elevator to the second floor. There, they stood at a window that overlooked the Moma, and surveyed the scene below.

Three uniformed cops had been posted in front of the Moma to keep the crowd at bay. Half a dozen police cars were parked along the curb on University Drive just west of the Moma, their bubble lights strobing. A cop stood next to one of the cars, speaking urgently into his radio.

The Moma's front door opened and another cop emerged and hurried toward one of the cars. In the brief interval before the front door closed again, Calvin and Cynthia caught a glimpse of a man in a black suit talking to a uniformed cop in the Moma's lobby.

Calvin and Cynthia remained at the window for nearly two hours, watching. They saw the coroner's van arrive. They saw a pair of paramedics wheel out the sheet-shrouded corpse. They saw cops interviewing students in the crowd. They saw news vans arrive. They saw no sign that the police had found anyone in the building aside from the dead man.

"That doesn't make any sense," Calvin said. "We were sitting right in front of the Moma; we would've noticed it if someone came out that way. And Brandon would've noticed someone leaving by the upstairs door. And the back door was locked from the inside."

"Maybe the killer's still in there. Maybe he just found one hell of a good hiding place."

"I suppose that's possible."

"Or maybe Brandon wasn't on the couch the whole time. Maybe he got up to go to the bathroom, and while he was in there, the killer slipped out of the stairwell."

"Maybe. We should've thought to ask him about that."

"Or, hey, maybe Brandon's the killer."

Calvin laughed. "What, you think maybe the dead guy was a part-time art critic, and he dissed Brandon's work?"

"Sure, why not? At least it would mean this isn't some horrible locked-auditorium mystery, right?"

Calvin watched a cop emerge from the Moma with the chubby girl's bag of props in his latex-gloved hand.

"Somehow I have a sinking suspicion that's exactly what this is," he said with a sigh.

Chapter 2

The murder was the lead story in the next day's *Daily Ames Record*, the campus paper. Calvin and Cynthia sat reading it in Lecture Hall 2 of Chandler Hall while they waited for World History I to begin.

According to the paper, the dead man was Judd Skerrit, 52, a campus maintenance worker. Skerrit's supervisor, a man named Lou Guglio, said that Skerrit was supposed to have been in the Student Center's basement replacing a light fixture at the time the murder occurred. Guglio had no idea why Skerrit had been in the Moma.

Robyn Blair, the girl who found the body, claimed she thought she had heard someone moving around in the Moma when she first entered, but the police searched the place thoroughly and found no one. The coroner estimated that Skerrit had been dead for no more than five or ten minutes before Miss Blair arrived.

The police were interested in talking to two students, a male and a female, who had been seen entering the Moma shortly after the body was found.

"Aw, crap," Calvin muttered.

"What, did you get to the part about the two students?" said Cynthia, who had just finished the article and was folding up her paper.

"Yeah."

"Well, keep reading. You'll like the next paragraph even better."

The detective in charge of the investigation was Lee

Anderson.

"Oh, shit," Calvin said.

The paper had run an article about Detective Anderson two weeks earlier. He had just received something called the Ames Distinguished Service Award, which was reserved for public employees whose accomplishments were particularly notable in some way. In Anderson's case, his notability rested on the fact that he had solved every single case to come across his desk in his ten years as a detective.

"Then again," Calvin said, "he probably won't be able to track us down. I mean, there are thousands of students at Ames. How's he gonna find us?"

"I hope you're right," Cynthia said.

Calvin put his paper into his backpack, then looked around the room. It was ten forty-four—a minute till class started—and the room was nearly full, but there was no sign of Professor Byrne. Usually Byrne arrived early to set up his notes on the podium at the front of the room. Today, though, the podium was empty. It would be surprising if Byrne didn't show up; this was supposed to have been the first class in a week. Byrne had canceled last Thursday's class because he was flying to Milan, Italy, that morning to take part in a three-day medieval history symposium. He was supposed to have been back by now, but maybe there had been some kind of delay. Or maybe he had decided he liked Italy better than dreary old Ohio and had ripped up his return ticket.

As Calvin looked around, his gaze fell on a blonde girl who was just coming in through the door at the back of the room. His jaw dropped at the sight of her, all thoughts of Professor Byrne and murdered maintenance men and everything else vanishing in the blink of an eye.

She was gorgeous. Long blonde hair. Smooth tanned skin. High cheekbones. Eyes the color of smoke. She was tall and slim yet still sported healthy curves in all the right places. Her high, firm breasts strained roundly against her black tank top, and the small hard bumps of her nipples and the way her breasts quivered with every step provided ample evidence she wasn't wearing a bra. Her low-rise skinny jeans hugged her legs and hips like a second skin. A gap between the bottom of her shirt and the top of her jeans exposed a breathtaking expanse of her flat, tanned belly, in the center of which a gold navel ring glinted like a doubloon on a tropical beach.

"Whoa," Calvin said.

"What?" Cynthia said. She followed his gaze. She saw the girl. "Whoa."

They watched the girl settle into an aisle seat near the back of the room and pull a notebook and a pen from her backpack. They found themselves envying the long-haired dude who sat next to her, and with whom she exchanged a few words as she settled in.

"She must be new," Calvin said. "I've never seen her in here before."

"It could be that we just never noticed her," Cynthia said. "It is a pretty big class, after all."

"Trust me, I would have noticed her."

Cynthia eyed the girl a moment longer, then sighed and nodded. "Yeah. Same here."

They were forced to wrench their eyes from the girl when the side door near the front of the room opened and Professor Byrne strode in. He was a short, wiry, fortyish man with prematurely gray hair and a neatly trimmed mustache that still had some pepper mixed with the salt.

As he headed to the podium, his eyes scanned the sea

of faces in front of him as if he were searching for some-one. His expression was tight, closed.

He set a sheaf of notes atop the podium and began to shuffle through them.

"I, uh, I believe I left off with Attila the Hun," he said.

A puzzled murmur ran through the crowd. Byrne noticed it and glanced up.

"No?" he said.

"Constantine's conversion to Christianity," someone called out.

"Oh. Right. Of course." Frowning to himself, he re-shuffled his notes.

The ensuing lecture was in the same vein: fumbling, distracted, disorganized. Midway through it, Cynthia leaned in and whispered to Calvin, "Wow, he must have the worst case of jetlag ever."

"I'm surprised he isn't talking about his trip," Calvin said. "He's usually eager to share his extracurricular projects with us. I mean, remember how he spent nearly a whole class talking about his research into Dagobert II?"

"Maybe the symposium didn't go very well. Maybe his paper got hissed, or something."

"I don't think academics hiss each other. They just write vaguely snotty rebuttals in online journals."

Apparently realizing his ineffectuality, Byrne ended class ten minutes early. As Calvin and Cynthia stepped out of the lecture hall and into Chandler's main hallway, they saw the blonde girl striding away toward the building's side door, her breasts and backpack bouncing. She pushed open the door and vanished into the rectangle of bright daylight outside.

Calvin and Cynthia wished they could follow, but their route, alas, took them out the main door, which was in the opposite direction.

"That was one stunning girl," Cynthia said as they crossed campus toward Duffy Hall, their dorm.

"Maybe next time I see her I'll ask her out," Calvin said with a mack-daddy waggle of his eyebrows.

Cynthia barked out a laugh. "Oh, like you'd have the balls to even talk to a girl like that. She's out of your league, my boy. She's hitting homers in the World Series while you're still playing around with your whiffle-ball bat."

"Like you're any better! You're not even in the bush leagues yourself!"

"I never said otherwise. I'm more realistic about these things."

"Since when? And besides, what do you even know about 'these things' anyway? Your luck with girls isn't much better than mine. I mean, aside from a brief trip to first base with that girl at the dorm party last spring—what was her name? Candy? Bambi?"

"Mandy," Cynthia mumbled.

"Yeah, Mandy. I mean, aside from that, your love-life's been about as unexciting as mine. Nothing but strikes and ground outs. And I don't think Mandy was actually gay or bi anyway. I think she was just trying to freak out her boy-friend."

Cynthia rolled her eyes. "You're never gonna shut up about that, are you?"

"Probably not. At least not until I get Alzheimer's and forget it ever happened."

"I'd better start putting aluminum shavings in your food, then."

They arrived at their dorm. They checked their mail-boxes, threw away the junk mail they found therein, and then headed to the elevator. While they waited for the elevator to descend, a man's voice behind them said, "Ah, just the two fine young students I'm looking for."

They turned and found themselves face-to-face with a tall, dark-haired man in a black suit and tie. Calvin and Cynthia recognized him instantly. They had seen his picture in the paper. It was Detective Anderson. He was smiling. Or at least his mouth was. Despite the broad grin and the wall of dazzlingly white, even teeth it revealed, his eyes were as cold and pitiless as a raptor's.

He pulled a badge from his inner jacket pocket and flashed it at them.

"Detective Lee Anderson," he said. "Ames Police."

"Um, hi," Calvin said, trying to sound pleasant yet baffled, as if he couldn't for the life of him understand why a policeman would want to speak with him. "Nice to meet you."

"Yeah, same here," Cynthia said, adopting the same tone.

"Why don't the three of us chat for a minute?" Anderson said, taking each of them by the arm. His voice was calm and friendly, but his grip was like iron. He led them to a quiet corner nearby.

"So how can we help you?" Cynthia asked innocently.

"Cut the shit," Anderson said, his smile already a memory. "I know you two were in the Moma yesterday. I've got five witnesses who saw you going in."

"Us?" Calvin said, feigning surprise. "I think you're mistaken. It wasn't us. It must have been two other students."

"Uh-huh. Right. If you can point me to another skinny young male with short blond hair and blue eyes and a skinny young female with long red hair and green eyes, both of whom are frequently seen in the company of each other on campus, I would be more than happy to talk to them too."

"Um…"

"There was a piece of paper sitting in a puddle of blood. I get the impression the paper didn't get there on its own. Do you know anything about that, by any chance?"

"No," Calvin and Cynthia said in unison. They very carefully did not look at each other.

Anderson eyed them in steely silence for a moment. They could tell he could tell they were lying.

"Do you know what the punishment is for tampering with a crime scene?"

"Um, no," Calvin said.

"Well, I'll tell you right now, if you ever again tamper with a crime scene in this locality, you are going to find out. Do you understand?"

Both of them felt an urge to continue protesting their innocence. But they knew it was futile.

"Yes," they said.

"Did either of you tamper with anything else, or take anything?"

"No," they said.

"Did either of you see or hear anyone in the building?"

"No."

"Do either of you have any other information that might be useful to this investigation?"

They immediately remembered Calvin's certainty that he had seen the viny pattern before in some context connected with anomalous phenomena. But they said, "No."

Anderson's eyes narrowed. He seemed to suspect another lie but was less certain of it this time around.

"Are you sure?" he said.

They nodded.

"What would we know?" Calvin said. "We're just students. We were just, you know, looking. That's all. Curiosity. We won't do it again."

"We promise," Cynthia said.

Anderson regarded them in silence for a moment, his raptor's eyes darting back and forth between them.

Then he said, "You'd better *not* do it again." He leaned forward. His eyes narrowed. "Especially at one of *my* crime scenes. Are we clear on that?"

"Um, yeah," Calvin said.

"Yes, sir," Cynthia said.

"Good," Anderson said. He motioned at the elevator. "Now you two little lovebirds move along and get on with your educations, or your partying, or whatever it is you kids do these days, and leave the criminal investigations to the professionals."

"Lovebirds?" Calvin muttered.

Cynthia waved an arm at Anderson. "Hello! Lesbian!"

Anderson blinked at her a moment. Then with a small frown he looked at Calvin. He opened his mouth as if to say something, then stopped himself and shook his head. "Whatever."

Without another word, he turned and walked away. Worried that he might change his mind and come back, Calvin and Cynthia lost no time in vamoosing. Rather than wait for the elevator, they bolted through the door to the stairwell.

"Why are we always getting in trouble with the cops?" Cynthia asked as they plodded up the stairs to Calvin's room on the fourth floor.

"It comes with the territory," Calvin said. "Remember

what Mr. May told us: When you're investigating phenomena that lie beyond the boundaries of what society accepts as normal, you often have to cross those boundaries yourself. Which can lead to trouble."

"Yeah," she said. "But one of these days we might not get off with just a warning. We might wind up with criminal records."

"It's a risk we have to accept, I guess."

They reached Calvin's floor and headed to his room. Like Cynthia, he had a single room. Given their outré interests, it seemed wisest to pony up the extra cash for one. Many folks would look askance upon a roommate who stayed up half the night downloading photos of spontaneous human combustion victims and first-hand accounts of anal probing performed by little gray aliens. Besides, the two of them wanted to maintain a low profile. Cynthia in particular harbored an intense dread of waking up one morning to find their photos in the paper under the headline "The Real X-Files!" She valued her privacy and her dignity. Calvin, on the other hand, wasn't quite as concerned about such things, caring only that they be able to do their work without interference.

Another thing he wasn't terribly concerned about was housekeeping. As usual, his room was a mess. The bed was unmade. The desktop was a jumble of papers, books, notebooks, gadgets, pens, and countless other things. A computer sat in the midst of this jumble like a car in a snowdrift. Books on anomalous phenomena overflowed the numerous shelves and were heaped ten-high on the floor. Atop one of these heaps sat a Starbucks cup that contained half an inch of cold coffee overlain with a thin film of dust. The closet door stood open a crack and from the gap extended a single white sock, an outlier of the mountain of dirty clothes that lay inside.

Calvin plucked a used T-shirt from his futon so Cynthia could sit there, then tossed the shirt into the closet. He sat down on the desk chair, facing the futon.

"Have you heard about these newfangled contraptions called vacuum cleaners?" Cynthia asked as she brushed cracker crumbs from the futon's seat. "I hear they're all the rage these days." Having created a crumb-free space, she sat down.

"Sorry. I keep meaning to clean up in here. I'll get around to it sooner or later."

"Yeah, probably when you move out."

"Hey, at least I'm not anal-retentively neat like some people."

"I'm not anal-retentive. I'm just well-organized."

"Uh-huh. You have your self-delusions, I have mine."

Cynthia noticed an odd assemblage of items on a small table next to the futon: a multi-head screwdriver, a tape measure, a Mini Maglite, scissors, tweezers, and a box of latex gloves.

"What's all this stuff?" she asked.

"Oh, yeah!" Calvin's face brightened with excitement and pride. "After that whole lack of tweezers thing yesterday, I decided to put together an investigator's kit, with basic items we might need in the course of our work. I still need to get a few more things, though. Especially some small vials for collecting samples. Maybe a compass, too."

She smiled and shook her head. "It's like your own little Batman utility belt."

"You may mock, but if we're going to be investigating stuff, we need the proper tools. I refuse to be caught tweezerless again. Honestly, I always planned to put something like this together, but I figured I'd do it after we graduated and started investigating weird stuff full time. I didn't think I'd need it this soon. I didn't think we'd stumble onto our first real case here in college."

Her smile faded. Her expression clouded. "If Detective Anderson catches us nosing around again, he'll come down on us like a ton of bricks."

He grinned. "That just means we'll have to be super-careful from here on out."

Instead of returning the grin as he had expected her to do, she said, "Are we sure it's worth it?"

"What do you mean?"

"I mean, are you sure about that vine pattern being from something connected with anomalous phenomena? We spent, like, three hours last night going through your books and browsing the internet in search of the pattern, and we didn't find squat. I don't want to wind up with a criminal record only to find out Judd Skerrit was murdered over an old and rare but hardly anomalous book."

"I'd say I'm about ninety percent sure I saw that pattern in relation to something anomalous. I just can't remember any specifics."

"It was probably something from the Collection."

"Maybe. But you've been going through that stuff with me. The pattern doesn't ring any bells with you?"

"No, but that doesn't mean much. We've looked at thousands of objects and read through thousands of files. And there's still over a thousand more we haven't gotten to yet. The pattern might be from one of those. It might have been something you saw while browsing through the Collection by yourself one day."

"Yeah." He sighed. "Well, let's finish looking through these books tonight and then search some more on the internet. If we don't find anything, then tomorrow after class we can head to May and start hunting through the Collection. But we should start doing more than that, too. I mean, it might take a long time to find the source of the pattern, if we even find it at all. We can't just wait until we do. We have to be more proactive. We have to start investigating."

"Investigating what, exactly?"

"Judd Skerrit, for one thing. We need to find out more about him. Maybe if we learn his interests, we'll figure out what the viny pattern is from."

She nodded. "Makes sense. We can start on that tomorrow, too." She looked around the room at the stacks of books, then heaved a sigh. "I guess we'd better get to work…"

Chapter 3

Clad in an extra-large T-shirt and panties, her usual sleep-wear, Cynthia sat down on the edge of her bed for the last act of her nightly routine: She squirted out a dollop of hand sanitizer from the bottle on the bedside table and rubbed it thoroughly over her hands.

She knew that if Calvin knew she did this, he would claim it was another proof of her supposed anal retentive-ness. But it wasn't anal retentive. It was called having good hygiene. It was called being civilized. If Calvin in his slobbish, guyish way couldn't see that, then so much the worse for him. At least she didn't live in the college equiv-alent of a pigsty like he did. No, she kept her room neat and tidy. The carpet was vacuumed and as stain-free as she could reasonably get it. Her dirty clothes were stashed safely out of sight in a laundry bag in her closet (whose door was always closed except when she was getting something out of it). The books on her bookshelf were sorted alphabetically. Her computer was fully visible atop her desk, which shone from the regular dustings she gave it. Her homework was stacked beside the computer, ar-ranged in the order it needed to be done. Her pens and pencils were corralled in an Ames U coffee mug. She knew where everything was and didn't have to go rooting through a veritable trash dump in search of anything.

Her hands well-sanitized, she pulled back the sheet and climbed into bed. She stared at the latest issue of *Fortean Times* on the bedside table and debated whether or not to read a little before going to sleep.

No, she decided. She was tired. Her eyes ached. Like last night, she and Calvin had spent hours scouring books and websites in search of that vine pattern, and they had found exactly nothing. When she had finally shuffled off to her room on the floor above his, he was still searching, though he conceded that he was probably wasting his time and that a trip to May was almost certainly in the cards.

She switched off the light and settled back in bed, ready for sleep.

Sleep wouldn't come. Alone in the dark with nothing to distract her, she found herself replaying their encounter with Detective Anderson that afternoon. Especially the part where Anderson had automatically assumed she and Calvin were a couple. "Lovebirds," he had said. Jesus Christ.

This wasn't the first time that had happened. A lot of people assumed she and Calvin were a couple simply because they hung out together all the time. Which was ridiculous. And presumptuous. And yes, she knew that Calvin had once harbored romantic feelings for her, but that had been a long time ago, and he was over that now. Their relationship had evolved. Now they were best friends and anomaly-investigating partners. Which inevitably meant they spent a lot of time together. And that was fine.

Except it wasn't. Not entirely. If Anderson's erroneous assumption irked her so much, it was because it struck a little too close to home. The truth was, she was spending way too much time studying anomalies with Calvin. Yes, she wanted to investigate strange phenomena with him, but she wasn't nearly as single-minded about the subject as he was. At times she got the impression he would be more than happy to make it the sole focus of his existence. She, however, wanted more than that. College was supposed to be a time of socializing and adventure and experimentation. And yet her life had somehow become a wearying routine of classes and homework and trips to May to study the Collection. She wanted a more well-rounded life.

Most of all, she wanted a girlfriend. She wanted someone to touch and kiss. She wanted a warm body to wake up next to. She wanted someone she could share her thoughts and feelings with. Because despite what Calvin might believe, she certainly wasn't comfortable sharing all her thoughts and feelings with him.

Her thoughts and feelings on this very subject were a perfect case in point. If she told him how she felt, he would just blather on about hormones and genes and how love and romance are just masks of lust, and how what she was feeling was simply a glorified sexual instinct, or something like that. And sure, there was a sexual element involved. But the sex would hopefully be part of something bigger and deeper and more meaningful, something more than genes and genitals.

She could at least console herself that she had a little more experience in these matters than Calvin. Not much, admittedly, but more than the Mandy incident that Calvin was always alluding to. One night last year, when Calvin was out having a birthday dinner with his mom, Cynthia had attended a meeting of the campus's LGBT group. The sad fact was, she went simply because she hoped to meet someone special, not because she cared about the politics or the lifestyle issues. And although she felt a bit guilty that she didn't care, her guilt didn't change her feelings, or lack thereof, one bit.

She realized almost from the outset that she shouldn't have come. Virtually all of the members of the group were

Gender Studies majors, and their discussion was dense with jargon and crass radicalism. Cynthia barely said a word the whole meeting. She couldn't wait to get out of there.

Still, when the meeting broke up, she found herself chatting with the group's secretary, a cute brunette named Jen, who wore an army jacket and a khaki cap with a red star on the front. Half an hour later Cynthia was in Jen's dorm room, letting herself be plied with cheap red wine and lots of strident talk about political activism. Cynthia didn't particularly like Jen, but she knew Jen wanted to fuck her, and the thrilling awareness that she could finally get laid had seized hold of her, making her horny, making her stupid. When Jen finally abandoned all pretence of conversation and kissed her, she kissed back. When Jen pawed her breasts, she pawed back. But when she felt Jen's fingers fumbling at the button of her jeans, it was like a dash of icy water over her lust-fevered brain. She realized she didn't want her first time to be some crude and hasty act done simply for the sake of getting her virginity out of the way. She wanted it to mean something. She wanted it to matter. And if that made her old-fashioned or idealistic, then so be it. Scrambling to her feet, she mumbled some half-assed excuse about a test she had to study for, then bolted. She pretended she didn't see the hurt and disdainful look in Jen's eyes. Suffice it to say, she never attended another LGBT meeting.

Calvin knew nothing about any of this, of course, and hopefully he never would. She wanted parts of her life to remain private. Especially her love life.

Assuming she ever had one.

As if her thoughts had evoked the reality, she became aware of the squeak of bedsprings from the room next door, punctuated by an occasional female moan.

Oh, for fuck's sake. Ashlee-with-two-Es was at it again. ("Ashlee with two Es" was how she invariably introduced herself. It was as if she thought everyone she met would be writing her name in their diary later on). Cynthia wondered what tonight's young dude looked like. He was probably muscular and hairy. Most of them were. And there were lots of them. Cynthia had never seen the same guy go into Ashlee-with-two-Es' room twice.

As she listened to the steadily loudening sounds from next door, Cynthia tried to tell herself that she felt disgusted at Ashlee-with-two-Es' mindless promiscuity, that she even felt sorry for Ashlee-with-two-Es, who clearly felt compelled to sleep with a large number of men out of some pathetic psychological need for attention or fulfillment or something like that. She tried to tell herself that there was nothing sexy about such wanton behavior, that it was demeaning not only to Ashlee-with-two-Es but to the guys involved.

But even as she thought all this, Cynthia's hand crept under the waistband of her panties and sought out the warm, sensitive flesh hidden therein. While her fingers began to rotate slowly atop her clitoris, she fantasized that it was she herself who was eliciting those sounds from Ashlee-with-two-Es, who was indeed quite a cutie. Cynthia envisioned herself kissing Ashlee-with-two-Es' full red lips, running her fingers through Ashlee-with-two-Es' long black-dyed locks, licking her way down Ashlee-with-two-Es' trim body, burying her tongue in the pink folds between Ashlee-with-two-Es' legs.

Her fingers moved faster and faster. She swapped out Ashlee-with-two-Es for the blonde girl she had seen in World History I that morning. She imagined her own naked body pressing against the blonde's. She imagined sucking the blonde's pert nipples, fingering the blonde's sodden pussy, feeling the blonde's agile tongue flicking vigorously across her clit…

She came with a groan, her hips rising off the mattress as her fingers blurred across her throbbing clit. Then she sank back down with a sigh, her body filmed with sweat.

Ashlee-with-two-Es cried, "Harder!" The bed next door rattled faster.

Cynthia rolled onto her side and stared into the lonely darkness.

"Shit," she muttered.

Chapter 4

Calvin sat back in his desk chair and rubbed his aching eyes. He glanced at the clock, then grunted. Two a.m. already? No wonder he felt like crap.

He had spent the last four hours scouring the internet in hopes of identifying the viny pattern on the piece of parchment in Judd Skerrit's hand. He had turned up more interior decoration websites than he ever suspected existed, but no useful info whatsoever.

He got up and stretched. His back and butt were sore from sitting for so long. One of his feet was half asleep. He paced about to get his circulation flowing again.

A door slammed and footsteps scuffed swiftly down the hall to the bathroom. The fact that Calvin could hear footsteps at all on this normally noisy floor was testament to how late it was. The dorm was dead silent.

No, wait: As he listened he faintly heard the rapid squeak of bedsprings from the room directly above his. Every now and then a woman groaned for more.

Great. That was the girl Cynthia was always complaining about. Cynthia said the girl was only a freshman but had already fucked enough men to fill the bleachers at the stadium.

Calvin's mood curdled with envy. He was still a virgin, which seemed quaint and embarrassing and somehow ridiculous for a twenty-year-old guy who had no qualms about premarital sex. He wanted to get laid, of course, wanted a girlfriend, but he considered his study of strange phenomena much more important. It was his life's work, after all, and right now he needed to learn and understand as much as he could about that work. Later there would be time to share his life and his bed with others. But not now.

And normally he was comfortable with that. Normally he barely spared a thought for sex and romance. Normally he was too busy researching anomalous phenomena to even notice his dorm-mates' boisterous sexual liaisons.

But right now he couldn't help it.

Detective Anderson's comment was the cause. His assumption that Calvin and Cynthia were a couple had stung Calvin's heart in a way nothing else could, for that had long been Calvin's fondest desire.

He had fallen for Cynthia when they were seniors in high school. She was smart and beautiful and funny and everything he had hoped to find in a partner. She was his dream girl brought to glorious life. He imagined many happy futures for the two of them.

And then he learned she was gay.

After that he tried to rid himself of his feelings for her and move on. And for the most part he succeeded. He and Cynthia became the best of friends and developed a beautiful working relationship. But every time he felt sure his unrequitable romantic feelings had been conquered once and for all, Cynthia's face would catch the light in just the right way, or she would give that thoughtful frown that made the skin between her eyebrows buckle into the little W that Calvin always found so endearing, or she would make some comment that was brilliantly apt and incisive and unlike anything anyone else would ever say, and all of those seemingly quashed feelings would rise back up and squeeze his heart till it ached.

Thankfully, these setbacks were happening less and

less often as time wore on. He supposed they would happen even less often if he didn't associate with Cynthia so much, but their friendship and the importance of their work trumped the occasional emotional pain. He also suspected that the feelings would vanish for good if he ever finally got laid and/or got a girlfriend. Which, alas, didn't look likely to happen anytime soon.

The squeak of the bedsprings upstairs grew faster, the girl let out a long, wavering moan, and then the squeaks abruptly stopped.

Calvin stared at the ceiling with a mix of bitterness and arousal. Then he glanced at his window to make sure the curtains were fully closed. They were. He sat back down at his computer and hunted through his browser's bookmarks for the Red-Hot Redheads website...

Chapter 5

The next day, Calvin and Cynthia read the latest *Daily Ames Record* while they sat in room 131 of Chandler Hall and waited for Introduction to Philosophy to start. The paper devoted nearly a whole page to the murder of Judd Skerrit, but managed to do nothing more than recap everything that had already been said.

"I notice there's still no mention of the piece of parchment Skerrit was holding," Cynthia said. "We know the cops know about it."

"Yeah," Calvin said. "They're probably withholding that information deliberately. Cops like to do stuff like that. They're sneaky that way."

The door opened, and Professor Kranhauser, their philosophy teacher, strolled in. Kranhauser was a tall, stooped, seventyish man whose face was a collection of droops. His lank white hair drooped down over his forehead. His forehead itself was a stack of fleshy folds that drooped over each other like the layers of some viscous, slowly oozing semisolid. His nose drooped down so far he could probably touch the tip with his tongue. His fleshy jowls drooped pendulously from his jaw. But in the midst of all this droopiness, half-hidden behind tufts of white eyebrow hair, were a pair of sapphire-blue eyes that were quick and alert and sharp enough to spot every dustmote.

Kranhauser's personality was as lively as his eyes. He was entertainingly cranky and often delivered snarky diatribes against philosophers he didn't care for (which sometimes seemed to consist of all of them except Nietzsche), and he took perverse delight in shocking his students with controversial statements, ostensibly to get them to think about things in new ways, but probably really only because he enjoyed getting a rise out of them. He had been born and raised in Germany, and he still retained an accent. Usually this accent was barely noticeable, but when he grew excited, as he often did when discussing the finer points of philosophy, the accent became more pronounced. If the topic was particularly important to him, his words were nearly indecipherable.

Kranhauser took his place at the desk at the front of the room, then watched in silence as Calvin, Cynthia, and several other students folded up and put away their newspapers. When all the papers had been stashed and all eyes were upon him, Kranhauser's mouth contorted into a rueful grimace.

"I have a confession to make," he said in a solemn voice. He raised his eyes to the ceiling as if speaking to God. "I am…a murderer. I have taken an innocent life."

He looked out at his students again. Some were smiling, sure that this was another of Kranhauser's stunts. Others weren't so sure, and eyed Kranhauser and each other with worried expressions. A few looked ready to scramble for the exit should Kranhauser's comments prove to be the prelude to a psychotic meltdown.

After waiting a moment to let the suspense and uncertainty build, Kranhauser slapped the back of his hand to his forehead and in a faux-woeful voice exclaimed, "I killed…a spider."

Smiles blossomed into laughs. Tense shoulders slumped in relief. One girl clucked her tongue and shook her head.

"I saw it creeping up my bedroom wall," Kranhauser went on, "so I crushed it in a Kleenex. Its body popped like an overripe pimple, squirting white guts everywhere."

A curly-haired brunette in the front row shuddered with a gleefully grossed-out squeal. Kranhauser grinned at her, pleased with the reaction he had elicited.

"I do not wish to belittle the tragic death of poor Mr. Skerrit," he said, "but I must ask, why do we regard insect and animal life as less than ours? Why is not the crushing of a spider, or the grinding up of a cow for hamburger, why is that not a tragic murder too? It is the ending of innocent life, is it not?"

Hands shot up. Voices called out comments about souls and intelligence and necessity. Kranhauser cackled and dove into the debate.

Normally Calvin and Cynthia would have enjoyed Kranhauser's performance and the ensuing discussion, but today their minds were on their investigation and more importantly their impending interview with Lou Guglio, Judd Skerrit's supervisor. Calvin had phoned Guglio two hours earlier, claiming that he and Cynthia were reporters who had been assigned to write a memorial article on Skerrit for the *Ames Buckeye*, the quarterly student magazine, and that they hoped to get some input from Guglio about his deceased coworker. Guglio agreed to meet with them, but the only time he could spare was during his dinner break at five-thirty, which meant Calvin and Cynthia would have to hustle straight to the Maintenance Department the moment Intro to Philosophy ended.

Indeed, when Kranhauser terminated his rant about the "simpering squishiness" of postmodernism and announced that class was done for the day, Calvin and Cynthia were the first ones out the door. They booked down the hall to Chandler's main lobby, strode across the lobby toward the double exit doors and the sunny afternoon outside…

And then they slowed to a crawl.

The blonde girl they had seen in World History I was sitting on the bottom step of the staircase that led to the second floor. She had a notebook open in her lap and was jotting something in it, a small frown of concentration on her face. Calvin and Cynthia's gazes remained fixed on her as they passed, their heads swiveling to keep her in view like sunflowers tracking the path of the sun.

Perhaps sensing their attention or their sudden change in speed, the girl glanced up. When she saw them looking at her, she smiled.

Their hearts leaped. They smiled back.

The girl's smile widened a fraction more, then she returned to her notebook. At the same time Calvin and Cynthia had to look away so as not to run into anyone in the busy lobby.

Picking up their pace again, they exited the building. The moment the doors clacked shut behind them they looked at each other with giddy grins.

"She smiled at me." Cynthia said.

"She smiled at *me*," Calvin said.

She rolled her eyes. "At *us*, then."

"If only we didn't have to go talk to Lou Guglio right now."

"Yeah." Cynthia's heart sank at the thought. Once again, the promise of romance hung just out of reach. Once again, other things took precedence.

One of these days that would change, she vowed to herself.

One of these days.

Chapter 6

The Maintenance Department was located next to the loading docks in back of the Student Center. It was one long concrete corridor lined with workrooms, offices, and storage cages. Lou Guglio's office was the first door on the right. The office was so tiny and cramped there wasn't any room for chairs besides Guglio's creaky metal desk chair, which meant Calvin and Cynthia had to stand to chat with him. To be polite—and perhaps also to underscore his desire to hurry up so he could have his dinner—Guglio stood, too.

Guglio was an obese balding man clad in a white shirt with the sleeves rolled up, black jeans, and steel-toed work boots. There were sweat stains at the shirt's armpits. A pair of leather work gloves jutted from one of the jeans' back pockets. Guglio's skin was a bright, waxy shade of pink that screamed hypertension.

"It's nice that you guys're doing an article on Judd," Guglio said. "I'm sure he would've appreciated that."

"Yeah," Calvin said. He tried not to squirm with guilt too openly.

"So what is it you want to know exactly?" Guglio said.

"We're just hoping for some general information. You know: what Mr. Skerrit was like, what his interests were, things like that."

"Judd was an okay guy. Frankly, I don't know a whole lot about his home life. He was kind of quiet on that score. Kept his personal life personal, you know? I know he was never married. He had a dog. He liked football. He liked visiting the new casino in Kingwood. He liked movies—war movies, westerns, stuff like that. Stuff with shootouts and explosions. Guy movies, you know? I mean, Judd was a normal, everyday kind of guy. He was a hard worker. Never complained. Rarely missed a day. Reliable, you know? He'll definitely be missed around here. It's shocking to think that something so awful could happen to someone like that. Just shocking." He shook his head.

Calvin hid his annoyance. So far Guglio hadn't said anything beyond the safe trivialities and bland platitudes one is supposed to say about the recently deceased. That wouldn't do. Calvin wanted truth. He needed to find some way to get Guglio to talk about what his underling was really like.

Calvin glanced at the door as if to make sure no one was listening, then leaned toward Guglio slightly and said in a low voice, "Off the record, I have to admit we've heard some interesting things about Mr. Skerrit. We heard that sometimes he could be a little, you know, *odd.*"

That was a safe bet. Everybody in the world had a few oddities of one kind or another. It would give Guglio a place to start talking about the real Judd Skerrit.

Guglio licked his lips and likewise glanced at the door. His eyes were agleam with the excitement of a gossiper with a whole sackful of beans to spill.

"Off the record?" he said.

"Of course!" Cynthia said. "We would never publish anything that might put anyone in a negative light."

"Yeah, we'd probably get sued," Calvin said.

Guglio chuckled. "I hear ya." He glanced at the door again, then said, "Judd was a real fuckin' weirdo, let me tell you. He used to tell everyone he was a Green Beret in Vietnam."

"But he wasn't?" Calvin said.

"Hell, no. He was way too young for Nam. But that didn't stop him from making up stories about mowing down Vietcong by the hundreds. Plus, he was always pursuing these hare-brained get-rich-quick schemes. None of 'em ever worked, of course. One time he tried to convince everyone who worked here to join him in investing in some venture capital thingie. It was based out of one of those African countries. I forget which one. Zimbabwe or Cambodia or some shit. He really seemed to think it was gonna make him rich. It didn't, of course. Anybody could see it was a scam. Another time he kept going on about how there might be Indian treasure buried somewhere around here. It was all based on some vague reference he read in a book somewhere. Nothing came of that, either. Hell, I remember one time he was talking about how to rob the Brinks truck that picked up the money at the First Federal Bank across from campus. He insisted it was just a thought exercise, but I wasn't so sure."

"Wow," Cynthia said. "He sounded like quite a character."

Guglio snorted. "You can say that again. I mean, not that I can blame him for wanting some easy dough, you know? Honestly, who wouldn't love to be rich and not have to work their butt off for a living? But Judd..." He shook his head. "Judd was something else."

"Did he ever run into trouble with his schemes?" Calvin asked. "Piss off the wrong people, or something?"

"Not as far as I know. You're wondering about the murder, right?"

"Yeah."

"The cops asked the same thing. But there wasn't much to tell them. I mean, he talked big and dreamed big, but to my knowledge, he never did anything that would've stepped on anyone's toes."

"Had he been acting strangely lately?"

Guglio laughed. "The cops asked that too. And I'll tell you what I told them: He was the same old Judd as always." He checked his watch. "Look, I gotta get going. My bologna and cheddar sandwiches are callin' me. Anything else you guys need to know quick?"

"Yeah, was Mr. Skerrit interested in strange phenomena by any chance? Someone we were talking to suggested he might have been.

Guglio shrugged. "Sometimes he went on about some of that crackpot conspiracy nonsense. You know, the government being controlled by the Illuminati, Masonic symbols on the dollar bill, stuff like that."

"What about, like, weird happenings? Ghosts, UFOs, anything like that?"

"Judd? No way. He wasn't into anything like that."

"Was he into art? Painting?"

Guglio laughed. "No. Not unless you count those Vargas girls as art." He checked his watch again. "Sorry, kids, but that's all I got time for right now."

"That's cool. I think we've got enough to work with. Thanks for your time."

"Happy to help. And good luck with your article."

As they headed back to their dorm, Cynthia said to Calvin, "Are you thinking what I'm thinking?"

"Probably." Calvin said. "What are you thinking?"

"That Judd Skerrit came up with a new get-rich-quick scheme that turned into a get-dead-quick scheme."

Calvin nodded. "Yep. That's pretty much what I'm

thinking. Trouble is, we don't have a clue what that scheme might have been."

"Let's hope we find some answers in the Collection." She sighed. "We'd better grab some coffee on the way. I have a feeling this is gonna be an all-nighter."

"Maybe we should ask Donovan and Violet to help us look. It'll save time. And after all, they do keep saying they want to help with the investigations."

She groaned. "I don't know. I'm pretty sure the only reason they want to help in the first place is because they think it'll be a big lark. Besides, do you trust them not to fuck up? I mean, they'll probably be too wasted to notice that viny pattern if it was tattooed on the backs of their hands."

"I think you're being too hard on your brother."

"Maybe it's because I know him better than you do."

"Look at it this way: If we ask them to help and one of them finds what we're looking for, then that's great. And if they don't find what we're looking for and we feel obliged to re-search everything they already searched, then it's not like we'll be doing any extra work. I mean, we won't be searching anything we wouldn't have had to search on our own anyway."

"I suppose you're right." She got out her phone to call Donovan. As she dialed she shook her head. "I still think we're gonna regret this, though."

Chapter 7

Forty-five minutes later Calvin and Cynthia arrived at Calvin's house. Set in a large round clearing in the woods south of downtown May, the house was an imposing Second Empire structure with four wings, a mansard roof, and a central tower. As Calvin drove his rattletrap Honda Accord up the long driveway, he and Cynthia spotted Cynthia's brother Donovan and Donovan's girlfriend Violet O'Donohue—both of them juniors at May High—sitting on the porch steps, waiting. Calvin parked the car, then he and Cynthia headed up the front walk to the porch.

Donovan rose as they approached. He was tall and lanky, with long red-brown hair pulled back in a ponytail. Like usual, he was wearing a black trench coat and round sunglasses even though the temperature was mild and the sky was overcast.

"Hey, guys," he said. "What's up?"

Violet remained seated. She, too, wore round sunglasses, and she peered over their rims and through her overhanging locks of dark-brown hair at Calvin and Cynthia.

"You guys're late," she said.

"That's because we have lives that involve more than skipping class and smoking weed," Cynthia said.

Violet shrugged. "Sucks to be you, then." She stood up and planted her hands on her hips. "So what is it you need our help with?"

Calvin headed past them and up the steps. "Come on

in and I'll explain."

The Collection filled five rooms on the house's upper levels. Each of these rooms contained rows of tall shelving units like the stacks in a library, and each of the shelves was crowded with objects that Mr. May had gathered in the course of his investigations. The objects ranged from the seemingly mundane—a baseball, a hand mirror, a pair of brown Hush Puppies—to the utterly bizarre—a pickled fetus with angel wings, a vial of luminous goo that kept changing colors, a book bound in leather made from human faces.

After Calvin explained what they were looking for and handed Donovan and Violet copies of the viny pattern, the quartet began their search in a room in the east wing on the second floor. Each of them was assigned an aisle, and Calvin supplied each of them with a stool so they could more easily examine the items on the higher shelves (especially Violet, who was only five-foot-two).

The next half hour was marked by the thump of shoes stepping onto stools, the thump of shoes stepping off stools, the rumble of stools being dragged to new spots on the hardwood floor, and occasional spates of conversation about some of the items the quartet ran across. Calvin and Cynthia took mental note of the areas Donovan and Violet searched in case they needed to search those areas again later on.

They didn't find anything in that room, so they moved on to another Collection room in the north wing. They hadn't been searching for five minutes when Donovan called out, "I think I found them."

"Them?" Calvin said. He hopped off his stool and hurried over to where Donovan was. Cynthia and Violet followed close behind.

Donovan stepped down off his stool and motioned at the top shelf.

"Yeah, there're three of them," he said. "Right up there. Between the *Little Mermaid* video and the melted cheerleader trophy."

"The Little Mermaid?" Violet said with a snicker. "What the hell're you doin' with that?"

"I haven't watched it yet," Calvin said distractedly as he stepped up onto the stool to look at the top shelf, "but supposedly there's a single frame somewhere in the middle of this particular copy that shows Satan's face."

"Whoa," Donovan said, casting a worried glance at the videotape.

On the top shelf Calvin found three small paintings roughly eleven inches tall and eight inches wide. Each had been done on a sheet of thick, stiff parchment and was sealed in a clear, acid-free plastic sleeve. He picked them up and stepped down off the stool. The others crowded around him to look.

The paintings were done in a crude yet naturalistic style that involved lots of bright colors and intricate detail. Each image was surrounded by a border of intertwined flowering vines that matched the design on the shred of parchment in Judd Skerrit's hand. The back of each sheet of parchment was painted black with a twelve-pointed star in the center. Patches of flaking paint and the brownness and brittleness of the parchment testified to the paintings' great age.

The topmost painting showed a little girl with black hair and a tattered white dress. She had a bouquet of flowers clasped in her hands. She stood atop a giant's severed head, her feet buried in its long, tangled hair. Blood pooled out across the ground around the head. In the middle of the viny border at the bottom of the painting was a box with the Roman numeral IX in it.

The second painting depicted a black-haired young woman sitting on a rough-hewn stone throne. A wolf crouched at the foot of the throne, its red eyes fixed on the viewer. A dolmen stood directly behind the throne like a gateway. It was night, and in the black, starless sky hung a bloated pock-marked moon. This painting likewise sported a box at the bottom. The number within it was XVIII.

The third painting showed a green, blue, and brown globe with a winged serpent coiled around it. Cracks zig-zagged out across the globe from beneath the serpent's coils, as if the hapless orb were being crushed. The snake appeared to be smiling. Stars shone in the background. The painting's number was XXIII.

"These look like Tarot cards," Calvin said.

"Yeah," Cynthia said. "Except don't Tarot cards have names?"

"So, are these, like, magic pictures?" Violet asked. "Do they come alive or something?"

"I don't know," Calvin said.

"What're you gonna do with them?" Donovan asked.

Calvin shrugged. "I don't know yet. Maybe nothing."

"What do you mean nothing?" Violet said. "What the hell were we looking for the damn things for, then?"

"I just needed to remember where I'd seen this viny border before. I came across it in a different context, and I couldn't recall exactly where I knew it from."

"That's it?" Violet said. "You dragged us all the way over here cuz your memory sucks? Dude, when does the cool stuff start? When're we gonna get to, like, shoot zombies, or fuck Bigfoot, or whatever?"

"Bigfoot?" Donovan said, blinking at her. "What?"

"Technically we're not even supposed to be open for business yet," Calvin said, trying to pretend he hadn't heard the Bigfoot comment. "Not till Cyn and I finish college. This case just sort of fell into our laps. And we're not even positive it's a valid case yet. We need to do a lot more research."

As Calvin had hoped, the word "research" had the same effect on Donovan and Violet that garlic has on vampires. They glanced at each other and started backing away.

"Uh, well, maybe we should leave you guys to that, then," Donovan said. "I don't think research is really our thing, you know?"

"Yeah," Violet said. "We're doers, not researchers. We leave that sitting-on-your-ass stuff to folks more suited to it."

"But, hey, let us know if you need our help with anything else."

"Especially if it involves doing stuff that isn't totally boring."

"Do you want me to see you out?" Calvin said.

"Nah, we got it," Donovan said, already disappearing out the door.

As he and Violet headed away down the hall, Calvin and Cynthia heard him ask, "What's this about Bigfoot?" Thankfully, they couldn't hear Violet's reply.

"That was more painless than I thought it would be," Cynthia said. "I was afraid we'd have them tagging along with us all the way back to campus." She nodded at the trio of paintings in Calvin's hand. "Now let's find out what these are."

On the shelf in front of each item in the Collection

was a sticker with a number on it. The number directed one to the case file Mr. May had written up on the anomaly in question. When Calvin stepped back up onto the stool to check, he found that the paintings' number was 2391.

"No wonder I didn't recognize them," Cynthia said. "That's way past where we currently are in the files."

"Yeah, that's gotta be from sometime in the 1980s. I must've seen these paintings while I was browsing around one day."

They headed across the hall to a room filled with metal file cabinets. After a short search through one of them, Calvin pulled out a folder labeled "2391."

He and Cynthia sat down at a small table in the southwest corner of the room, opened the file, and began to read.

File #2391
9/21/81

On August 25, 1981, I, Robert May, received a phone call at approximately 9:30 p.m. from a man who identified himself as Oliver Kidwell. The name sounded familiar, though I couldn't quite place it until Mr. Kidwell explained that while we had never met face-to-face, we had been in contact in the letter column of *Mystery Magazine,* a periodical devoted to strange phenomena that had been published from 1935 to 1972. I had contributed several articles and countless letters to the magazine, and had engaged in numerous letter-column discussions and debates with its other readers.

Once Mr. Kidwell mentioned this, I immediately recalled various letter-column exchanges I had had with him. He was an electrician from Northern California with a fascination with occult topics. He had always struck me as a kind and decent man, though a bit too trusting and gullible and ready to believe in things without sufficient evidence. For instance, for a period in the late sixties, he belonged to a small cult led by a fellow who called himself Umko-Arthok and who claimed to be in touch with a race of aliens called the Merkins. Mr. Kidwell's decision to abandon the cult was due in no small part to my pointing out that a merkin was a pubic wig and that Umko-Arthok was actually a fellow named Pat Haines, who was wanted by the authorities for numerous crimes including fraud, extortion, tax evasion, and indecent exposure.

Because of my help, and also because of the nature of my contributions to the magazine, Mr. Kidwell thought quite highly of me, and having learned from my letters that I collected material related to anomalous phenomena, he was calling to see if I possessed and/or knew anything about what he called the Ur-Tarot. I had never heard of the Ur-Tarot and asked him what it was. He proceeded to relate the following story.

Sometime around the year 900, a psychic monk in a monastery in Bavaria experienced a series of twenty-four visions concerning the end of the world. For each vision he created a small painting, or oversized card, depicting its key elements. He gave these cards no titles but labeled each with a number that denoted its placement in the sequence of visions. He asserted that the cards would soon be scattered far and wide, and that when all were gathered together again, the end of the world would be at hand. Shortly after completing his work he committed suicide by plunging a dagger into his heart.

The cards passed into the possession of another monk at the monastery who believed that the visions and the cards had been a wondrous gift from God. He made copies of the cards for a few fellow monks and scholars scattered throughout Europe so that they could have their own sets of eschatological flash cards to meditate on. Over the next few centuries, still more copies were made and distributed to still other monks and scholars, some of whom likewise made copies, and so on and so on until, as is to be expected when copies of copies are being made by parties unfamiliar with the original source material, the images on the cards bore only the roughest resemblance to the psychic's paintings. The copies had gradually grown smaller over the years, and the number of cards being copied also grew smaller, shrinking from twenty-four to twenty-two. It isn't clear whether the two missing cards were omitted by accident or on purpose.

In the early fourteenth century, copies of the cards began to trickle out of the monasteries and universities and into the hands of the general public. At the same time, the cards' purpose became garbled. Though they had been created as representations of the future, they were now seen as a method of divining the future, and were soon little more than a form of entertainment. Since the cards were similar in size and form to playing cards, which had recently entered Europe and become popular, the two decks merged and became the modern Tarot.

But whither the original cards? The sad truth is that virtually nothing is known of their whereabouts from the tenth century, when they were in the possession of their original copyist, until the late thirteenth century, when nearly a dozen of them turned up in the possession of a Hungarian nobleman who dabbled in the black arts. After studying the cards, he proclaimed that they possessed some ill-defined occult power that could be tapped and utilized. Alone, each card's power was negligible, but the power would increase exponentially with each additional card. Possession of the entire deck would grant one the magical equivalent of an atomic bomb.

Thus began one of the bloodiest and least-known scavenger hunts in history. Over the next six hundred years various kings, scholars, adventurers, criminals, and self-styled sorcerers scoured the world for the cards.

The Hungarian nobleman who started the whole thing became the hunt's first victim. A year after he announced his belief in the cards' powers, he was murdered in his bed in the dead of night and his cards stolen from his castle.

To follow the history of each card would be impossible, for they changed hands faster than a fifty-dollar bill at a pickpockets' convention, and most of them soon dropped out of sight anyway. Various cards were reported to have been possessed by such notables as Dr. Dee, Elisabeth Bathory, Louis XV, Catherine the Great, Cagliostro, Benjamin Franklin, Eliphas Levi, Aleister Crowley, Adolf Hitler, and William Randolph Hearst. The cards are also rumored to have been connected in one way or another with various historical events such as the Inquisition, the French and American Revolutions, the rise of Freemasonry, World Wars I and II, and the disappearance of Judge Crater.

The cards have become a sort of Holy Grail in occult circles, and certain unsavory characters will go to any lengths to acquire them. Lives have been lost, reputations destroyed, and livelihoods decimated in the pursuit of a single card.

The current whereabouts of most of the cards are unknown. Those who own cards are understandably unwilling to make their ownership a matter of public knowledge. However, Mr. Kidwell revealed that he and his brother Marvin had recently come into possession of three cards, though he refused to reveal how they had acquired them. He had been hoping that I, during my investigations, had learned of the cards and, more specifically, how to access their "cryptic powers." Alas, since I did not, he gave me his phone number, urging me to contact him should I ever come across such knowledge, then thanked me for my time and hung up.

On September 14, I received a second call from Mr. Kidwell, this time at three in the morning. I knew from the moment he spoke that something was wrong, for his voice was urgent and frightened. He explained that two days earlier Marvin had been found dead in his home, apparently the victim of a self-inflicted gunshot wound to the head. That, at least, was what the police and coroner concluded. Mr. Kidwell, however, didn't believe that his brother had killed himself. Marvin had shown no signs of depression, and more importantly, a week before his death he received a phone call from a man who had a thick foreign accent that he was trying to disguise with a poor imitation of an American accent. The man, who called himself Mr. Smith, was aware that the Kidwell brothers had come into possession of some of the Ur-Tarot and wanted to know if they would be willing to sell them. Marvin told the man that the cards weren't for sale, and hung up.

Oliver Kidwell was convinced that this enigmatic foreigner had murdered his brother and would soon be gunning for him. The brothers had been keeping the cards in a safe deposit box, but Oliver now feared that that wasn't secure enough. He wanted to completely eliminate any chance of these purportedly powerful cards falling into the hands of evil men, hence his call to me.

"Nobody knows I know you," Mr. Kidwell said. "And you're nearly a continent away. So if you're willing, I was thinking maybe you could hold onto the cards for me until this blows over. I know you're a reliable, trustworthy kind of guy, and I know you have experience dealing with things like this. I'm sure you have, you know, special procedures and stuff." (Alas, I didn't have the heart to tell him that my "special procedures" mainly consisted of giving the Collection a quick once-over with a feather duster every other week.)

I found his readiness to trust me—a man he had never actually met—to be a painful testament to his gullibility, and I felt that the cards would indeed be safer in cannier hands. Thus, I told him to send the cards at his leisure. And he did. Two days later I received a package via Express Mail. Inside were the cards, along with a note thanking me once again and telling me to call him to let him know I received the cards. I immediately dialed the number. No one answered. I tried the number again a few hours later. This time the phone was picked up by a man who identified himself as a police lieutenant. He told me that Mr. Kidwell had been tortured and murdered the previous night and his apartment torn apart as if someone had been searching for something. I told the lieutenant that I was an old friend of Mr. Kidwell's and that Mr. Kidwell recently told me that he believed his brother had been murdered and he feared he would be next. I mentioned the call to Marvin Kidwell by the mysterious foreign man, though I pretended not to know the precise object of the call, nor did I tell the lieutenant about the cards. The lieutenant thanked me for my help and assured me that they would do all they could to apprehend my "friend's" killer.

There followed a lengthy and detailed description of the cards, which Calvin and Cynthia only skimmed. And then:

ADDENDUM (4/15/82):
I followed the case in the papers for as long as I could, but information soon dried up. Police had no sus-

pects or leads, and the investigation eventually petered out. Apparently Mr. Kidwell's killer(s) did not learn what he had done with the cards, for I have had no problems with intruders, trespassers, threats, etc.

Calvin closed the file.

"Great," Cynthia said. "Supernatural artifacts. Psychic monks. Deception. Murder. This all sounds like something out of some horrible Dan Brown novel. What have we gotten ourselves into?"

"I think it's fascinating," Calvin said. He examined the trio of cards on the tabletop before them. "I'm guessing the one with the wolf and the moon is the one that later turned into The Moon. I mean, the modern card doesn't have a chick on a throne in it, but the other stuff's about the same, and it has the same number: eighteen."

"Yeah. And I'll bet the one with the little girl on the giant head is the one that became Strength."

Calvin examined the card with a frown. "You think?"

"Sure. It's the same basic symbolism: a female figure standing triumphant over a brutish masculine power symbol."

"True. But if it is the same card, then its number changed somewhere along the way. In the Ur-Tarot it's number nine, but in the modern decks Strength is number eight."

"Except it used to be...what, number eleven or something?"

"Yeah, until the Golden Dawn switched it around with Justice." He held up the last card, the one with the snake on it. "The numbering's off on this one, too. I mean, this has to be The World, but in the modern decks it's always twenty-two. Here, it's twenty-one."

"Did they know the world was a globe in 900 A.D.?"

"I guess the psychic monk did. If he even understood what he was seeing." Calvin shook his head. "Man, I wish I knew what the rest of these things looked like. Especially the two missing cards that aren't represented in the modern Tarot."

"Just don't become one of the homicidal nutballs obsessed with tracking them all down."

"Meh. I'm not the aggressive type."

"Oh, so you'd just be a nonviolent nutball then, huh?"

"Precisely."

"What I want to know is, what was a maintenance worker doing with a rare and priceless Tarot card?"

Calvin shrugged. "Lou Guglio said Skerrit was always on the lookout for ways to make money, so maybe he got hold of one of the cards somehow and was trying to sell it. Or maybe he stole it from someone and was ransoming it. Maybe it originally belonged to a professor or something."

"That would make sense. A scholarly type would be more likely to own something like this."

"Yeah." He stood up. "Come on. I want to scan these and make copies to take back to campus. I don't want to take the real ones out of the house."

"Just make sure you keep the copies under close watch," she said with a nervous laugh. "If the wrong person sees them, we could end up just like Judd Skerrit."

Chapter 8

"I wonder if the cops know about the Ur-Tarot yet," Calvin said, his voice low. It was the next morning, and they were in Lecture Hall 2 again, reading the latest update on the murder investigation in the *Record* while they waited for World History I to start. The article didn't have much to report. When asked about the investigation, Detective Anderson said only that things were "moving forward at a satisfactory rate."

"I sincerely doubt they know anything," Cynthia said. "I mean, it's not like Anderson has some of the cards sitting around his house like you do. And even knowing about the cards hasn't helped us much. I mean, there's hardly anything about the Ur-Tarot online. The few people who even know about them seem to regard them as a quaint historical myth."

"Yeah, no kidding. I was searching online, too, remember? I'm still spacey from staring at my computer screen half the night."

"Same here. I am definitely going to have to take a long nap this afternoon."

"Me too. I don't even like naps, but— "

"Excuse me," said a female voice behind them.

They turned.

In the seat behind Cynthia's was the blonde girl they had been seeing around Chandler Hall the last couple of days. She was smiling at them, her vibrant gray eyes bopping back and forth between the two of them as if she couldn't decide who she wanted to focus on more. Once again, the bumps of her nipples were faintly visible under her light-green tank top. The tank top's scooped neck showed off the inner curves of her breasts and the deep, dark slit of cleavage between them.

"Um, hi," Calvin said, giving her his best smile.

"Hi," Cynthia said, doing likewise.

"Hello," the girl said. "My name is Kaarina." She had a thick accent neither Calvin nor Cynthia could place, and she spoke slowly and with great care as if she had to keep her mouth from taking the words in directions they weren't supposed to go. "I am new student here, and I am needing for someone to show me notes from older classes in semester. I thought two of you would be good persons to ask." Her smile grew wider and one blonde eyebrow rose up, knowing and flirty. "I remember two of you from yesterday. Next to steps."

"Yeah," Cynthia said with a vigorous nod, hoping she didn't sound quite as dazed and giddy as she felt. She couldn't believe that this girl was actually talking to her. (Well, okay, and to Calvin, too, unfortunately.) "I remember you, too. I'd be happy to help. My name's Cynthia."

"I'm Calvin," Calvin interjected, not wanting to be left out. "I'd be happy to help, too."

"Maybe we could meet up after class and go over the material, if you have the time," Cynthia said.

"The three of us," Calvin said.

Kaarina nodded. "I am liking that very much. Thank you."

"I love your accent," Cynthia said. "Where are you from?"

"Finland, originally. But I travel much and have lived in many other places, too."

"Ah, Finland," Calvin said with a nod, wanting her to think him knowledgeable and cosmopolitan. Actually, he wasn't even sure he could find Finland on a map. All those Scandinavian countries ran together to him.

"Yes," she said. "You are much familiar with Finland?"

"Um…"

He was saved from answering by the arrival of Professor Byrne, who emerged from the side door and headed to the podium. The chatter that filled the room quickly diminished.

"We'll talk later," Calvin whispered to Kaarina.

"After class," Cynthia added.

"I cannot wait," Kaarina said.

Byrne cleared his throat. The room fell silent.

"Now, then, we left off at the Dark Ages," Byrne said. He seemed to be back to his usual calm and well-prepared self, all trace of jet lag long gone. "Let's see if we can't shed a little light on them, shall we?"

There were a few polite chuckles. Then they forged ahead into the darkness.

Chapter 9

After class, Calvin, Cynthia, and Kaarina headed to the Student Center and sat at one of the picnic tables in the plaza, Calvin and Cynthia on one side, Kaarina on the other. The plaza was noisy and bustling with the usual lunchtime crowd, but Calvin and Cynthia barely noticed. Their enraptured attention was fixed on Kaarina.

The moment they were seated, Calvin unzipped his backpack and whipped out his World History I notebook.

"Here," he said, handing it to Kaarina. "Have a look at my notes."

Beside him, Cynthia stopped unzipping her own backpack and suppressed a scowl at having been beaten to the draw.

Her ill humor vanished a moment later when Kaarina flipped through a few pages, then shook her head.

"I do not know what writing says," Kaarina said.

"What?" Calvin said.

"This is crazy person writing. It is messy boy writing. I do not know how to read these words."

Smiling, Cynthia pulled out her own notebook.

"Here," she said, handing it to Kaarina. "You can use mine instead. My writing's legible."

"Mine's legible," Calvin protested.

"Only to yourself and the criminally insane."

Calvin reluctantly took back his notebook while Kaarina examined Cynthia's.

"Ah, yes," Kaarina said with a nod. "I read this okay."

Cynthia beamed. Calvin rolled his eyes.

Kaarina spent the next few minutes flipping through Cynthia's notebook. She paused half a dozen times to jot a few short notes in her own notebook. Then she shut Cynthia's notebook and handed it back.

"Thank you," she said.

"You hardly took any notes," Cynthia said.

"Much of notes are things I know already."

"Wow, you must be, like, super smart or something."

Kaarina waved a hand modestly. "Oh, no. I am simply possessing excellent education. Schools in Finland are nothing to be sneezing your nose at."

"How long have you been in the U.S.?" Calvin asked.

"Two weeks."

"What made you decide to come here?" Cynthia said.

"I needed change. I lived most of last two years in Tokyo and felt need to move on to new place and meet new people.

"Tokyo, wow," Calvin said, impressed. He had always dreamed of traveling the world. "I'd love to visit there someday."

Kaarina nodded. "Tokyo is fun place. But even fun place becomes old place after long enough. Because of work my father does, I spend much of my life traveling with him, so traveling is now my normal. I cannot stay in one place too long. The world is big, and there is much to see. I want to see all of it. I do not understand how any person is happy seeing only small part of it. I want to see everything. I want to experience everything."

"Really?" Cynthia asked. She couldn't help but wonder if one of the things Kaarina had experienced was sex with another girl. And if she hadn't, if she would be interested. "So what is it your father does?"

"He is engineer for bridges."

"He must be really good at it if they want him all over the world."

"Yes," Kaarina said. "He is famous for bridges." She shrugged. "At least to people who know such things."

"Where is he now? Is he in the U.S., too?"

"Um, no. Not yet. He is in Europe now, finishing project. But his next project is here in U.S. That is other reason I choose to come here. He will be here soon, too."

"Ah."

Kaarina slid her notebook into her backpack and stood up.

"I am sorry to run away so quickly," she said, "but I have much things to do." She cocked her head and raised her eyebrows hopefully. "Maybe we can meet again later. I would like to get to know two of you much better, if you are liking idea."

"Oh, I'm certainly liking idea," Calvin said.

"Yeah," Cynthia agreed. "What about tonight? Are you busy tonight? We could meet up at the Root Cellar."

"Tonight is good," Kaarina said. "I can be meeting after eight o'clock. But I am not knowing Root Cellar."

"It's a hangout in the basement of the Student Center. They try to make it like a bar, with greasy food, live bands, and a sort of dim, cozy atmosphere. But instead of alcoholic beverages, they've got root beer. It sounds kind of dorky, but it's actually not bad." While she had been talking, she had taken out her phone and gotten online to check the Root Cellar's Upcoming Events page. "Tonight they've got a band called The Black Lodge, which they characterize as 'alternative prog rock,' whatever *that* means. The show starts at eight-thirty, so if we meet up around eight that should give us plenty of time to hang out and talk beforehand."

"And if it turns out the band really sucks, we can just leave and do something else," Calvin said.

Kaarina nodded. "That is good plan. It sounds like much fun."

They traded phone numbers. Then Kaarina slung her backpack over her shoulder.

"I will see two of you tonight at eight o'clock." She flashed them a smile, then strode away.

They watched her go with unblinking, unwavering gazes, not wanting to miss a nanosecond's glimpse of her fantastic body: Her ponytail swishing back and forth across the bare skin of her upper back, the luscious swells of her hips and ass in their denim sheath, her long slim legs scissoring swiftly as she walked.

She rounded the corner of the Student Center and was gone. Calvin and Cynthia kept gazing at the corner with dazed and dreamy smiles for a moment. Then they looked at each other.

"I think we just made it to the World Series," Calvin said.

Chapter 10

When Calvin arrived at the Root Cellar at eight on the dot, Cynthia was already there. She stood beside a square brick pillar a dozen paces inside the entrance, her eyes on the slow but steady trickle of newcomers. When she saw Calvin she waved him over.

He wasn't surprised she was already there. That was normal for her. She was one of those people who always leave extra-early for wherever they have to be just in case there's a delay, and invariably wind up arriving extra-early as well. But he *was* surprised at how she was dressed. Instead of her usual jeans and T-shirt, she wore a tight, black, long-sleeved V-neck shirt with ruffled cuffs, plus a pair of tight white bell bottoms and black suede peep-toe wedge pumps. Her red hair had a gentle wave to it and shone like something out of a shampoo commercial. Sterling silver butterfly earrings dangled from her earlobes. Most of amazing of all, she had put on makeup: dark red lipstick and light-green eye-shadow. The last time Calvin had seen her wear makeup was at their senior prom.

She saw him staring at her outfit and squirmed nervously.

"Do I look okay? Is something weird?"

"Nuh…" He cleared his throat. "No, it's…you look great."

She smiled, relieved.

He sniffed the air.

"Is that perfume?" he asked.

"It's *oil.* I don't wear perfume."

"Oh, I see." Actually, he didn't. There was a difference?

He looked around the cavy, low-ceilinged room. Roughly half of the wooden tables and booths were occupied. There was a short line at the food counter, behind which student workers bustled about preparing orders. Food sizzled on fryers. Cooler doors clacked open and thumped shut. The air was filled with the scents of salsa, grilled chicken, mozzarella cheese, root beer. At the far end of the room the low stage was already set up for the band, with microphones on stands, a drum kit, amps, and countless wires snaking everywhere, all of it lit by the overhead spotlights. Big white papier mâché replicas of theatrical comedy and tragedy masks hung on the brick wall behind the stage. Of the band itself, there was no sign.

"Kaarina's not here yet?" Calvin asked.

"No. She——"

And then there she was, pushing through the glass entrance door. She wore a tight light-green dress cut low enough on top to display the upper hemispheres of her breasts and high enough at the hem to show off nearly the entirety of her long, tanned legs. On her feet were silver high-heel gladiator sandals. A silver ring glinted on the second toe of her left foot. She wore cherry-red lipstick and silvery eye-shadow. From one shoulder hung a small silver purse that matched her sandals.

When she spotted Calvin and Cynthia, a smile lit her face, and she strode toward them with enough vigor to make her breasts jiggle hypnotically. Calvin and Cynthia had to exert every ounce of willpower they possessed to keep their eyes on Kaarina's face.

"Hello hello!" Kaarina said to Calvin and Cynthia as she joined them.

"Hi," Cynthia croaked.

"Hi," Calvin croaked. He glanced at Kaarina's outfit, then at Cynthia's, then at his shlubby jeans and T-shirt. Then he shrank down as if he wished to dwindle away into nothing.

"Two of you have not been waiting long for me, have you?" Kaarina asked.

"No, only a minute or two," Cynthia said. "Come on. Let's go get some food and a table."

At the food counter they bought a root beer apiece, plus a jumbo order of nachos to split among them. Food and drink in hand, they turned to face the room.

"Where should we sit?" Cynthia asked. "Do you guys want to sit close to the stage, or what?"

"No," Kaarina said. "Let us find nice quiet place. We need privateness for talking." She motioned with her root beer bottle at a small unoccupied table in a corner at the back of the room. "What about there?"

"Looks good to me," Calvin said.

They threaded their way through the room and sat down at the table.

"This is nice," Kaarina said, looking around. "It reminds me of basement club I much visited when I lived in Germany."

"You lived in Germany, too?" Calvin said.

"Yes. For almost whole year as teenager. I lived in many places. Germany and Italy and Egypt and Australia and Japan."

"Wow! It must be great to travel so much."

Kaarina nodded. "It is. I am very lucky to have father who takes me around world with him when he travels."

"I'll say."

Kaarina picked up her bottle of root beer and sniffed it. "This is beer, but not with alcohol, you say?"

"No, no alcohol," Cynthia said. "It's root beer. It's more like a soft drink, like Coke or something. Sort of."

"Oh." Kaarina took a sip, then smacked her mouth a few times and frowned at the brown glass bottle. "I am not knowing what this is. This is not tasting like roots *or* beer."

"It's just a name, that's all. You don't like it?"

"It is okay taste. But it is not what I expect."

"Well, have some nachos," Calvin said, nudging the basket of nachos toward her. "Nachos improve the flavor of everything."

Kaarina took a nacho, scooped up a shiny orange blob of melted cheese with it, then popped it into her mouth.

"So," she said between bites, "what do two of you do for fun?" She gestured at the room around them. "Aside from music and beer from roots."

Calvin and Cynthia glanced at each other. They didn't want to tell Kaarina about the Collection and their interest in strange phenomena, at least not until they were sure they could trust her to keep mum. But what should they tell her instead? They should have discussed this.

"Just, you know, the usual," Cynthia said. "Movies. Reading. Stuff like that. Just hanging out." She shrugged. "Frankly, our classes keep us pretty busy most of the time."

"Ah, and what do two of you study?"

"I'm majoring in Environmental Studies right now," Cynthia said. "But I think I'm gonna switch to something else."

"Why?"

"I don't know. It just doesn't feel right for me. It's not quite grabbing me the way I thought it would."

"So what will you study instead?"

"I don't know yet. I keep trying to think of something, but…I don't know."

"And you?" Kaarina asked Calvin.

"I've got a double major," he said, trying not to sound too boastful. "Physics and Psychology."

"Oh!" Kaarina gave him a sidelong look of mock alarm. "You are not psychologizing me now, are you? Probing my brain to learn my secret thinkings?"

"No. I'm not that good at it yet. Actually, the main reason I wanted to study both subjects is because in a sense both fields are what underlie all other fields."

"Oh, here we go," Cynthia said. "He tells this to everybody," she told Kaarina. "It's his shtick."

"See, physics deals with the root phenomena of the material world," Calvin went on, ignoring her. "Everything that exists is based on physics. But all that stuff is known only via our minds. So you could argue that it's our minds that are actually the underlying reality of reality. But of course our minds are made up of matter, which is physics again. But of course the matter is known to us only via our brains, which is psychology again."

Kaarina nodded. "It is like chicken and chicken egg."

"Exactly! So I decided to study both of them."

"Very impressing. You are seeker after truth. But which will you look for career in?"

"Uh…" The truth was, he and Cynthia planned to investigate anomalous phenomena full time once they were done with college. Mr. May had left them enough money to make normal jobs unnecessary, at least as long as they handled that money wisely. "I haven't decided yet."

"So what about you?" Cynthia asked Kaarina. "What's your major?"

"I am in same boat with you," she said. "Before I move here, I study Criminal Justice. But now I do not think it is right choice for me. My mind is changing lately. My interests are changing. I still very much like to solve crimes and mysteries, but there are many other things I very much like, too."

"Crimes and mysteries, huh?" Calvin said.

"Oh, yes. I actually solved crime once when my father and I lived in Germany."

"Seriously?"

"Yes. We were staying in hotel in Berlin, and somebody stole envelope full of money from businessman's room. The businessman was very important, and police made big investigation. Nobody was allowed to leave hotel while police searched and asked questions. I became curious and started to make investigation of my own. I think best suspect is one of hotel's workers because they have keys to all rooms, and businessman's room was locked when money was stolen. So I follow workers and try to learn what I can about them, but that does not work so well. They see me watching and get mad and tell me to go away. But then I have good thought: Where is excellent place to put envelope where it will not be noticed?"

"Uh, with other envelopes?" Cynthia said.

"Yes! In mail! I tell this to police, and they look inside all mail that is waiting to be sended out. And there it is! One of maids had taken envelope from room and put stamp on it and written her own house address on it so it will be sended to herself."

"Wow, that's pretty clever. Not just the maid, but you for thinking of it."

"Thank you. I received reward, too. One hundred Euros. The hotel detective told me I have talent for solving mysteries. It is funny: When I tell my father I am going to America, he warns me. He says: Be careful, there is much gun violence in America. I tell him not to be a silly. But then, when I get here, there is man murdered on campus! My father is now very upset. But he tells me: Maybe you should solve crime for American police, Kaarina. You do it before in Germany." She shrugged. "Maybe I should try."

"Huh," Cynthia said with a meaningful glance at Calvin. "Maybe so."

"Still, I hope such things do not happen here too much?"

"Oh, no," Calvin said. "This is the first murder we've had here in over a week."

Kaarina frowned at him with mock poutiness. "You are having fun with me."

"Sorry. Just kidding. No, this is the first murder on campus that I've ever heard of."

"Are two of you from this area?"

"Not Ames itself," Cynthia said. "We're from a town called May. It's about a ten-minute drive south of here."

"Two of you come from same home town, then? You grow up together?"

"Yeah. Technically. We didn't really get to know each other very well until our senior year of high school. But once we did, we became best friends almost immediately."

"Friends, yes," Kaarina said, nodding. She scrutinized them with a small, thoughtful smile. "At first, when we meet, I think two of you are boyfriend and girlfriend. But I soon can tell that is not true."

"Yeah," Cynthia said with a laugh. "Definitely not

boyfriend and girlfriend. In fact, um…" She took a breath, hoping the truth didn't scare Kaarina away, hoping instead the truth drew Kaarina closer. "I don't like boys at all."

"Neither do I," Calvin said dryly.

Kaarina laughed. "Well, *I* do."

"Ah." Cynthia stretched a blithe smile across her face in hopes of masking her disappointment.

"But I like girls, too," Kaarina went on. Cynthia's heart leaped like a landed fish. "I like individuals. The things they have between their legs are not important." She paused a moment, reconsidering, then flashed an impish smile. "Well, they are important, of course, but they are not main thing. Point is, I do not believe in limitations. Every person is unique. Every situation is unique. And they must be treated as such, not as repeat of old things. And you can never know for certain if you will like something until you do it. You know?"

"Yeah, I guess," Cynthia said. Though she had been forcing a smile a moment ago, now she had to struggle to keep a goofy grin from stretching across her face. "With an outlook like that," she told Kaarina, "you must have led a pretty interesting life."

Kaarina nodded. "Interesting is good word for it, yes."

"Ohio must seem kind of boring to someone who's traveled the world and experienced so much," Calvin said. "I mean, what made you choose Ames? Why not somewhere a little more…interesting?"

Kaarina grinned at him. "Maybe that is exactly why I choose it. Maybe I have not experienced boring place like Ohio before." She grabbed another nacho, loaded it with cheese, and took a bite. "But, really, boring is only state of mind. I think you see it as boring because you have familiarness with Ohio. To me, it is new and strange and wonderful."

"You're very wise," Cynthia said. "You have a really positive, upbeat way of looking at things."

Kaarina gave a modest shrug. "I try to look on bright side. I try to find right ways to look at things. It is important for me. Lately I am studying much of meditation and things to grow my consciousness."

"Grow your consciousness?" Calvin said. "How do you mean?"

"I am investigating mysticalism and magic, and I try to develop my psychical powers." She laughed a little self-consciously. "You probably think I am a silly."

"No! Why would I?"

"Because you are science man, with physics and psychology. You probably think magic and ghosts and telepathicness is from stupid brains."

"Not at all!" Calvin said. "On the contrary, I think there's ample evidence for strange phenomena, but too many in the scientific community choose to look the other way because it doesn't jibe with their prejudices."

Kaarina raised her eyebrows at him. "Oh, my. You have much opinions on this."

"Oh, um…" Calvin shifted in his seat. It was looking more and more likely that he and Cynthia would be able to take Kaarina into their confidence without any worries, but he didn't want to reveal anything until he and Cynthia had had a chance to discuss it. "Well, you know, it's just a sort of personal interest of mine."

"Mine, too, actually," Cynthia chimed in.

"Really?" Kaarina sat forward eagerly. "Have two of you had any psychical experiences?"

"No," Calvin said. "Not as such. Not yet anyway."

"I have! Once I make pendulum move with my brain.

And I have had dreams. Dreams that become truth. But never about anything important."

"I had an aunt who was psychic," Cynthia said. "She could read objects' pasts by touching them, and sometimes she had visions of the future, too."

"Ooh! Was she famous? Did she make herself rich?"

"Well, no. Her powers were kind of erratic. They happened only when they wanted to. She didn't have a lot of control over them."

"I see. But what of you? Do you have visions, too? They say that psychical powers run in families."

"Not in my family. As far as I know, my aunt was the only one. What about your family?"

"My grandmother—my father's mother—she was powerful psychic. People came from very far to visit her and learn future. I never met her, though. She died long ago, before I was born. My father tells me I look much like her when she was young. He says that maybe I have some of her powers, too. He often asks me to tell him where he will be hired next. It is mostly joke, but I try anyway. Usually I am wrong."

"What about your mom? You never mention her. Are they divorced or something?"

A shadow settled over Kaarina's face. She looked down at her root beer. "She is dead. She died when I was nine."

"Oh, I'm sorry. She must have been pretty young."

She nodded. "Yes. She was young and strong and healthy. But then suddenly she was sick, and she died. It was very quick."

"What was wrong with her?" Calvin asked.

"It was cancer in her ovaries."

"I'm so sorry," Cynthia said. "I know what it's like to

lose a close family member. My little sister Emily died just a couple of years ago."

"I am sorry. Was she sick?"

"No. She was murdered."

Kaarina gasped. "That is terrible! Did they catch person who did it?"

"Oh, yeah. He's dead now, too. It's...a long story."

A susurrus ran through the room. Calvin, Cynthia, and Kaarina looked around. The Black Lodge had emerged from a door behind the stage. There were four members of the band, two men and two women, none of whom looked much older than their college-age audience. The lead singer was a pale, chubby-cheeked man with long dark-brown hair. He was dressed in a black suit and tie with a purple trench coat. The guitarist was a petite brunette girl in a black cat suit with cat ears on her head. The tip of her nose had been colored black at the tip in imitation of a cat's nose, and three whiskers had been drawn across each cheek. The bassist was a heavyset girl with glasses and brown hair that hung down to her waist. She was dressed like a cowgirl, complete with a neckerchief, rhinestone-studded black cowboy boots, and a black ten-gallon hat. The drummer was a Native-American guy with a spiked Mohawk. He wore a black leather vest, black leather pants, black leather boots, and black leather wristbands with silver studs.

"What the hell?" Calvin muttered. "It's like the Village People meets Josie and the Pussycats."

"It is...interesting," Kaarina said.

"Greetings," the singer said into the microphone. "We are..." He spread his arms. "The Black Lodge."

Scattered applause.

"Through our music tonight we shall explore the

masks of society…" He paused for effect, then cocked one eyebrow and added, "And the society of masks."

"And the pretentiousness of pseudo-intellectuals," Calvin said, adopting the same melodramatic tone as the singer, but making sure he wasn't loud enough for anyone to hear him beyond the confines of their corner table.

"C'mon, be nice," Cynthia said, unable to help smiling anyway. "They haven't even started playing yet. They might be good."

"I don't know. I've got a bad feeling about this."

The lead singer snapped his fingers and the band unleashed their first number. Despite Calvin's fears, the music itself was decent. As advertised, the band was striving for a sound that was somewhere midway between prog rock and punk. Many of the songs were very long, with hard, fast verses that shot by like bullets and then gave way to lengthy, elaborate instrumental sequences. The lyrics were often something of a mystery since the singer had a problem with enunciation, and given his propensity for prancing about on the stage and gesturing dramatically, he kept getting either too close or too far from the mike. Judging by the lyrics that were decipherable, the songs traced a person's progress through life, from birth to school to love to work to death, all the while comparing life to a sinister masquerade where everyone's true faces and intentions remain unknown behind the masks society requires them to wear. The opening song's conclusion made this fairly explicit:

> *Plastic faces, rictus grins*
> *Hiding hopes and hates and sins*
> *Masks are smiling as you howl*
> *And vice-like fingers hold you down*

Your own expression's pressed in place
Welcome, child, to the masquerade.

"They're not too bad," Cynthia said to Calvin during a brief break between songs.

"They're good," he conceded. "Good but not great. I'm not sure the whole prog-punk mashup works very well for them. It's kind of schizoid. I think they're aspiring to something they're not really ready for. They need a few more years practicing in the garage." He took a swig of root beer, then turned to Kaarina. "What do you think?"

"I think it is fun," she said. "It is experience." She waved her arm in a gesture that encompassed everything: Calvin, Cynthia, the food, the band. "Whole night is experience. I like it all."

Cynthia nodded. "I think that's a very healthy attitude to have. It beats being cynical and judgmental." She said this latter sentence with a pointed glance at Calvin.

He rolled his eyes. "There's a big difference between being judgmental and having standards."

"A big difference or a fine line?"

Calvin never got a chance to answer—if he was even going to—because just then the Black Lodge let loose with their next song, a rapid-fire, tongue-twisty chant called "Second Guessing":

Oh, she says she is
But said she wasn't
So since she said she wasn't but was
Maybe since she says she is she isn't
Or maybe she said she wasn't but was
And knew she was
Or perhaps she says she is

And knows she isn't
And knew she wasn't
Like she said.

The concert went on for another half an hour and culminated in a slow waltz-like number about death, which in the context of the masquerade theme was more of a blessing than a curse:

Your mask flaking, breaking, crumbling to bits
Reduced to worthless prismatic dust at your feet
And so you exit as you came
Naked and alone
Finally free of the endless ambiguities
Of this tragicomic masquerade.

The band bowed to moderately enthusiastic applause. The cat-girl announced there were shirts and CDs for sale. Some people stood up and headed toward the stage. Others stood up and headed toward the exit. Most remained seated and continued eating, drinking, talking.

Kaarina downed the last of her root beer, then stood up. "I am getting shirt."

"You are?" Calvin and Cynthia said in unison.

"Of course! It will help me remember this wonderful night."

"Wow," Calvin said, smiling. "That makes me want to get a shirt too."

"Same here," Cynthia said. "Maybe even a CD."

"I don't know if I'd go that far."

The three of them joined the small crowd beside the stage. Up close, the lead singer's chubby face was shiny with sweat, no doubt from spending over an hour capering around under the bright, hot stage lights clad in a suit and a trench coat. He stank of B.O. and wet cotton.

"Hope you enjoyed the show," he said to the trio.

"I will never be forgetting this night," Kaarina said.

"Glad to hear it," the man said with a smile. His eyes wandered over her cleavage.

All three of them bought T-shirts that had the band's name emblazoned above cute manga-style cartoon images of the four band members in their costumes. Calvin and Cynthia got medium tees in black and white, respectively, while Kaarina got a light-blue cropped baby doll tee. Cynthia also bought a CD, whose cover sported the comedy-tragedy masks.

With their new loot tucked under their arms, Calvin, Cynthia, and Kaarina exited the Root Cellar, then went upstairs and into the plaza. The night was warm, and stars twinkled overhead. A boy and a girl were making out at one of the picnic tables. The rest of the picnic tables were empty. A few students were strolling through the plaza on their way elsewhere. The fountain had been turned off, and the resultant quiet was jarring. Calvin and Cynthia were rarely here this late.

"Which way are you going?" Cynthia asked Kaarina.

Kaarina pointed north, the direction opposite Duffy Hall.

"I go that way," she said. "I must hurry, too, I am sad to be saying; I have many things to do early tomorrow. I must have much sleep."

"Yeah, it is pretty late for a school night. At least for those of us who attend classes."

"Which I think is only a fraction of the student population here at Ames," Calvin said.

"Yeah." Cynthia turned to Kaarina. "Do you want us

to walk you home or something?"

"Oh, no, thank you," Kaarina said. "I am fine. I live in little apartment on very edge of campus. It is not far."

"All right. If you're sure."

"I must tell you, I have great time tonight," Kaarina said, beaming at them. "You say Ohio is boring, but it is not true: Two of you are here. And two of you are great! Most smart and interesting people I meet in very long time. I am so happy I meet you."

"So are we," Cynthia said, beaming right back at her.

"Yeah," Calvin agreed, likewise beaming.

"We must meet again soon!" Kaarina said.

"What about tomorrow?" Cynthia asked. "Are you free tomorrow night? We could do something then. We don't have any plans." She glanced at Calvin for confirmation. He nodded.

"I think I will be free," Kaarina said, "but I am not certain. I will know tomorrow afternoon. Call me then, and we set up plans."

"Will do."

"Until tomorrow, then." She waggled her fingers in a little wave, then turned and strolled away, humming snatches of one of the Black Lodge's songs as she went. Calvin and Cynthia watched her go, big smiles still stuck on their faces. They felt as if they would never stop smiling. Kaarina rounded the corner of the Student Center and vanished from sight. The sound of her humming remained audible for a few seconds, echoing faintly off the buildings that surrounded the preternaturally silent plaza. Then it, too, vanished.

"Wow," Calvin said.

"Yeah," Cynthia said. "Wow."

They floated all the way back to their dorm.

Chapter 11

When Calvin met up with Cynthia for lunch in the Food Court the next day, she had already gotten her food and sat down and was immersed in a book that lay open on the table next to her spinach casserole.

She looked up at him as he sat down across from her with his plate of Szechuan Shrimp.

"Mitä kuuluu?" she said.

"Huh?"

"Mitä kuuluu?"

"What is that? Tagalog, or Venusian, or something?"

"It's Finnish for 'How are you?'" She tilted up the book so he could see the cover: *Teach Yourself Finnish.* There was a yellow Ames University Library sticker on the spine.

"Oh, come on," he said. "What, are you hoping to impress Kaarina with your sudden familiarity with her native tongue? That's just sad."

"No!" she said, reddening. "I was—I just—I was in the library for...for something else, and I just thought I'd find out what the language was like. You know, just to try to understand our new friend and her background a little better. That's all. Turns out it's a really fascinating language. Very mellifluous."

"Mellifluous, my ass. This is just a lame ploy to impress a hot girl."

She rolled her eyes, then pulled out her phone.

"Speaking of the hot girl," she said, "we should probably call her, now that we're both here."

"Yeah." He watched her dial Kaarina's number with a small frown. "I could've called her, you know."

She shrugged. "I'm already halfway done with lunch. You just sat down." She nodded at his food. "You should eat."

"How magnanimous," Calvin muttered, then speared a shrimp with his fork.

Kaarina answered her phone on the second ring.

"Yes?" she said.

"Hi, Kaarina," Cynthia said. "This is Cynthia. From last night, remember?"

"Of course. I will remember last night until I am old woman. And tonight, too, I hope! I am happy to say I am okay to meet tonight. Any time after seven o'clock."

"Awesome." She put a hand over the receiver and relayed the news to Calvin, who gave a thumbs up.

"Is that Calvin you talk to?" Kaarina asked.

"Yeah," Cynthia said.

"Oh, good. Tell him hello for me."

"Kaarina says hi," she told him.

"Hey, Kaarina!" he said, loud enough for Kaarina to hear him.

It was also loud enough for nearby diners to glance over. Cynthia shrank down in her seat, embarrassed. But then she heard Kaarina giggle, and she couldn't help but smile at the sound.

"So, is there anything in particular you want to do tonight?" Cynthia asked.

"No more beer from roots," Kaarina said. "We must have real beer."

"Beer?" Cynthia said.

Calvin looked up, a forkful of rice frozen halfway to

his mouth. He shrugged.

"Actually, we, uh, we're not old enough to drink," Cynthia told Kaarina. She felt a little reluctant to admit it, as if their not being of legal age were somehow a character flaw that would diminish their greatness in Kaarina's eyes. "The drinking age here is twenty-one, and we're still about a year away from that."

"I see," Kaarina said.

"I mean, we do drink," Cynthia hastened to add so that Kaarina wouldn't think they were total squares. "Once in a while. It's just, we wouldn't be able to meet up at a bar or buy beer."

"That is okay. I can buy."

"Wait, how old are you?"

"I am twenty-one. But is there place we can meet where we will not be troubled by police or blabbing mouths? I would say my apartment, but everything is in boxes, and I have very few furnitures. It is no good for guests."

"We could always meet in my dorm room," Cynthia said.

"Or mine," Calvin said, his voice muffled by a mouthful of shrimp and rice.

Cynthia shook her head and waved a hand to shush him.

Calvin frowned. "What?"

"That is fine," Kaarina told Cynthia. She hadn't heard Calvin. "Your room would be perfect. We will have peace and quietness."

"Okay, then. Why don't we make it eight o'clock in my dorm room?" Again, she looked at Calvin as she said it, asking both of them.

Calvin nodded grudgingly.

Kaarina said, "Yes! It is good!"

Cynthia gave Kaarina directions to her dorm.

"They keep the front door locked," Cynthia added. "And non-residents are supposed to be let in by whoever they're visiting. But at that hour, there're so many people coming and going, you should be able to just walk right in. But if you do need me, just call my number and I'll come down and get you."

"You will get me," Kaarina echoed. "Very good."

"Do you need money for the beer, or—"

"No, no! Beer is my treat. You supply room, I supply beer. It is good trade."

"All right," Cynthia said. "See you tonight."

They hung up.

"So how come we have to meet in your dorm room?" Calvin asked. "Mine would have been just as good."

"First, because I was the one who was on the phone. And second, because your room looks like a landfill. I'm doing you a favor. And Kaarina, too; she'd probably wind up with tetanus, or something."

"Your wit sparkles like cubic zirconia."

They ate in silence for a while. Then Calvin asked, "So have you given much thought to the investigation and what we should do next?"

"Not really. I mean, I haven't had much time. I was pretty tired last night after we got back from the Root Cellar." She didn't want to admit that she had actually spent over three hours online researching Finland, then another hour trying to go to sleep but failing thanks to various dreamy fantasies about Kaarina, many of them involving naked bodies snuggling close in a hot sauna. "What about you? Any bright ideas?"

"No." He shrugged. "Same story as you." He spoke

truer than he knew. He, too, had spent hours lost in dreamy fantasies. In them, he and Kaarina traveled the globe investigating anomalies while looking fantastic, trading quips, and fucking like bunnies in a variety of exotic locales.

He frowned slightly and licked his lips. "You know, I was thinking…"

"Did you hurt yourself?"

"Har har. No. About Kaarina. I mean, I was thinking, seeing as how she's obviously very bright, and she likes solving mysteries, and she has an interest in the paranormal—"

Cynthia nodded. "We should see if she'd be interested in joining the team."

He stared at her in surprise. "Yeah!"

"I agree. She's ideal. I was thinking the exact same thing."

He grunted. "I thought for sure I'd have to do more to convince you."

"Why?"

"Well, you're the one who's the privacy freak and wants to keep everything all hush-hush top-secret."

"Privacy freak?"

"You do seem to have major concerns on that score, yes." He smiled. "But I guess Kaarina's different." He gestured at her book. "You're already eager to master her tongue."

She rolled her eyes. "Now who's the cubic zirconia?"

They finished eating. Calvin picked up a heap of salt packets that had been sitting on his tray and unzipped his backpack to put them inside.

"What are you doing?" Cynthia asked.

"They're for my kit."

"Salt?"

"Yeah."

"Why?"

"Salt could be useful. I mean, if you're trapped somewhere or in a desert or something, you need salt to survive. And more importantly, a circle of salt is said to keep certain occult entities at bay. It's practically a necessity for any paranormal investigator."

She shook her head. "I think you're going a little overboard with this whole kit thing. I mean, at this rate, you're gonna need a U-Haul for all this stuff."

"You never know what you might need."

As he stashed the packets in his backpack, Cynthia spotted a familiar yellow sticker on one of the books therein. Feeling sure she knew what it was, she lunged across the table and plucked the book from the backpack before Calvin knew what she was doing.

"Hey!" he cried.

She peered at the book's title. As she thought: *Learn Finnish Now.*

"What's this, eh?" she said with a smirk.

He snatched the book back from her.

"It's mellifluous, damn it," he said.

Chapter 12

Calvin showed up at Cynthia's dorm room at five to eight that night. When she answered the door and invited him in, he couldn't move for a second. He had dressed in a manner he considered commensurate with what the girls had worn the night before: a dark-blue sport shirt, black jeans, and black Chelsea boots. Alas, Cynthia had one-upped him outfit-wise. Or maybe ten- or twenty-upped him. This time she was actually wearing a dress. A dress! A very flattering and sexy dress. It was a floral-print ruffled surplice neck dress whose hem fluttered at mid-thigh. Never before had Calvin seen so much of her long, slim legs. On her feet were a pair of brown wedge sandals that showed she had painted her toenails dark red. Her hair was as shiny and wavy as last night, and she wore the same eye-shadow. Her lipstick matched her toenails. An onyx pendant hung on a silver chain around her neck. She was cocooned in the scent of the same oil she had worn in the Root Cellar.

"Are you gonna come in or are you just gonna stand there ogling me?" Cynthia said, a touch frostily.

"Sorry," he said, stepping inside. "But since when do you wear dresses? I mean, when you're not attending some kind of ceremonial event, that is?"

"Since when do you wear shirts with buttons on them?"

He shrugged. "Since about ten minutes ago."

"I rest my case."

Calvin was amazed to see that her room looked even neater and cleaner than usual. Every surface gleamed. Not a single spot of lint marred the carpet. The bed had been made with military precision, all straight lines and taut plains. Even the plastic light covers on the ceiling had been cleaned of dust and bug husks.

When he went to sit down on the edge of the bed, she shook a hand at him. "Don't. You'll mess it up. I just made it."

"Where am I supposed to sit, then? All you've got is a desk chair."

"I don't know." She looked around, then sighed. "I should have gotten a futon like you."

"Maybe we should've met in my room, after all."

"No. No, it's…it's fine. You can sit there, I guess. But just don't mess it up too much."

With an exasperated sigh, he perched himself gingerly on the edge of the bed.

Cynthia looked around the room, checking everything one more time. And just like the last five thousand times she had checked, everything looked fine. Except…

"Aw, crap!" she said. "I should've emptied the waste-basket!"

"Why?"

"Cuz there's trash in it."

"Uh, it's a wastebasket. It's supposed to have trash in it."

"Yeah, but it looks skuzzy. I want everything to look nice. I don't have guests very often. Except you."

"What, and I don't merit a wastebasket-emptying? Thanks."

"You know what I mean."

"Yeah, I don't count as much because you're not trying to get in my pants."

She clucked her tongue. "Why do you make everything about sex?"

"Because pretty much everything *is*." He gestured at her. "I mean, what, you doll yourself up like that for all your new friends?"

She opened her mouth to deliver a withering rejoinder, then realized she didn't have one.

There was a knock on the door.

Cynthia took a deep breath, brushed her hands down the front of her dress even though it was already perfectly wrinkle- and lint-free, and opened the door.

"Hello!" Kaarina said. She wore a tight white tube top, a silver miniskirt, and the same gladiator sandals as last night. Her fingernails and toenails were painted bright pink. Over her shoulder hung her backpack, which bulged with something big and heavy and boxy.

Calvin and Cynthia couldn't help but be acutely aware that more of Kaarina's body was exposed than concealed. And that Kaarina seemed perfectly comfortable with that. She strode into the room with the casual, unselfconscious grace of lioness. Calvin and Cynthia had never seen a woman who was so clearly at home in her own body. Cynthia, who kept fighting the urge to tug down the hem of her dress, couldn't help feeling envious and somehow juvenile in comparison.

"Um, I hope you found your way here okay," Cynthia said.

"Directions were perfect," Kaarina said. "And you were right: Boys downstairs let me in with no questions. Only problem was they make whistles at me and want to talk at me and slow me down."

"I can see why," Calvin said. "You look great."

"Thank you." She gestured at his outfit. "You do, too." She turned to Cynthia. "And you, too. Very nice dress. You look very pretty."

Kaarina took off her backpack and dropped it onto the bed. The backpack's weight tugged the sheets askew, but Cynthia barely noticed and cared less. Her soul was still resonating from the word "pretty." She couldn't remember the last time anyone had called her that.

Kaarina unzipped the backpack's main compartment and extracted a case of Molson's.

"It is time for party," she announced. She opened the case and handed beers to Calvin and Cynthia, then took out one for herself.

"Here, let me put the rest in the fridge," Cynthia said. She set her beer down, then moved in beside Kaarina to get the case. Kaarina smelled strongly of vanilla. The yummy aroma roused Cynthia's appetite in more ways than one. She felt an insane urge to lean over and lick Kaarina's neck to see if she tasted as good as she smelled.

As Cynthia bent down to pick up the case, she contrived for her bare arm to brush Kaarina's. The brief touch of silky skin sent an electrical tingle coursing through Cynthia's body. She glanced at Kaarina, but was a little disappointed to see that Kaarina was focused on zipping up her backpack and seemed not to have noticed the touch.

Cynthia carried the case to her mini-fridge. She opened the fridge and began to redistribute the items therein—mostly bottled water and fresh veggies—to make room for the beer.

"Where is good to sit?" Kaarina asked.

"Oh, um…" Cynthia looked over her shoulder. Calvin had risen when Kaarina entered, and now the two of them were just standing in the middle of the room, unopened beers in hand. "I guess wherever you want. You're welcome to have the desk chair. It's probably the most comfortable seat. Or there's the bed, if—"

"Floor is good." Kaarina began to kneel down.

"Are you sure?"

"I am used to sitting on floor. Like I tell you last night: My little apartment has no furnitures. Only bed and two tables."

"I feel like a bad host," Cynthia muttered. Having cleared a suitable cube-shaped space in the middle of the mini-fridge, she slid the case of beer inside, then shut the door.

"The carpet looks clean," Calvin said, sitting down next to Kaarina. "Hell, it's your carpet, so it's probably the cleanest carpet in the whole dorm."

"It's not like I had it steam-cleaned or something, but if you guys are okay with it…" She shrugged, then grabbed her beer and sat down alongside them so that the three of them formed a triangle on the floor.

Calvin and Kaarina had already cracked open their beers and were drinking away. Cynthia didn't really care for beer, but she didn't want to look like an utter milquetoast in front of Kaarina, so she pulled the tab and took a swallow. The bitter taste made her wince.

"Books," Kaarina exclaimed. She was looking at Cynthia's bookcase, which stood nearby. "You have many, many books." She leaned over to read some of the titles on the spines. As she did so, her legs sprawled out a bit, and the bottom of her skirt inched up, which enabled Calvin and Cynthia to glimpse the pale shape of her panties in the shadows between her thighs. Kaarina either didn't realize this, or simply didn't care. Calvin and Cynthia tried to pretend they didn't notice, but couldn't keep their eyes from flicking down there every few seconds.

"There are many fictions," Kaarina said. "And…" She squinted and leaned over a little more. The skirt rose a fraction higher. *"Sex and the Paranormal?"* Kaarina looked over her shoulder at Cynthia.

Cynthia tore her eyes from Kaarina's crotch. "Oh, um, yeah. It's—it's an interesting book."

"I am sure it is," she said with a lascivious grin. She returned to the shelf. "Oh, and you have *Complete Books of Charles Fort!* I have been wanting to read that for very long time."

Cynthia and Calvin looked at each other. Calvin raised his eyebrows questioningly. Cynthia nodded. This was the perfect opportunity to segue into their work as anomaly investigators.

"You're interested in paranormal stuff like that, huh?" Calvin asked.

"Oh, yes!" Kaarina said. "Very much!"

"Well, can you keep a secret?"

Kaarina sat up straight, all attention, the bookshelf forgotten. Darkness reclaimed the space between her legs.

"Of course!" she said earnestly. "I keep many secrets."

"Well, Cyn and I—we plan to investigate strange phenomena once we're done with school."

"Actually, we kind of already do, a little bit," Cynthia said.

"Yeah."

Kaarina looked back and forth from one of them to the other. "You are being true with me?"

"Yep," Calvin said. "Totally true."

A huge grin spread across Kaarina's face. "Wow! I knew two of you were something special, but this is much more than I expect. You must tell me more! How did you get into this? And why? And what investigatings have you already done?"

"Uh, well..." Calvin glanced at Cynthia. "I guess we should just start at the beginning."

"Yeah," Cynthia said.

They spent the next half hour telling Kaarina the whole story. They told her about Cynthia's sister Emily's abduction, about their unofficial search for Emily, about befriending Cynthia's reclusive neighbor Robert May and learning about the Collection, about the death of Emily's killer and the strange events that surrounded it, about Mr. May's own death and how he had bequeathed his house, the Collection, and a million dollars to Calvin, plus a hundred thousand each to Cynthia and several other people.

"You are millionaire," Kaarina said, regarding Calvin with surprise. "I am impressed."

Calvin shrugged. "Well, technically I'm not a millionaire yet. Thanks to certain stipulations in Mr. May's will, I won't come into full possession of the inheritance until I graduate from college. And when I do get it, taxes'll strip away enough of it that I won't actually be a real millionaire."

"Even so, it is very impressing. So what are some of objects in Collection?"

"Um..." Calvin looked at Cynthia. "What's something cool?"

"The Porsche," Cynthia said. "Part of the Porsche James Dean crashed and died in. It's said to be cursed. Uh, you know who James Dean is, right?"

"Yes, American movie star," Kaarina said. "Very handsome."

"Plus there's a severed green human hand that supposedly can travel through time," Calvin said.

"Green hand that travels in time?" Kaarina said. "For serious?"

"Maybe," Cynthia said. "We read the file on it three times and I still don't entirely understand what it was all about."

"Neither do I," Calvin said. "And I don't think Mr. May did either, frankly. Oh, and there's also what's supposed to be a Yeti pelt. It's kind of dirty white, with gray streaks."

"And it smells like old cat piss."

"Yeah. And there's a copy of the *Necronomicon*. You know, that tome of ancient magical lore that H. P. Lovecraft wrote about?"

"But that was lie," Kaarina said. "It was fiction. It was story he make up in his brain."

"That's what I always thought, until we found an old worm-eaten copy in the Collection. According to the file, Mr. May ran across it while investigating a bizarre murder in Mexico in 1966. It sure looks real. If it's not, someone went to a whole lot of trouble to produce a really amazing fake."

"And what about two of you? You said you have done investigatings of your own already?"

"Actually, you know the murder a few days ago?" Cynthia said. "We're investigating that."

Kaarina cocked her head and gave a puzzled frown. "But that was only murder. Is there strangeness involved?"

They filled her in on the investigation, starting with the discovery of the body and ending with their perusal of Mr. May's file on the Ur-Tarot. Calvin handed Kaarina the copies he had made of the cards and the file, and she examined them while Calvin and Cynthia watched and drank their beers.

"Amazing," Kaarina said, handing the folder back to Calvin. "Can I see real cards and Collection?" She gave him a cutely beseeching smile. "Please?"

"Of course," Calvin said. "But not right now. Not tonight." He held up his beer can and shook it back and forth. The liquid inside sloshed. "No drinking and driving. Besides, it'll take a while to show you the whole Collection. How about tomorrow? We could make an afternoon of it."

Kaarina bounced in place excitedly, her eyes and smile huge, her breasts jouncing distractingly in their cotton sling. "That would be great!" Her smile faded and she frowned with concern. "But what about investigation? I do not want to stop you from catching crook and finding new card."

"Frankly, we're at kind of an impasse. We're not really sure what to do next." He shrugged, a little embarrassed. "I mean, this *is* our first real investigation, after all."

"I can help!" Kaarina said. "I am investigator, too, remember? I solve hotel crime. I take many criminal justice classes."

"Oh, that's right," Cynthia said. "Maybe you're just what we need."

She nodded vigorously. "I think I am. It is destiny that brings us together."

Cynthia smiled. "I think you might be right."

"So do you have any thoughts about what our next move should be?" Calvin asked Kaarina. "We've told you all there is to tell. What do you suggest?"

Kaarina sipped her beer in silence while she pondered this. Finally she said, "Go back to beginning. Return to scene of crime and look for clues that were missed first time. And there is question about how killer got out of building, yes? Maybe killer did not leave out of front door or upstairs door. Maybe he left other way."

"The only other exit we saw was padlocked," Cynthia said.

"What about roof exit?"

Calvin and Cynthia looked at each other.

"There's a roof exit?" Calvin said.

"I do not know," Kaarina said. "I am saying to look. And basement, too. Does building have basement?"

"Beats me."

Kaarina slapped her palm on her bare knee. "Then we must go there and look."

"You mean right now?" Cynthia said.

"Why not? It is short walk."

"I'm not sure, they might have reopened it already. It might be in use tonight. And even if it's not, it might be locked tight."

Kaarina shot to her feet. "Let us find out."

Chapter 13

A cluster of dreadlocked students were hacky sacking right in front of the Moma, making it impossible to go in through the main entrance without being seen, so Calvin, Cynthia, and Kaarina went into the Student Center and headed up to the second floor. As expected, the couches in the long hallway were only lightly tenanted, and no one at all was sitting near the door to the stairwell that led to the Moma's lobby. As they strode down the hallway, Calvin and Cynthia kept fearing that Brandon's head would pop up over the back of one of the couches, as had happened the other day, but they made it to the stairwell without incident.

They paused at the top of the stairs and listened. They could faintly hear the hacky sackers laughing in the plaza, but the Moma itself was dead silent.

They crept down the stairs as quietly and cautiously as possible. They paused again at the door that led to the lobby and listened. They heard nothing except the hacky sackers. They cracked the door and peeked through it. The lobby was empty. They crossed the lobby to the door that led to the auditorium. Calvin tried the knob. It was locked.

"Crap," he said. "I guess they've started locking things up a bit more carefully."

"Can you blame them?" Cynthia said.

"No, but it kind of kills our plans. What do we do now?"

Kaarina had brought her backpack with her. Calvin

and Cynthia assumed she had done so because she might want to head straight home after their investigation of the Moma. But now they found that wasn't the reason at all: While they had been talking, Kaarina had taken off the backpack, unzipped the compartment in front, and pulled out a small black leather case.

"What's that?" Cynthia asked.

"Watch," Kaarina said.

She knelt down in front of the door, then unzipped the case and laid it open on the floor. Inside were rows of skinny metal implements that looked a lot like dentists' tools.

"Are those what I think they are?" Calvin said.

"Probably," Kaarina said.

"You've got a lock-picking kit?" Cynthia asked.

"It is good thing to have for solving of mysteries." She examined the tools, then pulled out two of them. She began to work them into the keyhole.

"And you have experience using them?" Cynthia said.

"I am full of surprises."

Calvin looked at Cynthia and said, "She is full of coolness, too."

"Much coolness," Cynthia agreed.

The lock clicked.

"It is done," Kaarina said.

"That was fast," Calvin said.

"It was not good lock." She put the tools back into the case, zipped it shut, and put it back into her backpack. "Now let us look at crime scene."

The auditorium was a lot darker than it had been the last time Calvin and Cynthia were in here: The only lights that were on now were the guide lights on the steps that led down to the stage and a row of dim work lights above the stage.

"We probably shouldn't turn any lights on," Cynthia said. "Someone might notice."

"How?" Calvin asked. "I don't think there are any windows in the auditorium, are there?"

"No, but don't forget, there're the front and back doors. Someone might see light through the cracks. Besides, I think we can see well enough, so why risk it, right?"

They descended the steps to the edge of the stage. Like before, the curtain was up, but this time the stage was bare. The stench of some kind of citrus-scented cleaning product overhung everything. The floor in the center of the stage was slightly lighter than the rest of the stage floor. From the right angle and with the light hitting just right, they could make out the curving lines from a cleaning brush in the finish on the stage floor.

"It's weird to think that a dead guy was right there just a couple of days ago," Calvin said, staring at the lighter patch of floor.

"Yeah," Cynthia said.

Kaarina planted her hands on the stage floor, then pushed herself up and hooked one leg over the front edge of the stage. The leg she had lifted was the one closest to Calvin and Cynthia, and as she boosted herself onto the stage with a grunt, they got a brief but very clear view up her skirt. Her panties were pink, they saw. And they were thongs. Calvin and Cynthia blinked in awe at the scrap of pink fabric pulled taut across the contours of her pudendum, and at the full, round globes of her ass trembling with her exertions.

Kaarina stood up and patted dust from her hands and legs, then glanced back at Calvin and Cynthia. "Are you coming?"

"Practically," Calvin muttered.

Cynthia choked back a laugh and elbowed him lightly in the ribs.

"Knock it off," she whispered. Then to Kaarina she called out, "We're on our way."

They followed her up onto the stage. The three of them spent a while examining the floor in search of debris or marks or stains, but there was nothing to see.

Kaarina led them backstage. Back here it was much darker. The dim glow from the work lights faded to virtually nothing. The props and scenery were visible only as vague dark shapes against a deeper darkness.

Kaarina took off her backpack again and this time pulled out a small silver flashlight.

"It looks like she's already got her own Batman utility belt," Cynthia told Calvin.

"I bet she doesn't have salt, though," Calvin said.

"I don't know if I'd brag about that."

They began to explore backstage, Kaarina in the lead as she slowly swept the flashlight beam back and forth, Calvin and Cynthia following close behind. Things hadn't changed much since Calvin and Cynthia had been back here the other day. The padlock was still on the exit door. Kaarina checked it anyway. It was locked tight.

They moved on. Soon Kaarina stopped dead, the flashlight beam trained on a door in a far corner.

"Where does that go?" she asked.

"I don't know," Calvin said. "We didn't notice that before."

They headed over to the door. Up close, they saw that there was a small sign on the wall next to it that read, "Basement."

Kaarina tried the knob. The door was unlocked. She opened it and shone the flashlight down the staircase on the other side. All they could see at the bottom was a stretch of concrete floor and a large cardboard box with the word "GELS" scrawled on the side in black marker. There was a light-switch on the wall at the top of the stairwell. Calvin switched it on. Fluorescent lights stuttered to life down below.

"Should we really be turning the lights on?" Cynthia said.

Calvin shrugged. "Why not? The light from down there won't be visible under the doors. Besides, if we're gonna search this whole place, it'll take forever with just a single flashlight."

"Yeah, I guess."

They went down. The basement was a labyrinth of theater-related items—boxes of spotlight bulbs, coils of rope, folded-up curtains, wardrobes full of old costumes, shelves full of props, bits of sets from former plays. Many of the items were gray with dust and had clearly been sitting down here untouched for many years. In one area they came across a stack of half a dozen old mattresses. They couldn't figure out why the mattresses were there until they looked up and saw a hinged trap door in the ceiling overhead. A short metal ladder hung down next to the trap door.

"Door could have been used by killer," Kaarina said. "Perhaps he surprised dead man by going up through it. Or perhaps he used it to flee away."

"Maybe," Cynthia said. "But where would he have gone from here?"

"We keep looking."

They did. Soon they rounded the corner of a long

wooden wardrobe and saw a metal door in the far wall. A sign on the door read, "Mechanical Room - Authorized Personnel Only."

Calvin tried the door. It was locked. He looked at Kaarina. "Think you can work your lock-picking magic again?"

"Of course," she said, taking off her backpack. "I am girl of much magic."

She was right. The door was open in less than twenty seconds. They went inside and turned on the lights. The room contained a generator, an air conditioning unit, and several other large machines. Along one wall were steel shelves bearing tools and paint and rags. Along another was the building's electric panel. Thick insulated pipes and electrical cables extended along the ceiling toward the far wall where they exited the room over the top of a chain-link gate. Beyond the gate the pipes and cables stretched away down the slanted ceiling of a stone stairwell and disappeared into the blackness beyond. A metal sign on the gate read, "Main Tunnel."

"Tunnel?" Cynthia said.

"Oh," said Calvin. "So *that's* how he got away."

"A tunnel?"

"The steam tunnels. Remember? Miss Starr, our Freshmen Orientation instructor—she talked about them."

"Oh, yeah! That's right. I forgot about that." She stared at the chain-link gate in wonder. Then the wonder transformed into dismay. "They lead all over the campus, though, don't they?"

"Yeah. Pretty much everywhere."

"What do we talk about?" Kaarina said. "Steam tunnels?"

"They were constructed way back when the campus was built nearly a hundred years ago," Calvin said. "They provide access to the pipes that supply all the buildings with heat. They lead from the Heating Plant to pretty much every other building on campus."

Kaarina nodded. "We must look in them, then."

"Yeah, but..." Cynthia shook her head. "I mean, they're vast. We could get lost in there."

"They connect with other basements of other buildings, yes?"

"Well, yeah, but—"

"Then if we find us lost, we go up at different basement and I get us out. I can get us through any door we find."

"You make a persuasive argument."

The chain-link gate was locked, but Kaarina swiftly changed that. After putting away her lock-picking kit, she pulled out her flashlight and swung open the gate.

"Be careful with the flashlight," Cynthia told her. "Don't shine it up too much. I remember Miss Starr telling us that those grates that you see in the ground next to the campus sidewalks—those lead straight up from the tunnels. So if we're not careful someone might be able to see the light down here."

Kaarina nodded. "I will be careful."

They descended the stairs. The air grew warm and humid and suffused with a damp, earthy odor. When they reached the bottom of the stairs, they paused and Kaarina shone the flashlight around.

They stood in an old brick tunnel whose sides were lined with insulated pipes, some as thick as tree trunks, others as thin as baseball bats. Here and there valves and meters protruded from the pipes. The bricks in the walls were cracked and stained, and the mortar between them was crumbled and in some places missing entirely. Cobwebs festooned the bare, dusty light bulbs that hung from the ceiling at fifteen-foot intervals. The corners of the plain cement floor were littered with the husks of countless generations of beetles and spiders. In either direction the tunnel extended away into darkness, its ends beyond the flashlight's reach. On the wall next to the stairwell that they had come down was a large metal sign that read, "39M."

"This is creepy," Cynthia muttered.

"Yeah," Calvin said with a grin. "I can totally see why people would play *Dungeons and Dragons* in places like this."

"*Dungeons and Dragons?*"

"Yeah. I remember hearing about some big incident in the seventies or eighties where some college students at MIT or someplace were playing *D&D* in the steam tunnels under their campus, and one of them went crazy and killed himself down there." He shrugged. "Or something like that. I don't remember all the exact details. But I can totally see why they'd want to play in a place like this. I mean, I'm half expecting zombies or giant rats to come lunging out of the darkness."

Cynthia shot him a cold, humorless glance. "Could we not talk about stuff like that right now?"

"Sorry."

"Let's just—"

A series of loud, sharp bangs echoed out of the darkness. All three of them jumped and looked wildly around. Kaarina's swiftly moving flashlight beam sent long, sharp shadows veering everywhere. Before they could even tell which direction the sounds were coming from, the bangs stopped.

"Shit," Cynthia hissed. "Someone else is down here."

"But where?" Kaarina said. "I do not—"

A ticking sound grew audible nearby. Kaarina aimed the flashlight at the spot the sound was coming from. It was a pipe.

"Oh, I get it," Calvin said. "It's just the pipes. They must be, like, expanding and contracting with the heat."

As if to confirm this, the ticking pipe emitted a clank loud enough to make them jump again.

"Oh, this is gonna be loads of fun," Cynthia said.

"We'll get used to it," Calvin said. "I hope."

"Which way should we go?" Kaarina asked. She shone the flashlight left, then right. The corridor looked more or less identical in either direction.

"Right," Calvin said. "That's north, and there are more buildings that way. To the south, there're only some dorms and the math and science buildings."

"And the library," Cynthia said.

"Yeah, but just about everything else is to the north, so I think that would be the most logical way to go."

"We go that way, then," Kaarina said. "We go slowly, and we look out for recent signs of people down here. Clues."

"Gotcha."

They headed north down the tunnel. Some of the pipes stuck out a few feet from the walls, and many of the pipes were hot enough to burn, which meant that the three of them had to travel single file down the center of the tunnel. Kaarina went first with the flashlight, then Calvin, then Cynthia. Even though they stayed as far from the hot pipes as possible, they were soon filmed with sweat.

The pipes continued to emit sporadic clanks, clicks, groans, hisses, and bangs. Despite what Calvin had said earlier, it wasn't easy to get used to the sounds. Not in a dark, isolated tunnel with a murderer at large. Not when mistaking the tick of a furtive footfall for the tick of a hot pipe could literally be a matter of life and death. Cynthia, who was at the rear of the line, had it worst, with only shadows at her back and no flashlight to illuminate them. She couldn't help glancing over her shoulder every few seconds, half sure she'd see a sinister figure shambling out of the murk. Why the hell had Calvin had to mention zombies? Damn it.

Periodically the darkness beyond Kaarina's flashlight was broken by a cluster of small squares of dim light in the tunnel's ceiling. These were the grates Miss Starr had mentioned. The light was the radiance from the nearby dorms and the cast-iron pole lamps that lit the campus paths. On the tunnel floor beneath each grate was another, smaller grate to catch the rain and snowmelt that dripped down from above. Kaarina shone her flashlight through a few of these floor grates and found that they drained into a shallow stone channel thick with slime. The floor grates were all cemented into place and impossible to remove.

Here and there side tunnels branched off from the main one. Some of them were of the same dimensions as the main tunnel. Others were narrower and had ceilings so low an average person would have had to stoop to go down them. The trio decided to ignore these side tunnels for now and stick only to the main tunnel.

Occasionally instead of a side tunnel there was a stairwell that led up to another metal gate that led to another mechanical room. On the wall beside each stairwell was a large metal sign with a number and the letter M on it like the one next to the stairs that led to the Moma's mechanical room. The numbers were decreasing as they headed north toward the Heating Plant.

"Must be a code that signifies which mechanical room the stairs lead to," Calvin said. "Each building must have its own number."

"Why not just list the building's name?" Cynthia said.

"I don't know. Maybe it's in case they change the name of the building. Remember how they changed the name of the Financial Affairs Office to the Chalfont Center when President Chalfont retired last year? This way, using just a number, they don't have to make up a new sign."

"That makes sense. Though it implies a lot more foresight than you would expect from college bureaucrats."

After nearly fifteen minutes of slow, careful exploration, during which the trio saw no signs of recent activity, Kaarina let out a gasp, then switched off her flashlight and flung out a hand to stop Calvin. Cynthia, suddenly in darkness, bumped right into him.

"What are you—" she began.

"Shh," Kaarina whispered. "Look."

Two hundred feet ahead, a large, hazy circle of light shone on the brick wall on the left-hand side of the tunnel. The light slowly grew smaller and more focused, and Calvin and Cynthia spied a faint glow emanating from a side corridor across the tunnel from the circle of light. The light, they realized, was coming from a flashlight shining into the main corridor. And the way the circle was getting smaller and tighter, and the glow from the side corridor was growing brighter, whoever was holding the flashlight was approaching the main tunnel.

The trio had stopped beside a stairwell marked "17M," and now they quickly ducked into it, then peeked around the corner to watch.

The person holding the flashlight emerged into the main tunnel. Whoever it was was just a vague shadowy shape behind the light. He or she paused briefly, the beam still trained on the brick wall across the tunnel. If the person turned south, Calvin, Cynthia, and Kaarina could be in big trouble. Even as skilled as she was, Kaarina probably wouldn't be able to pick the lock at the top of the stairs before the flashlight-bearer reached them.

After one long, tense moment, the person turned north and headed away from them, his or her figure a black mass backlit by the flashlight, like the moon during a solar eclipse. He or she moved quickly, with the swift-footed assurance of someone familiar with the tunnels.

"We must follow," Kaarina whispered.

"It might just be a maintenance man," Cynthia said.

"At ten o'clock at night?" Calvin said. "And carrying a flashlight, when there are light-bulbs every fifteen feet? No, this is someone who wants to advertise their presence about as much as we do."

"It could be one of your suicidal D&D players."

"Could be. Let's find out."

They slunk forward. They tried to keep pace with the mystery man or woman, but it was impossible. Because turning on their flashlight would alert the mystery person to their presence, they had to travel in darkness, which meant they had to move slowly and with great care lest they scald themselves on a hot pipe. As a result, the mystery person swiftly drew farther and farther ahead of them.

Suddenly the distant flashlight beam swerved sharply to the left and vanished. Or so it seemed at first; peering into the darkness, they could just make out dim radiance lighting up a stone archway, apparently the mouth of a side tunnel. The radiance grew dimmer and dimmer and then disappeared completely. A faint bang echoed down the tunnel. It didn't sound like a pipe. It sounded more like a door.

"Come on," Kaarina said. She switched her flashlight back on, but kept the beam trained on the floor a couple of feet ahead of them, which produced just enough light for them to navigate by but not enough to be seen by anyone in the side corridor up ahead.

As they drew near the spot where the flashlight-bearer had vanished, Kaarina said, "Hold on," then switched off the flashlight.

Blackness swallowed them. The only visible light was the faintly glowing squares of a ceiling grate a hundred yards behind them. There wasn't the slightest trace of light from the archway the flashlight-bearer had headed through. They heard no sounds except for the occasional clunk or click of a pipe.

"I think it is safe," Kaarina said.

She switched the flashlight back on, and they hurried to the archway.

It wasn't a tunnel, they discovered. It was one of the flights of stone steps leading up to a mechanical room. The metal sign on the wall next to the stairs read, "14M."

They went up the steps. The gate at the top was locked, but Kaarina picked it quickly, and they entered the mechanical room, which was pretty much identical to the one in the Moma's basement. Though the room was kept at a fairly warm temperature, it felt blessedly chilly after the hot tunnels. The trio's sweat swiftly cooled and dried, and goosebumps rose up on their skin. The girls' nipples stood out like bullets under their clothes.

They crossed the room to the door that led to the main part of the basement of whatever building they were in. Kaarina turned off the flashlight again. No light shone under the crack at the bottom of the door. She turned the light back on. Calvin flipped the latch and opened the door, and Kaarina shone the flashlight through the doorway.

The basement was full of old desks, chairs, file cabinets, and other articles of bland institutional furniture. No one was in sight. They soon found a stairwell leading up to a door.

They paused at the door, and once again Kaarina turned off the flashlight. This time light shone through the gap at the bottom of the door. They put their ears to the wood and listened. They heard nothing.

Kaarina grasped the knob, turned it slowly and quietly, then cracked the door. They peered through the crack. Their eyes widened.

They were looking at the main first-floor hallway of Chandler Hall. To the right of the door was the drinking fountain Calvin and Cynthia had stopped at countless times for a sip of water. Never once during all of those sips had they taken any notice of the plain wooden door an arm's length away. Across the hallway and about ten feet to their left was Chandler's lobby. At its far end a pair of glass doors looked out onto the parking lot, a sea of dark asphalt lit by rows of sodium-vapor lamps. On the left side of the lobby were the stairs where Kaarina had been sitting the other day. No one was in sight. Everything was silent.

Kaarina opened the door wider to step out into the hallway, but then immediately gasped and pulled it back until it was open only a crack.

"What's wrong?" Cynthia whispered.

"Look," Kaarina said, pointing at the stairs.

The stairs ascended toward the far side of the lobby, but then reversed direction at a half-landing halfway up. A man was descending the upper flight of stairs. He wore a dark-brown overcoat and a fedora, and held a black briefcase in one hand. A fringe of lank white hair was visible under the fedora's brim. From the doorway where the trio watched, the man's face could be seen only in one-quarter profile, but even so, Calvin and Cynthia found his white hair and droopy jowls strikingly familiar.

"Is that who I think it is?" Calvin said.

Indeed, just then the man reached the landing and turned to descend the lower flight of steps, which brought his face into full view.

"Professor Kranhauser," Cynthia said.

"Who?" Kaarina asked.

"He teaches our Intro to Philosophy class," Calvin said.

"Maybe he was just working late," Cynthia said.

"Maybe. But I think we should follow him."

When Kranhauser reached the bottom of the stairs, he turned, presenting his back to them, and headed for the entrance. He pushed through the glass doors and vanished outside.

Kaarina started to open the door again, then promptly drew back inside again.

"Another one," she whispered.

A second man, this one gray-haired, was creeping down the stairs. He wore a white shirt with the sleeves rolled up, and black slacks. He moved with great care, planting his feet on each step as softly as possible to keep from making any noise. When he rounded the landing and headed down the lower flight of steps, the trio goggled in surprise.

"That is Professor Byrne," Kaarina whispered.

Byrne stopped three steps from the bottom and slowly and cautiously peered over the railing at the entrance. Seeing no one in sight, he leaped down the last few steps and hurried over to the doors. He flattened himself against the wall next to one of the doors, then peeked outside.

In the parking lot an engine roared to life. Byrne ducked out of sight a moment before headlights swept across the doorway. A big gray SUV drove past the doors and headed out of the lot. Byrne peeked outside again, then opened the door and darted out. Ten seconds later a car door slammed and a second car zoomed out of the lot, streaking past the doors so fast it was identifiable only as small and red.

After waiting a couple more seconds to make sure no other professors would creep into view, Calvin, Cynthia, and Kaarina emerged from the doorway and crossed the hall to the lobby. They looked out the doors. The parking lot was empty.

"What the hell was that all about?" Cynthia asked. "Do you think it was one of *them* in the steam tunnels?"

"I think yes," Kaarina said. "But which one? And why does Professor Byrne follow your philosophy professor?"

"I don't know," Calvin said.

"Offices of professors are upstairs. We could take quick look inside."

"They're probably locked," Cynthia said.

"That is not problem." Kaarina patted her backpack.

"Yeah, don't forget we've got the lock-picking queen on our side," Calvin told Cynthia.

Cynthia gave a soft, grunting laugh. "Why does it seem like every time we investigate something, it winds up involving illegal trespass?"

"Occupational hazard," Calvin said.

They ascended the stairs, moving slowly and quietly in case any other professors were working late, though that didn't seem likely given the lack of cars in the parking lot. The second floor was as still and silent as the first. The hallway stretched away in either direction, its walls lined with wooden doors sporting frosted-glass windows with brass nameplates underneath.

Professor Byrne's office was directly across the hall from the top of the stairs. While Calvin and Cynthia stood watch, Kaarina squatted down and got out her lock-picking kit.

This time her magic didn't seem to be working. The seconds ticked past while she labored at the lock. Then the seconds turned into a minute. Kaarina scowled and muttered a few words in Finnish that Calvin and Cynthia felt fairly certain they wouldn't find in the vocabularies in their Finnish books. Kaarina swapped out one of the tools that she had been using for another with a finer and more acutely angled tip. Another minute ticked past. Calvin and Cynthia were beginning to wonder if Kaarina would have to give up in defeat when the lock clacked. Kaarina let out a breath and stood up.

"That was very hard one," she said. "Much newer and better lock. Professors need more secureness than pipes and machines, it would seem."

After a last glance up and down the hallway, Kaarina opened the door. The office was dark and unoccupied. They slipped inside, shut the door, then switched on the light.

Byrne's office was neat and tidy and almost Spartan. His books, most of which were about the Early Middle Ages, were arranged alphabetically on the bookshelves.

The desk was practically bare, with only a computer, a sheet-a-day calendar, and a coaster occupying its spotless surface. The few decorative knickknacks—a snow-globe containing the Tower of London, a pewter knight on horseback, a little man made of pipe cleaners—were stationed in out-of-the-way corners. A framed print of a woodcut of Saint George battling the dragon hung on the wall behind the desk.

"Wow," Calvin said to Cynthia. "I think he's even more anal-retentively neat than you are."

"You think anyone who's less of a slob than you are is anal-retentive," she replied.

They searched the office. A file cabinet next to the door contained only class-related paperwork. The wastebasket was empty. Nothing was marked on any upcoming day on the calendar. Most of the desk drawers contained nothing of interest—more paperwork, sundry office supplies, a pair of leather driving gloves, a bag of cough drops—but in the bottom drawer, atop a stack of printouts of articles about the Merovingians, were copies of every issue of the *Daily Ames Record* that had been published since the murder of Judd Skerrit. The latest one had been folded open to the article about the murder.

"Interesting," Calvin said. "He seems to be avidly following the murder."

"So is half the campus, though," Cynthia said.

"Yeah, but he's saving copies of the paper. They say killers like to keep track of the police investigations of their crimes."

"Maybe. But that seems like kind of a leap based on pretty scanty evidence. And it doesn't explain why he was following Kranhauser."

"Maybe we find something in Kranhauser's office that

will explain," Kaarina said.

They left Byrne's office, making sure to turn out the light and lock the door behind them, then headed to Kranhauser's office at the far north end of the hallway. Every office along the way was shut tight, and the frosted glass windows were dark. Calvin, Cynthia, and Kaarina seemed to be the only people in the building.

At Kranhauser's door they repeated the procedure, with Calvin and Cynthia standing guard while Kaarina worked at the lock. All of the offices used the same kind of lock, and now that Kaarina knew how to pick it, the job took less than half the time it had taken with Byrne's lock.

They went in and shut the door and flicked on the light. The layout was the same as in Byrne's office, but Kranhauser's office was more cluttered and more heavily decorated. A black metal bust of Nietzsche glowered on the right front corner of the desk. Several framed prints of posters for various Wagner operas—all in German—hung on the walls. A small German flag in a black plastic flag holder sat on the windowsill. The desktop was laden with unruly stacks of papers, scattered pens and pencils, a computer covered with Post-It notes bearing scribbled phrases in German, a coffee mug adorned with a cartoon of a big fish about to eat a littler fish about to eat a littler fish and so on all the way around the mug, and a dog-eared copy of Sartre's *Being and Nothingness.* Calvin flipped through the latter item and discovered that the margins were brimming with penciled annotations, all of them in German. Calvin couldn't understand much of it, but the word "dummkopf" cropped up repeatedly. The drawers in the file cabinet and the desk contained nothing of note.

The three of them were about to give up the search in frustration when Cynthia noticed a strip of paper jutting from the top of the campus phone directory, which sat on one of the bookshelves. On a whim she opened the phone book to the place marked by the paper.

The paper itself was blank. The pages it marked listed the addresses and phone numbers of various nonacademic university departments, such as the Heating Plant, House-keeping, and Maintenance.

"Look at this," Cynthia said. "He's bookmarked the page with the Maintenance Department."

"Does it give the names of employees?" Calvin said, hurrying over for a look. "Is Judd Skerrit listed?"

"No. It just lists managers and supervisors. It lists Lou Guglio, though."

"It gives number for Heating Plant, too," Kaarina said. "Did you not say that is where tunnels come from? Maybe he called them to learn about tunnels."

"Yeah, maybe," Calvin said.

"How does this all add up, though?" Cynthia said. "I mean, Kranhauser has significant phone numbers book-marked. Byrne is avidly following the murder investiga-tion. And he's following Kranhauser, too. But why?"

"I don't know. But remember: Byrne's specialty is Ear-ly Medieval History, which is when the Ur-Tarot cards were made, so he would have a definite interest in them, if only from an academic standpoint. Kranhauser, on the other hand, doesn't seem to have any obvious angle of interest."

"Not true," Kaarina said. She waved an arm at the Wagner posters and the German flag. "He has obvious interest in Germany. And file says cards were made there. Or at least what later became Germany."

"Yeah, that's right," Calvin said. "Good catch."

Kaarina gasped and shook an excited finger at them.

116

"File also says man who killed two brothers had foreign accent. That could be Kranhauser!"

"Holy crap! It could be."

"But what does that mean, then?" Cynthia said. "Did Kranhauser kill Skerrit? If so, why's Byrne following him?"

"Maybe he plays detective like us," Kaarina said.

"He doesn't seem the type. Maybe Byrne's the killer, and Kranhauser's playing detective, but Byrne realized it and now he's following Kranhauser to see how much he knows or to kill him or something."

"Kranhauser's even less likely to play amateur sleuth than Byrne," Calvin said.

"Maybe both do crime together," Kaarina said. "But Kranhauser betrays Byrne and keeps card for self, and now Byrne follows him to learn where card is."

"That's a possibility," Cynthia said.

Calvin shook his head. "There are still way too many unknowns at this point. I don't even want to start speculating until we have more information."

"And how will we get information?" Kaarina asked.

"That's something we'll have to work out." He glanced at the clock on the wall. It was already midnight. "We should probably call it a night. It's late, and I'm tired, and after that trip through the steam tunnels, I'm sweaty and stinky and I need a very long shower. Why don't we give the situation some thought overnight, then we can discuss it when we meet up to take a tour of the Collection tomorrow."

Kaarina grinned and clapped her hands. "I cannot wait! This is all very exciting! I feel like I am in movie!"

Cynthia sighed. "Yeah, well, let's just hope it's one of those movies where the good guys win in the end."

Chapter 14

When Calvin and Cynthia met for lunch in the Food Court at noon the next day, they were buzzing with anticipation. They were scheduled to meet Kaarina at one o'clock and drive her to Calvin's house in May. They couldn't wait to see her reaction to the Collection. More importantly, they couldn't wait to spend a whole day with her.

"I hope my brother doesn't show up," Cynthia said as she emptied a packet of ketchup onto her veggie burger. "Or Violet. Oh, God, if she pops up, it'll probably scare Kaarina away forever."

"I don't think so," Calvin said. "Besides, it's a Saturday, so Violet'll probably be sleeping off a hangover all day."

"Let's hope so."

He took a bite of his chicken soft taco, washed it down with a quick sip of Coke, then said, "So have you given any thought to what we should do vis-à-vis Byrne and Kranhauser?"

"Not really. Maybe we should—"

"Hey hey hey!" said an all-too-familiar voice.

They turned. Brandon Taylor stood beside their table.

"Hey, Brandon," Calvin said.

"Hi," said Cynthia.

"So what's up, guys?" Brandon asked with a small, knowing smile that implied he felt sure that something was indeed up.

"Uh…not much," Calvin said. "Classes and stuff. The usual."

Brandon nodded, that knowing smile still on his face. Then he bent close, and dropping his voice to a whisper, said, "How's the investigation going?"

They gaped at him.

"Investigation?" Calvin said. He looked at Cynthia. "Do you know what investigation he's talking about?"

"No idea," she said.

"Aw, c'mon guys," Brandon said. "I know what's goin' on. I know you're investigating the murder in the Moma." His eyes went distant and his mouth dropped open. "Hey! *Murder in the Moma.* That'd make a fuckin' awesome title. Nice and alliterative."

"Why on Earth do you think we would be investigating that?" Cynthia asked, trying to sound utterly baffled. She didn't think she was doing a very good job of it.

Brandon tutted like someone being forced to explain the obvious. "You guys popped out of the stairwell on the second floor right after it happened and were, like, asking me if I'd seen anyone and all that. I mean, at the time I didn't know about the murder, but once I found out, it all made sense. After all, I know you guys investigate weird shit."

"How do you know—I mean, what makes you think that?" Calvin asked.

"Dude, I'm an artist. That means I pay attention to the world around me. I *observe.*" He pointed at his left eye in demonstration. He reminded them of a leather-clad mime. "I *listen.*" He pointed at his left ear. "And I do it in such a way that I remain unobserved myself so as not to affect what I'm observing." He smiled as if he felt sure he had satisfactorily explained everything.

Calvin and Cynthia looked at each other again.

"I think you're gonna have to explain it a little better than that," Cynthia told Brandon.

"Well, during the course of my observations of the world around me over the years," Brandon said, "I happened to overhear bits and pieces of things you guys said at various times. A little here. A little there. Ever since our senior year of high school, basically. And over time, I was able to put these pieces together."

Cynthia's jaw dropped in outrage. "You've been eavesdropping on us?"

"I wasn't eavesdropping! I just put together little things you said to me, and things I heard you tell other people and each other, and *click*—the pieces formed a picture."

"And what was this a picture of, exactly?" Calvin asked.

Brandon looked around to make sure no one was eavesdropping (or "observing the world around them") and said, "You've got, like, an *X-Files* thing going on, right? You're just like Mulder and Scully." He waved a hand apologetically at Cynthia. "Uh, not that Scully liked the ladies or anything."

Calvin and Cynthia exchanged a glance. A lot passed between them in that glance, but the main thing was the recognition that it was futile to try to deny what Brandon was saying. It was clear that Brandon felt sure of his conclusions, and no amount of protestation would change his mind. All Calvin and Cynthia could do now was damage control.

"Yeah," Calvin said with a sigh. "You're right."

Brandon pumped a fist in the air. "I knew it!"

"But you can't tell *anyone*."

"Not a soul," Cynthia said. "Not even your own mother."

Brandon looked hurt that they would think him capable of such a thing. "I won't, guys. Your secret's safe with me. I mean, I didn't tell that detective guy anything."

"Who? Detective Anderson?"

"Yeah, that was his name. He showed up after I talked to you guys on the second floor the other day, right after the murder. He popped out of the stairwell about ten minutes after you left and was asking me who I was and what I was doing down there and if I'd seen anyone pass through recently."

"And you didn't tell him about us, right?" Calvin said.

Brandon tutted again. "I told you: I'm on your side. I told him I hadn't seen a soul. Well, except for that dude in the cowboy boots who went into the Moma. That's the guy who got whacked, right?"

"Yeah."

"I thought so. Anyway, I figured that the murder was probably an X-File, and that you guys were investigating, so I kept mum. My suspicions were confirmed when I saw you heading back into the Moma last night."

"You saw us?" Cynthia said.

"Yeah. I was up on the second floor again, slacking off in my usual spot down at the end there. And I had to get up to pee, right? And when I came out of the bathroom, I saw you two and this totally smokin'-hot blonde chick disappearing through the door that leads down to the Moma. That was twice I'd seen you nosing around the Moma. I figure this must be one major X-File. So what is it? Men in Black? An organ-sucking mutant serial killer? A mind-altering fungal lifeform?"

"Nothing quite that exciting," Calvin said. "Just a deck

of ancient Tarot cards whose creator was supposedly psychic."

"Psychic, eh? Do the cards show events in the present or something? Does one of them, like, show you guys looking at the card, which shows you looking at the card, and so on in some kind of creepy *Twilight Zone* infinite regress?"

"No. They seem to be just annoyingly vague symbolic pictures like regular Tarot cards."

"Oh. Well, do you need my help for anything? I mean, like, I'd be an asset in certain situations. I can pull my own. I'm smart. I'm clever. I'm lateral-thinking. I mean, I figured out what you guys were up to, didn't I?"

"That you did. But to be honest, the case is kind of on pause at the moment. We're not quite sure where to go from here. If anywhere."

"Oh." Brandon seemed to deflate for a second. Then he perked up again and said, "Can I ask one thing?"

"Sure."

He licked his lips. "Who was that girl? The blonde. Is she, like, seeing anyone?"

Calvin glanced at Cynthia. "Uh…"

"What, is one of you going out with her?"

Cynthia felt her face start to redden, though she wasn't entirely sure why it should. "Not exactly."

Brandon's eyes went wide and a lascivious grin split his face. "Whoa, are you *both* going out with her? Is this, like, some kinky *ménage a trois* kind of thing?"

Cynthia wrinkled her nose. "Ew. No. We're not—it's just—I like *girls*, remember?"

"Yeah, and she's a girl. So?"

She jerked a thumb at Calvin, who was just sitting there with a dreamy, faraway look in his eyes. *"He's* not."

"Well, you don't all have to be involved at the exact same time," Brandon said. "You could, like, take turns or something."

Cynthia stared at him with her mouth agape, too aghast to speak.

Calvin snapped out of his reverie and shook his head. "It's not like that," he told Brandon. "She's just a friend. At the moment." He gave the last three words added weight, hoping Brandon would get the picture.

He did. "Oh! I get it. Still striving for the big score, huh?"

"Basically."

"And you don't want me horning in." He frowned and eyed them with suspicion. "Is she helping out with the case?"

"Kind of."

Brandon stiffened. "Oh."

Calvin had to make a supreme effort of will not to roll his eyes. Now Brandon's feelings were hurt. Lovely. "It's just that she has certain special skills we need."

"Oh?" Brandon's hurt feelings were softened slightly by curiosity.

"Yeah. I mean, for one thing, she knows how to pick a lock. She even has her own lock-picking kit."

"Whoa. That's pretty bad-ass."

"Yeah."

"Oh, I get it! You have, like, a whole bunch of potential operatives, and you call each one into play as you need them based on their strengths!"

Calvin stared at Brandon with an awestruck look.

"Yeah!" he said.

"It's like *Global Frequency*."

"*Yeah!*"

Cynthia eyed them dubiously. "What the hell are you talking about?"

"Global Frequency," Calvin said. "It's a comic book about this organization that helps save the world from various threats."

Cynthia shook her head. "Comic books again. Whenever you two start talking I should just put on headphones or something."

"No, but see, the organization is this network of people all over the world, and each person has some kind of special skill. Like, one's a brilliant biochemist and one's an expert marksman and one's an ace pilot and so on, right? And the different people get called into action only whenever their particular skills are needed."

"I get it now," Brandon told Calvin. "But, hey, you know, I've got lots of skills you can use. I can act, so I'd make a good undercover operative. And I can paint and stuff. And then there's my poetry. You never know when you might need to bring some poetry into play. And I write, too, so I could be your chronicler or something."

"Uh, we don't really want a chronicler," Cynthia said. "We're trying to keep a low profile, remember?"

"Yeah, but I could, like, mask it as fiction. Wouldn't that be cool?"

"Yeah!" Calvin said.

"No!" Cynthia said.

"Uh, we can discuss it later," Calvin said with a glance Cynthia. To Brandon, he said, "I wouldn't worry. I'm sure we'll need your particular skills eventually. It's just a matter of time."

"Awesome. Oh, and speaking of poetry, I've been working on a poem about the two of you."

"About us?" Cynthia said.

"Yeah. Well, more like *inspired* by you and by the crazy shit you guys investigate. I've actually been working on it for a while now, but I didn't want to mention it before since you guys didn't know I know what you do. But now that you know I know, I guess it's safe to tell you. I'm almost done with the poem, too. I'll read it to you once it's finished. It's gonna kick some major fuckin' ass."

"Uh, good. Cool. I can't wait to hear it."

"Well, hey, I gotta go. I'll see you guys later." He leaned toward them and melodramatically whispered, "And good luck with...*The Murder in the Moma.*"

As soon as Brandon was gone, Cynthia said, "You weren't serious about all that, were you?"

"About what?"

"Well, for one thing, that stuff about him being our chronicler?"

"Look, you know Brandon: He writes about everything. I mean, remember that time he wrote a play about our eleventh grade geometry class?"

She chuckled. "Oh, yeah. *The Great Pi Fight.*"

"Right. So you gotta figure that since he already knows about us, it's pretty safe to assume he'll wind up writing about this stuff eventually. This is a democracy, after all; we can't exactly stop him from writing. So ask yourself: Wouldn't you rather be working with him and therefore have at least some control over what he writes, as opposed to letting him work alone and fuck things up in ways we probably can't even imagine?"

"Okay, that is a valid point. But why do I get the impression you just like the idea of having fiction based on our investigations?"

"It has a certain charm, you have to admit."

"Um, no, I don't."

"Okay, fine." He frowned and popped the last of his taco into his mouth.

"And what was all that stuff about a team of operatives with different skills?"

"It's not a bad idea," he said through his mouthful of food. "It could work."

She shook her head.

"I'm serious!" he said. He quickly swallowed his food, then went on: "I mean, we could have someone with breaking and entering skills, like Kaarina. And we could have someone who's good at acting and undercover work. And we could have a guy with computer skills, like some super-hacker or something."

"What super-hacker are we talking about, exactly?"

"Well, no one in particular right now. I'm just saying, we could assemble a loose network of people with diverse skills. It could come in handy."

"And completely kill any chance of maintaining a low profile."

"Come on. We've already got a team of sorts. We've already got your brother and Violet—"

Cynthia snorted. "Yeah, so we've got the stoner and the drunken skank skill-sets accounted for."

"And then there's Kaarina. She's officially one of us now, right? And now Brandon, too."

"Yeah, and the bigger this gets, the more unwieldy it'll get, too. I mean, do you want to investigate anomalies or be an administrator? Because that's what you're gonna have to become if this thing keeps growing at this rate."

"You're exaggerating."

"Maybe, but not by much."

"No, by a lot. I mean, we're six people total. That's not much at all. And it's all friends and relatives. People we can trust. It's not like we're going crazy with it and handing out membership cards on street corners."

She finished off the last few bites of her veggie burger in thoughtful silence.

"I suppose you're right," she said finally. "But only as long as we keep it limited strictly to people we can trust…"

"We will."

"We'd better."

"We will."

She took a few sips of her iced tea, then gave him a sidelong look.

"So, we're both 'striving for the big score,' are we?"

Calvin shrugged.

"I don't know," he said. "Aren't we? I mean, I know I like her. I like her a lot. I certainly wouldn't say no to…whatever."

"Me too. But despite Brandon's little *ménage a trois* idea, there can be only one, you know. I mean, I don't want this getting ugly or anything."

"I know. I don't either. But…" He shrugged again. "I guess we should just agree to let the cards fall where they may, right?"

She laughed softly. "A very apt expression, all things considered. But, yeah, you're right. We need to be mature about this. Calm. Rational."

"Exactly," he said with a dignified nod. "There's absolutely no reason we can't act like adults."

Chapter 15

"And there's our old elementary school," Cynthia enthused, pointing out the passenger window of Calvin's car at the long, low brick building they were passing. She turned and grinned at Kaarina, who sat in the back seat. "That's where I used to beat everyone at the eraser march in second grade."

"What is eraser march?" Kaarina said.

"It was this silly little game Miss Twain would have us play. We had to walk around with chalkboard erasers balanced on our heads, and she would give candy to whoever could carry their eraser on their head the longest without it falling off."

"Yeah," Calvin said. "Cyn always won cuz she has a flat head."

"Shut up," she told him. She turned back to Kaarina. "I think it was Miss Twain's sneaky way to improve our posture."

Kaarina laughed. "That is funny."

Calvin and Cynthia smiled. They had been smiling almost nonstop since they got in the car. They made the drive from Ames to May at least once a week, and the trip had long ago become routine and robotic. They had ceased to really see the sites they passed. Now, though, it was as if they were seeing everything for the first time. The journey that had grown so dull through familiarity now seemed fresh and new because they were sharing it with Kaarina and viewing it through her excited eyes.

After passing the elementary school, Calvin drove them through downtown, most of which consisted of brick business blocks divided into shops and offices.

"There's my dad's bookstore," Cynthia said, pointing at a striped green-and-white awning that read, "Crow Books."

"Oh!" Kaarina said. "Your father owns bookstore. Now I see why you are book girl. Daughter follows in father's steps."

Cynthia laughed. "You can't escape your roots, I guess."

They passed out of downtown, heading south. A small park appeared on their right. A white gazebo sat at the near end of the park. Beyond it were flowerbeds and walking paths and a baseball diamond.

"Very lovely," Kaarina said.

"Yeah," Cynthia said. But her gaze was somber as she watched the park glide by. This was where her sister Emily had met her killer. Even after two years, the pain sometimes still felt fresh.

Calvin turned right onto Oaks Road. The south side of the street was occupied by a few large, widely spaced houses. The north side appeared to be one unbroken stretch of dense woods.

It wasn't entirely unbroken, though. Cynthia soon pointed out a gravel driveway that cut into the woods like a long, narrow scar.

"My parents' house is back there," she said, twisting around to look at Kaarina again. "That's where I grew up."

Kaarina peered into the woods.

"You can't see it from here," Cynthia said. "The woods are too thick, and it's pretty far back.

Kaarina gave Cynthia a smile. "Maybe one day I see

it."

"Yeah," Cynthia said, smiling back. "Maybe." She had a brief but vivid fantasy of introducing Kaarina to her parents as her girlfriend. She imagined her parents' shock and her own pleasure at showing off Kaarina. She imagined making love to Kaarina in her own childhood bedroom.

Kaarina's smile widened as if she somehow knew what Cynthia was thinking. Cynthia swiftly returned her attention to the road ahead of them before Kaarina could see how red her face got.

Farther down Oaks Road they came to a second driveway.

"Here's my place," Calvin announced. He turned down the driveway.

When the woods fell away and the house came into view, Kaarina gasped.

"This is your house?" she said. "It is bigger than I expect. And more beautiful. I am much impressed."

"Most people think it looks creepy," he said. "Like the house in *Psycho.*"

"There is beauty in creepy things."

He grinned over his shoulder at her. "You're my kind of girl."

She grinned back.

Cynthia frowned, not liking this exchange one bit. She reminded herself to be mature and to let the cards fall where they may. She was starting to suspect that was a lot easier said than done, though.

Calvin parked the car, and they headed up the walk to the front porch.

"I'll show you the Tarot cards and the Collection first, since those are the important things," Calvin told Kaarina as he unlocked the front door. "Then maybe if there's time, I can give you the full tour of the house."

They went inside, and Calvin led them down a long hallway lined with paintings. Kaarina regarded the paintings as they passed—rustic farmhouses, wooded lakeshores, golden cornfields—then scrunched up her nose.

"You have much liking for quiet country pictures, I am seeing," she said.

"Huh?" Calvin glanced back and saw what she was looking at. "Oh, no. Those were Mr. May's paintings. Like I told you last night, the house isn't fully legally mine yet, and won't be until I graduate from college. It's being held in a sort of trust until then. So I'm not going to be doing any serious redecorating until then."

"I see. First redecorating must be to get new paintings."

"Yeah, well, I'm with you on that."

The hallway ended at a circular area with a spiral staircase in the center. They headed up the staircase to the second floor, then down the north wing to the Collection room where the Ur-Tarot cards were stored. When Kaarina stepped inside and saw the plethora of weird items crowding the shelves, her jaw dropped.

"Uskomaton," she muttered.

Calvin and Cynthia watched with smiles as Kaarina examined some of the items on the shelves nearest the door: a purple scorpion-like creature in a formaldehyde-filled jar; a yellowed scroll written in an unknown language; a human skull with abnormally long, pointed canines; a jar full of kidney beans, each of which sported a tiny and apparently naturally occurring image of Princess Di's face.

"This is nonbelievable," Kaarina said.

"Well, come on," Calvin said, motioning for her to follow. "Take a look at the Tarot cards first, then you can browse to your heart's content."

Calvin got down the three Ur-Tarot cards and handed them to Kaarina. She studied each one in turn.

"So these are what fussing is about," she said. "They are so old."

"Yeah. Over a thousand years, if Oliver Kidwell was right."

"Amazing." She handed the cards back to him with a grin. Still grinning, she turned and surveyed the room. "Collection is amazing. Whole house is amazing!" She turned back to Calvin and Cynthia. "And two of you are amazing! I know I say it before, but I must say it again: I am so happy I meet two of you!"

"Not as happy as we are," Cynthia said.

"Not even close," Calvin agreed.

The rest of the afternoon passed in the Collection rooms on the second and third floors, with Calvin and Cynthia showing Kaarina items of particular interest and Kaarina gushing nonstop and bustling from stack to stack and devouring countless files and generally behaving like a kid in a candy store. Calvin and Cynthia delighted in her delight. Their cheek muscles hurt from all the smiling they did.

As the day waned, Calvin led them up the last few twists of the spiral staircase to the room at the top of the tower. The room was level with the treetops, and Calvin had timed their visit so that the sun was touching the crowns of the westernmost trees, with the result that the lush green foliage was aglow with sunlight, while the world below was filling with gloom. The view was augmented by a few low clouds, which blazed pink and yellow in the sunshine. The three of them stood at the window and drank in the scenery.

"It is beautiful!" Kaarina said to Calvin. "Thank you for showing me."

"You are more than welcome."

"I love this house so much!" She laid a hand on Calvin's shoulder and leaned against him. "Can I move in with you, please?" she asked in a mock-pleading tone.

At first Calvin had trouble formulating a response. All he could think about was her warm hand pressing on his shoulder, her soft breast brushing his upper arm, her beautiful smiling face only inches from his. Her weight began to pull him toward her, and he instinctively placed his hand on the small of her back to keep his balance. A thrill raced through him when he realized what he had done. Most of his hand was on the fabric of her tank top, but his pinkie lay on her bare skin between the shirt's hem and the top of her jeans. She didn't pull away.

"Sure!" he said with an almost drunken laugh. "There's plenty of space. Way more than I can use." He knew she was probably only joking about moving in, but he desperately hoped he was wrong.

"It's not officially yours yet, don't forget," Cynthia said, fighting back an urge to tear them apart.

Perhaps sensing something in Cynthia's voice, Kaarina smiled at her and then draped an arm over her shoulders.

"You can move in, too," Kaarina said, tugging Cynthia toward her. "We all live together! Plenty of space."

"Uh…" Now it was Cynthia's turn to have her thoughts rattled by Kaarina's touch. She flashed back to Brandon's comment about a *ménage a trois,* and for one dizzying moment she actually entertained the idea. She had an image of Kaarina's face between her legs, Kaarina's tongue lapping vigorously at her clit, while Calvin fucked Kaarina from behind.

Wait. Calvin? Naked?

No. No way. She flung the image into the darkest depths of her mind. Kaarina might talk about needing to experience something before you can know whether you like it or not, but there were some things you didn't have to experience to know you would regret them for the rest of your life.

"Oh, you don't want to live here," Cynthia told Kaarina. "Trust me. I've seen his dorm room. Once he starts living here, this place is gonna be like a trash dump in no time flat."

"Hey," Calvin said. "It's one thing if it's a dorm room. I wouldn't treat my own house like that."

"Color me skeptical."

Kaarina listened to this exchange with a small smile. Then she released her hold on the two of them and patted her belly.

"Does house have food, at least?" she asked. "It is late, and I have great hunger."

"He's got Count Chocula and Funyuns," Cynthia said.

Kaarina cocked her head in puzzlement. "I do not know those things."

"Count yourself lucky. They're not even real food."

"They are so," Calvin protested. "Besides, like I keep saying, I don't actually live here yet, so it seems pretty silly to keep much food here."

"If you're really hungry, we could head to the River-wood Family Restaurant," Cynthia told Kaarina. "It's close by, right on the edge of downtown, and they have a pretty good selection of food, as long as you aren't looking for anything too exotic."

"I am not caring about exotic," Kaarina said. "I care only about putting food in my belly."

"Well, let's go there, then," Calvin said. "I could use some dinner myself. And then maybe we can finally discuss our next move regarding the Ur-Tarot situation."

"Actually," Kaarina said with a sly smile, "I already have idea about that. I will explain while we eat..."

Chapter 16

Three hours later Calvin, Cynthia, and Kaarina sat in Calvin's car, which was parked in the shadowy gap between two streetlamps on Hanley Court, a quiet dead-end street in east Ames. The car's lights were out, and the engine was off. The trio was eyeing 365 Hanley, a one-storey brick house a few doors down from where they sat. According to the Ames University Faculty Directory, the house was Professor Byrne's. The lights were on behind the living room curtains. The driveway was empty. The door of the one-car garage was closed.

"We ready?" Calvin asked. The nervous tremor in his voice suggested that he himself might not be.

"I am ready," Kaarina said with a firm nod.

"Same here," Cynthia said. "Let's do it."

Calvin dug into the pocket of his jeans and pulled out the folded-up sheet of paper on which was scribbled the script they had crafted over dinner. He unfolded the paper and laid it on his thigh. The paper bore a few small red spots of spaghetti sauce from Calvin's dinner. The spots reminded him of blood, which didn't help his nerves any.

He opened a plastic bag that sat in the seat well and took out the electronic voice modulator they had bought at Big Fun Costumes barely twenty minutes ago. The voice modulator resembled a small megaphone and enabled the user to make his voice sound like a monster, a space alien, or a psycho killer. They had tested it in the store and decided to use the space alien setting, which transformed

Calvin's normal tones into an eerie robotic buzz.

He got out his phone and set it to speaker mode. Then, after taking one last, shaky breath, he dialed Byrne's home number. His palms were slick with sweat, and the phone kept wanting to slide around in his grasp.

One ring. Two rings.

"Hello?"

Calvin put the voice modulator to his lips and spoke through it into the phone.

"Greetings, Professor Byrne," Calvin read from the sheet of paper. "Listen closely and listen well."

"What? Who is this?"

"I know about the Tarot situation."

There was an audible gasp from the phone.

"You will come to the Ames Student Center plaza immediately," Calvin went on. "You will sit on the bench around the fountain, and there you will await further instructions. Failure to do this will result in...unpleasant consequences. I look forward to seeing you, professor."

"Wait, I—"

Calvin hung up. He set down the phone and the voice modulator and wiped his palms on the legs of his jeans.

"I hope he falls for it," Calvin said.

"We'll see," Cynthia said.

They watched the house. After twenty seconds a shadow darted across the living room curtain. Thirty seconds after that, the garage door opened, and a red Toyota Camry backed out. In the light that spilled from the garage, they caught a glimpse of Professor Byrne behind the wheel, his face tense and troubled. As he backed out onto Hanley Court, the garage door began to close. Byrne sped off down the street. Calvin waited until the Camry turned north onto Brandywine Road and vanished from sight.

Then he picked up the phone and dialed Byrne's home number again. The phone rang five times and then an answering machine clicked on. Calvin hung up.

"I don't think anyone else is there," he said. "Let's go."

They got out of the car and strode toward Byrne's house. They looked at the houses around them as they went. Lights were on in most of them, but the drapes and blinds were shut, and no one was in sight.

Byrne's porch light was on, which wasn't good. It meant anyone passing by would see them standing at the door.

"You sure we don't want to try to slip in through the back door instead?" Cynthia said as they headed up the driveway.

"We already talked about that," Calvin said. "We'd look even more suspicious if we get seen creeping around the sides or back."

"We must look like we belong at house," Kaarina said. "It is best way. People often do not see what is in plain sight."

"If you say so," Cynthia said, not entirely convinced.

Kaarina smiled and gave Cynthia's shoulder a light squeeze. "Trust me."

Despite her worries, Cynthia couldn't help smiling in return.

They headed up the front walk and ascended the steps to the porch. Calvin rang the doorbell and waited. They knew Byrne wasn't married, but he might still be sharing his house with someone. If someone answered the door, they had a cover story prepared: They were members of the Libertarian Party and were surveying local residents about their political beliefs. They even had a few questions ready.

Calvin rang the bell again, then knocked for good measure.

The house remained silent and still.

"I guess we're good to go," Calvin said. He looked at Kaarina and gestured at the lock. "Work your magic, girl."

Kaarina bent down and studied the lock for a moment, then grunted.

"What?" Calvin said.

"This is new lock. Barely used. See how shiny it is. No scratches or wear."

"Will that make it harder to pick?" Cynthia asked.

"I do not know," Kaarina said. "We find out."

She straightened up and got her lock-picking kit out of her backpack. She took two tools from the kit. Rather than squatting down and keeping her face level with the lock as she had in the past, she remained standing while she inserted the tools into the keyhole. She was trying to look as if she were simply unlocking the door with a regular key. Calvin and Cynthia stood behind her, half shielding her from view from the street.

Kaarina turned and twisted the picks for a minute. Then another minute. Then another minute.

"Are you sure you have the right tools?" Cynthia asked.

"Yes, yes," Kaarina said. "Problem is, I am not used to doing locks at angle like this. I am used to being lower. Plus this is new model of lock, and it is very good model."

"Well, just keeping working at it," Calvin said. "And try to look casual."

The drone of an approaching engine grew audible. Calvin and Cynthia looked down the street. A blue pickup truck had just turned onto Hanley and was slowly heading their way. Kaarina glanced at the truck, then redoubled her efforts. She wiggled, she levered, she twisted. The lock remained locked.

The truck drew closer and closer, and its headlights grew brighter and brighter, bathing the porch in light. Despite Calvin's injunction to look casual, he and Cynthia stood stiff as statues, their eyes tracking the truck. Kaarina kept working at the lock.

The truck rolled past. They saw that the driver was an older guy with silver hair and glasses. His eyes were on the road ahead. He didn't seem to have noticed the trio on the porch. The garage door of one of the houses on the turnaround at the end of the block started sliding up on its track.

Calvin and Cynthia slumped with relief as the truck pulled into the garage and the garage door began to descend.

There was a sharp clack beside them.

"It is done," Kaarina said. She opened the door. They slipped into the vestibule.

They had had some lingering fears that someone might be at home, but the moment they heard the silence of the house's interior, they knew the place was unoccupied.

While Kaarina shut the door behind them, Cynthia spotted something on the floor right in front of the door.

"What's that?" She squatted down to look at it. A moment later Calvin and Kaarina joined her.

It was a playing card. The queen of spades. It lay faceup on the black welcome mat.

"That's weird," Calvin said. He turned and looked at the front door, thinking that maybe someone had dropped it through the mail slot. But there wasn't a mail slot. He remembered seeing a mailbox on a post beside the curb.

"That's a bad-luck card, isn't it?" Cynthia said.

"Yeah, unlucky queen of spades," Calvin said. He slid the tip of his fingernail under the edge of the card and flipped it over to see if there was anything on the back. There wasn't, except the card's normal blue-and-white Rider Back design which featured a double-ended image of a cherub riding a bicycle.

"Did he drop it, do you think?" Cynthia asked. "Or was this put here on purpose for some reason?"

"I don't know," Calvin said. He flipped the card back to its original position. "It seems somehow significant that it's a card, and we're investigating cards."

"Tarot cards, though. Not playing cards."

"Still."

They stood back up and looked down at the card on the mat.

"Just leave it, I guess," Calvin said. "Let's get to work."

They put on the latex gloves they had brought and started to search the living room. The general décor was similar to that of Byrne's office, with basic functional furniture, well-ordered bookshelves, and a handful of knick-knacks and decorations situated in out-of-the-way places. It was the home of a man who cares more about his work than about creature comforts. There was a TV and a DVD player, but the remote controls to operate them sat covered in dust in a corner of the TV cabinet. Most of the decorations were medieval-themed. On the living room walls were framed prints of medieval paintings, many of them images of saints and monks. The only personal photograph in sight was a framed 8x10 on top of a bookcase that was full of old issues of *The Medieval Review* and *Journal of Medieval History*. The photo showed Byrne with his arm around a smiling raven-haired woman with thick glasses. They stood somewhere outdoors with rhododendron bushes and a sundial in the background. It was an old photo; their clothing and hairstyles had a 1990s vibe, and more tellingly, most of Byrne's hair was still brown.

"It doesn't feel right, being in someone else's house like this," Cynthia said, staring at the photo.

"Yeah, but it's for a good cause," Calvin said. He opened a drawer in a side table. Inside was a jumble of rubber bands, fliers for lawn-care services, pens, shoelaces, and other miscellaneous items. "We're trying to solve a murder."

"I guess." She doubted the murder was really Calvin's top priority. Given his devotion to his work (much like Byrne, she reflected), he was no doubt far more interested in finding the card than in balancing the scales of justice. Still, if the end result was the same and justice was served, what did it matter?

They quickly but efficiently searched the house. With the three of them working together, they managed to search each room in only a few minutes. They opened drawers, flipped cushions, looked inside the refrigerator, and even fingered through the wastebaskets. They didn't find anything of much interest until they came to Byrne's home office, a small room at the back of the house where a computer sat atop an old, scarred cherrywood desk.

"Should we turn it on?" Cynthia said.

"It's probably password-protected," Calvin said. "But I guess we should check it out."

He pressed the power button. The computer whirred to life. When the main screen appeared, it indeed demanded a password.

"Knowing him, it's probably something from old European history," Cynthia said. "'Dagobert' or something."

Calvin typed in "Dagobert." It wasn't accepted. He tried "Clovis." Same result. He tried "Charlemagne" and "Visigoth" and "Beowulf." Nothing.

He glanced at Kaarina, who was searching through the desk's drawers. "I don't suppose your illegal entry skills include knowing how to hack into a computer?"

"No," she said. "I am sorry. I wish they did."

"The heck with it, then." He shut down the computer. "See?" he said to Cynthia. "Now's the time we could use that super-hacker I was talking about."

She rolled her eyes.

"Look at this!" Kaarina said. She pulled a folder from the desk's bottom drawer and began to flip through the papers inside

"What is it?" Cynthia asked.

"He travels to Italy recently, it seems."

"Oh, yeah," Calvin said. "He had some big medieval history symposium he attended last weekend."

"Oh, yes. I see. Most of folder is hotel bills and symposium papers and—" She froze, frowning at one of the papers. "There is email from...Doctor Enigma?"

"Doctor *what?*" said Cynthia.

"Yes, and..." She read a little further, then gasped. "Read this!"

Calvin and Cynthia crowded in behind her and read the paper over her shoulders.

> **From:** Doctor Enigma
> **To:** Andrew Byrne
> **Subject:** Briefcase
> **Date:** September 21

Professor LaFleur will be carrying the card in a Kenneth Cole Reaction Lock & Roll black leather briefcase. This model is readily available both online and in brick-and-mortar stores. You should have no trouble finding one.

LaFleur's briefcase is a fairly recent acquisition, and so should not have significant wear, and thus this should not be a concern. If you make the switch deftly, he will be none the wiser until the time comes for him to finalize his negotiations with the buyer on the last night of the symposium. By then, of course, you will be on your way home and under no suspicion.

I look forward to finalizing our own negotiations once you have returned from your trip.

—Doctor Enigma

"Holy crap!" Calvin said.

"And look," Kaarina said, holding up the piece of paper that had been underneath the email printout. "It is receipt for briefcase!"

"It was Byrne who got the card! He pulled a gypsy switch on some foreign professor who was gonna sell the card at the symposium!"

"But he was acting under the guidance of this mysterious Doctor Enigma," Cynthia said.

"But who is Doctor Enigma?" Kaarina said. "Could he be your Professor Kranhauser, perhaps?"

"It's possible, sure," Calvin said. "But that just begs the question—"

They heard the drone of a car coming up the street outside. They all tensed up, waiting, listening. The drone grew louder, then passed the house and began to recede into the distance.

"We'd better get out of here," Cynthia said. "We've been here almost half an hour already. If he decides not to wait around on campus, he could be back any minute."

"Shit," Calvin said. "You're right. Let's go."

As they headed out of the house, Calvin paused at the threshold to take one last look at the queen of spades on the welcome mat. The queen's humorless face stared off to her left and offered no answers.

He grunted and shut the door.

Chapter 17

Professor Hans Kranhauser lived outside of the city itself, in what was technically Ames Township. His house was in a hilly, wooded area south of town, and from Janus Road the only signs of habitation were the driveway stretching away into the trees and a few small squares of light barely visible amid the foliage.

"It is much like your houses," Kaarina said.

"Yeah," Cynthia said. "Except hopefully ours don't have teams of wannabe housebreakers lurking outside right now."

There was a wide grassy berm a couple hundred feet south of Kranhauser's driveway, and Calvin parked there with his lights off, facing the mouth of the driveway. Then he got out the script and his phone and the electronic voice modulator, and called Kranhauser's landline. The phone was picked up after just one ring.

"Jah? Who is it?" Kranhauser's voice was slow and thick. Calvin wondered if Kranhauser had been sleeping, or drinking.

Calvin read the script exactly as he had with Byrne. Then he hung up, and they waited.

A minute passed. Then two. Then four. Then six.

"Maybe he's not gonna bite," Cynthia said.

"Are you sure this is only exit from house?" Kaarina said.

"Well, not absolutely," Calvin said. "But according to the Google map, there's a big horse stable on the next road over. I doubt he'd have an access road through that."

"You never know," Cynthia said.

Just then they spotted a pair of headlights heading down the driveway. A moment later Kranhauser's gray SUV emerged onto Janus Road. The trio tensed up, ready to duck out of sight should the SUV turn their way. Which it shouldn't, assuming Kranhauser was heading to campus as intended. But in a situation like this it wasn't wise to assume anything. They breathed a sigh of relief when the SUV turned north and sped off.

The moment the red taillights vanished over the crest of a hill half a mile down the road, Calvin dialed Kranhauser's landline again. The phone rang eight times before the answering machine clicked on. Calvin hung up.

"All right. Let's roll." He started the car, turned on the lights, and headed up Kranhauser's driveway.

The house was an old stone farmhouse built atop a low, rocky hill. A few lights shone behind the house's closed curtains, including one in the front room.

The driveway ended at the mouth of a garage that was built into the hillside and was big enough to accommodate small farm equipment. Calvin parked front-first against the garage door and switched off the car. The sudden silence outside was near total. Very faintly they could hear trucks booming down Route 7 two miles east.

"Wow, this really is the middle of nowhere," Calvin said with a nervous laugh. "If he catches us here, he could, like, shoot us and bury us in the woods, and no one would ever know."

Cynthia scowled at him. "Why do you always have to say things like that?"

"Yes," Kaarina said. "We must be thinking positive thoughts instead."

"Sorry," Calvin said.

They got out of the car and headed to the front door. The wind picked up, bringing them the faint odors of hay and horseshit from the nearby stables. An owl hooted somewhere in the woods.

Calvin rang the bell and knocked. No one answered. He tried the knob. The door was locked.

"You're up," he told Kaarina, who was already getting out her lock-picking kit.

She squatted down and went to work.

"Oh, much better than Professor Byrne's," she said as she worked the picks. "Much older lock. Very easy." Even as she said this the lock clicked.

They went inside. The living room was high and spacious, with bare beams stretching overhead like in a hunting lodge. The décor was all deep reds and browns, giving the room a dark, earthy look. On the walls were framed posters of Wagner operas like the ones in Kranhauser's office, as well as a pair of crossed rapiers, an antique musket, and a broadsword. A stuffed grizzly bear was stationed next to the front door. A jacket and a scarf hung from one of its outstretched claws, and Kranhauser's fedora was perched atop its head.

"He's using a dead bear as a coat-rack," Cynthia said. "Somehow I'm not surprised."

They searched as quickly and methodically as they had at Byrne's. They didn't find anything of interest in the living room. But in the kitchen, of all places, Cynthia opened the bottom drawer of a cabinet to discover several boxes of 9mm ammo and a box for a Luger. The Luger itself was missing.

"I wonder if it was a Luger that killed Skerrit," Cynthia said.

"Could be," Calvin said. "And the fact that it's not here might mean Kranhauser disposed of it after the murder."

"But he would not keep everything else," Kaarina said. "He would dispose of boxes and bullets, too."

Cynthia stiffened. "I bet he's got the gun with him right now. Which means he'll have it when he gets back. Let's just hurry the fuck up and save the analysis for afterward."

"Agreed," Calvin said.

They hurried the fuck up. They found a few more items of vague interest: There was a bottle of Prozac nestled amid the antacids and stool softeners in the medicine cabinet; on the desk in the study was a stack of paperwork concerning a still-active lawsuit that Kranhauser had filed against the neighboring stable for "sanitation violations"; a shelf above an old phonograph at the back of the study contained a pristine set of LPs of Hitler speeches. But the trio turned up nothing related to the murder or the Tarot cards.

A rec room at the rear of the house contained half a dozen more stuffed and mounted animals, including a coyote and a wolverine, plus more antique weapons on the walls. Amidst the weapons hung numerous framed photos, some of them quite old. Most of them depicted Kranhauser's relatives. The likeness was unmistakable, especially among the older ones whose droopy skin and lank white hair were a perfect match for Kranhauser's. One old black-and-white photo showed Kranhauser at around the age of eight, posing with a dour, dark-clad couple, presumably his parents. In the background were fir trees and snow-capped mountains.

"It's weird to see him as a cute little kid," Cynthia said,

staring at the shyly smiling boy in the photo.

Kaarina shrugged. "Everybody was cute little kid at some point. Even worst of people."

Their search came to a screeching halt when they got to the bedroom. Calvin had opened the bedroom door and was reaching in to switch on the light when Cynthia gasped and yanked him backward by the collar.

"Wha—" he began, but then Cynthia clapped a hand over his mouth and pointed a finger into the room.

He followed the finger. The band of light that shone into the bedroom from the hallway fell partly across a king-sized bed, illuminating a set of sheet-shrouded feminine curves, a bare shoulder, a spill of long curly brown hair. Even as Calvin stared, goggled-eyed, the figure emitted a sleepy grunt and smacked her mouth and shifted a little on the bed. The shift brought a swath of her face into view. Calvin and Cynthia recognized her instantly. They didn't know her name, but she was in their Intro to Philosophy class. She was the one who had shuddered and squealed when Kranhauser talked about squishing the spider the other day.

Moving as quietly as possible, Calvin reached back into the room and slowly pulled the door closed.

"Someone's getting an easy A this semester," he whispered.

"We'd better get out of here right now," Cynthia said.

Calvin nodded. They still hadn't searched over half the house—in addition to the bedroom, there was the whole second floor, plus whatever basement or attic the place might have—but they couldn't risk staying here.

They hurried outside, locking the front door behind them as they went. No sooner had they gotten into Calvin's Honda Accord than they heard the hum of an engine behind them. Headlights appeared at the end of the driveway, casting the dim shadow of Calvin's car and of their heads within it upon the garage door.

"Shit shit shit," Calvin said as he jammed the key into the ignition and turned it. The engine rasped but didn't start. "God damn it!"

"We weren't even in there that long!" Cynthia said.

Calvin turned the key again and the car coughed to life. He put it in reverse, slammed his foot on the gas, and wrenched the steering wheel to the right as hard as he could. Thankfully the driveway here was so wide he was able to make a one-eighty without leaving the concrete, though his back fender bumped the frame of the garage door. He threw the car into drive, switched on his headlights, and floored the accelerator.

Kranhauser's SUV had just emerged from the corridor of trees, and in response to the sudden flare of headlights and the squeal of approaching tires, Kranhauser veered off the driveway and onto his lawn. Calvin's car barreled past him. Calvin and Cynthia caught a quick glimpse of Kranhauser ducking down in his seat, his forearm raised to shield his face from the light and/or a bullet or other projectile.

Calvin's car shot out onto Janus Road, narrowly missing a passing pickup truck, whose driver honked and shouted something. After fishtailing on the tarmac for a moment, the Accord straightened out, and Calvin sped back toward the university.

"Oh, my God," Cynthia said. She pressed one shaking hand to her chest to quell her galloping heart. She looked back to make sure Kranhauser wasn't following them. The mouth of his driveway was empty and unlit. They were already far enough away from his property that the lights of his house had vanished into the darkness. "I hope he didn't recognize us."

"I don't think he even saw us," Calvin said. "Not with our headlights in his face. I'm more curious as to why he came back so early. There's no way he could've made it all the way to the university and back."

"Maybe he suspected trick," Kaarina said.

"Yeah," Cynthia said. "Maybe he got concerned for the safety of the little student body in his bed." She shook her head in disgust. "She's our age! He's old enough to be her grandfather."

"Yeah, well, I guess it's one of those February-December romances," Calvin said. He drove in silence for a little while, then said, "So. What have we learned from our misadventures tonight?"

"Well, we know Byrne stole the card from another professor while he was in Europe last week. And we know he was in negotiations with this Doctor Enigma character, who seemed to be calling most of the shots."

"I wonder if Byrne even knew who he was dealing with, or if all the negotiations were done anonymously."

"But how did maintenance man wind up with card?" Kaarina asked. "Could he be Doctor Enigma?"

"I suppose so," Calvin said.

"Yeah, maybe this was one of his get-rich-quick schemes," Cynthia said.

"But who killed him, then?"

"At this point Kranhauser's the most likely suspect as far as a shooting is concerned, since we know he owns guns. We didn't see evidence of any firearms at Byrne's."

"Plus do not forget," Kaarina said: "Kranhauser has foreign accent like man who murdered two brothers in file. There is possibility he is same man."

"Right," Calvin said. "So he might have a history of homicide. Also, we saw Byrne following Kranhauser, which suggests that Kranhauser might have the card now, and Byrne's trying to get it back."

"Okay," Cynthia said. "So Skerrit, posing as Doctor Enigma, negotiates the transaction with Byrne, then Kranhauser somehow finds out about it and kills Skerrit and takes the card for himself and now Byrne's following him to get it back?" She frowned. "Wait a second." She turned and looked at Kaarina in the back seat. "Didn't you say the lock on the front door of Byrne's house was new?"

"Oh, yes," Kaarina said. "Very new. Very shiny. No scratches at all."

"Well, maybe that's it. Maybe Byrne replaced the lock because somebody broke in. Maybe Byrne and Doctor Enigma—whoever it is—plotted the theft of the card. But then once the theft was done, someone broke into Byrne's house and stole it. Maybe it was Doctor Enigma deciding he didn't want to share his illicit gains with Byrne. Or maybe it was someone else who found out about the deal and wanted the cards all to himself."

"Maybe that was Skerrit," Calvin said. "Maybe he found out about the whole thing by accident. I mean, maintenance men wind up having to access all kinds of places on campus, even the professors' offices. So maybe in the course of his job, he was in Byrne's office and he stumbled across email printouts similar to the one we saw in Byrne's house."

"But then why does Byrne follow Kranhauser?" Kaarina asked.

"Maybe Kranhauser was Doctor Enigma, and he caught up with Skerrit and shot him, but then decided to keep the card for himself? Or..." He shook his head and growled in annoyance. "Shit, I don't know."

"What?" Cynthia said. "I thought it was starting to make sense. Sort of."

"It is. But the problem is, you could rearrange these pieces in all kinds of other ways, too. I mean, even after what we did tonight, we still don't have enough information to put all this together yet. For all we know, the killer could actually be this Professor LaFleur dude, out to reclaim his card."

"So where do we get more information?" Kaarina asked.

Calvin stared out the windshield at the headlight-lit road for a moment. Then he said, "Now that we have a better idea of what this case is really about, I think we should have another chat with Lou Guglio about his dear, departed coworker."

Chapter 18

"I'm kind of surprised to see you folks here again," Guglio said when they met him in his office near the end of his lunch break the following day. He had just finished eating. The smell of bologna hung in the air, and there was a tiny orange-brown streak of dried mustard on the collar of his shirt. A wadded-up paper bag and a ball of plastic wrap sat in the trashcan next to his desk. A can of Diet Pepsi sat on the crumb-specked desktop in front of him. "I mean, how much info do you folks need for this memorial article of yours?"

"We have a certain amount of column inches to fill," Cynthia said. "And unfortunately we're coming up a bit short."

"Huh."

"We really appreciate your agreeing to meet with us again," Calvin said. "Especially on such short notice. We weren't even sure you'd be working on a Sunday."

"Normally I don't. But there's been a lot to do lately, especially with Judd gone." Guglio heaved a weary sigh. "I could use one of his get-rich-quick schemes myself right about now."

"Well, we'll try to keep this short, then. We only have a few questions."

"I'm not sure what there is I can tell you that I haven't already told you." Guglio's gaze drifted to Kaarina, whom he hadn't met before. His eyes swept up and down her tight cropped tank top and the bare belly below it. Guglio cleared his throat and hurriedly added, "But of course, I'll be happy to help you folks however I can."

"Thanks," Calvin said. "Now, um, we were talking to some other people who knew Mr. Skerrit, and they mentioned a few things that they thought they had heard about him—interests of his and stuff like that—but they seemed a bit unsure, and we wanted to try to confirm the information with you."

"Sure. Fire away."

"First of all, we were told he had an interest in Tarot cards."

Guglio chuckled. "Judd? Tarot cards? No way. I don't know who you were talking to, but they couldn't have known Judd very well. He wasn't into stuff like that."

"Did he travel much? We heard he might have taken a trip to Europe at some point. Maybe Italy?"

"No. I don't recall him ever traveling anywhere outside of Ohio. And if he went anywhere, it wouldn't have been Europe. He thought Europe was for liberals and fairies. I do remember him talking once about wanting to go to Thailand because of the, you know, the women and stuff." His eyes once again flicked to Kaarina. She smiled blandly back.

"What about history?" Calvin said. "Was he interested in history? Especially medieval history?"

Guglio shook his head. "No no no. None of that either. That's not Judd at all. He was very down-to-earth. He wasn't into any kind of intellectual stuff."

"So I take it that means he didn't associate much with members of the faculty?"

Guglio started to shake his head, then froze, his eyes distant, thoughtful. Calvin and the others sat forward expectantly, thinking that perhaps Guglio had recalled something significant. But then the distant look vanished and Guglio shook his head.

"No," he said. "No, I never saw him hanging out with any of the faculty guys. I mean, sure, occasionally he might exchange a few words with a professor or a TA or whatever. On a college campus, it's kind of hard not to, right?"

"Yeah, I guess."

Guglio glanced at the clock on the wall above the door, then pushed himself to his feet.

"Sorry, kids," he said, "but I'm out of time. I really gotta get back to work. Do you have any other questions, real quick?"

"Um…" Calvin glanced at Cynthia and Kaarina. They shrugged. "No. I think that should do it."

Guglio saw them to the door.

"Thanks again for your time," Cynthia said.

"No problem," Guglio said. "If any of you need anything else from me, feel free to ask." He flashed a smile that was aimed more at Kaarina than at Calvin or Cynthia, then shut the door.

The trio exited the Maintenance Department and circled around to the front of the Student Center. They found an unoccupied picnic table in the plaza and sat down.

"That was kind of a bust," Calvin said.

"I don't know," Cynthia said. "It looked like Guglio suddenly remembered something when you asked that question about faculty members, didn't it?"

"Yeah," Calvin said. "But the problem is, it might have been something totally unrelated to the murder. I couldn't think of a way to ask about it without arousing suspicion. I suppose we could investigate Guglio, too, and start following him around or something, but I don't want us to spread ourselves too thin based on nothing more than a momentary zone-out. Especially not when we have other, more solid avenues of investigation to pursue. I mean, if we—"

A shadow fell over their table and a familiar voice said, "And how are Hercules Poirot and Miss Marple on this fine sunny day?"

They looked up. It was Detective Anderson. He was smiling a big fake smile.

"Why, hello, detective," Cynthia said, giving him an equally fake smile.

Next to her, Kaarina emitted a small gasp, then bent over her backpack, which sat on the seat beside her, and began to rummage through it.

Anderson eyed her with amusement. "New member of the Baker Street Irregulars, I take it?"

"I have no idea what you're talking about," Calvin said.

"Mm." Anderson nodded slowly, his lips pursed. He looked at some students strolling past, at the blue sky, at the front doors of the Student Center. Calvin and Cynthia glanced at each other. They could tell he was letting the suspense build for some reason, but they weren't sure why. Kaarina kept rummaging.

Anderson turned his gaze back upon them. His fake smile widened. His blue eyes were like chips of ice.

"It's funny," he said. "Some doors in the basement of the Moma were found unlocked on Saturday morning. And the lights were on down there, too. I don't suppose you know anything about that, do you?"

"Why would *we* know anything?" Calvin said, feigning a look of utter bafflement.

"Maybe whoever killed Judd Skerrit did it," Cynthia

said.

Anderson laughed softly and shook his head. "No, no, no. See, if you're suggesting that the person who murdered Skerrit came and went via the basement, you might be right. But the thing is, if they did, they had a key, and they were smart enough to lock the doors and turn out the lights behind them as they left. They left no trace at all. Whoever it was on Friday night...well, they *picked* the locks. There were faint but tell-tale scratches on the metal. And they were *not* smart enough to lock the doors or turn out the lights behind them. A real amateurish job, if you ask me."

"Huh," Cynthia said. "I'm sure glad it wasn't us. I'd hate to be in the kind of trouble those amateurs are gonna be in when you catch them, as I'm sure you will, what with your exemplary record and your brilliant detective skills."

"Absolutely," Calvin said, nodding heartily.

Anderson stared at them a moment, still smiling that fake smile, then said, "I'll tell you, though: If I catch someone where they shouldn't be, maybe doing something they shouldn't be doing, like, say, picking locks at one of my crime scenes in a misguided effort to play Jessica Fletcher, those someones are going to be in so much trouble they'll almost certainly get expelled from school."

Calvin and Cynthia said nothing. They had to struggle mightily to maintain their fake smiles.

"Anyway," Anderson said, "I just thought I'd share that with you. Not that *you* have any reason to know that, of course. I don't know *why* I felt it necessary to tell you that. Must be going senile or something. Oh, well. Have a nice day."

He turned to go. Kaarina stopped rummaging and started to straighten up.

"Oh, wait," Calvin said.

Anderson turned back around. Kaarina grunted in dismay and began rummaging again.

"What," Anderson said.

"Two things, actually," Calvin said.

"What."

"What do you know about Tarot cards?"

Anderson looked blank for a moment. Then he gave a small shake of his head as if he thought he hadn't heard correctly. "Tarot cards?"

"Yeah."

Anderson looked from Calvin to Cynthia to Kaarina (still rummaging) and then back to Calvin again. "Not a hell of a lot, fortunately. Why?"

"Just wondering."

Anderson gave him a frowning sidelong look. "Why would you be wondering about that?"

"No reason. Just curious."

Anderson eyed him in silence for a moment, then said, "What's the other thing?"

"I'm just wondering what kind of gun was used to kill Judd Skerrit."

Anderson chuckled. "Yes, because the police frequently divulge such information to people who aren't involved in their investigations."

"It wasn't a Luger by any chance, was it?"

"Did you not hear what I just said?" He frowned. "Besides, what makes you think a Luger was involved?"

"Just a rumor we heard."

"A rumor."

"Uh-huh."

Anderson shook his head. "Look, just stay the hell out of this, okay? This is not your business. If I catch you snooping around again, your asses will be out of this university before you can say 'community college.' Got it?"

"We're not snooping," Cynthia said. "How are we snooping? We were just sitting here quietly. *You* came to *us.*"

He smiled thinly. "Just remember what I said." He turned and sauntered off.

Kaarina looked up from her backpack, saw that Anderson was gone for good, then straightened up with a long sigh. "You have met him before?"

"Yeah," Calvin said. "He's the cop in charge of the investigation into Skerrit's murder. He's a little too clever for my taste."

Kaarina gave a nervous laugh. "When you said he was detective, I get scared. I think we have extremely big trouble. I am sorry I did not help to make him go away faster."

"It's okay," Cynthia said. "It's not like you could've done much anyway."

"Judging by Anderson's reaction," Calvin said, "I'm guessing he doesn't know squat about the Ur-Tarot. Which means he still has no idea what this murder is even about."

"Wow. We're actually ahead of the mighty Detective Anderson. Yay us."

"And he didn't react at all when I mentioned the Luger. Did you notice that?"

"Yeah. It meant nothing to him."

"Yes," Kaarina said, "but I do not think police can identify types of guns from bullets. Many different guns use same kinds of bullets."

"Oh," Calvin said. "Is that right?" He looked at Cynthia. She just shrugged. "I could swear I've seen them do it on cop shows."

"Yeah, well, I hate to break it to you," Cynthia said, "but stuff on TV's not always real."

"Gosh," Calvin said, blinking with mock surprise. "How disillusioning."

Kaarina smiled and shook her head. "Sillies."

Chapter 19

That evening they hung out in Calvin's room. Cynthia brought down the rest of the beer that Kaarina had left in her fridge the other night, and they sat and chatted and drank, Cynthia and Kaarina on the futon, Calvin facing them in his desk chair. Calvin wasn't entirely comfortable with the girls sitting side by side like that, but since he was playing host tonight, it was only proper that he cede the best seat to the ladies.

The three of them hadn't dressed up and still wore the casual outfits they had worn around campus that afternoon. Thanks to their almost constant contact with each other over the last few days, they had grown comfortable enough around each other to no longer feel compelled to preen and display. They were all fast friends now. And maybe if they played their cards right, either Calvin or Cynthia would become something more to Kaarina.

Cynthia was amused to note that Calvin had made a rather pitiful effort to clean his room. The bed was made, though sloppily. The dirty clothes had vanished (she guessed they had merely been tossed into the closet, whose door was now firmly closed). The ancient Starbucks cup was now sitting in the wastebasket atop a heap of other freshly chucked trash. And the desktop was marginally less messy, some of the stray papers and office supplies having disappeared, probably into the desk drawers. The table next to the futon, on the other hand, was more cluttered than ever.

"Your utility belt is coming along, I see," Cynthia said, nodding at the items on the table. The newest additions included a compass, a magnifying glass, a waterproof pen, and a small waterproof notebook.

"Utility belt?" Kaarina asked. She scooted toward Cynthia and craned her head to peer over Cynthia's shoulder at the table. Her breasts pressed lightly against Cynthia's arm. Cynthia nearly spilled her beer.

"Yeah," Calvin said. "I figured that if we're gonna investigate anomalous phenomena, we should have field kits, with stuff we might need."

"Ah," Kaarina said. "That is good idea."

Much to Cynthia's disappointment, Kaarina climbed off the futon and headed over to the table for a better look.

"This is good selection," Kaarina said, examining the items. "Very good."

Calvin swelled with pride. "It's not quite done yet. I want to add a lock-picking kit like yours, and maybe a couple of other things."

"Don't add too much more," Cynthia said. "Otherwise you'll be lugging around a huge sack full of stuff, like Santa with his toys."

"Actually, I'm considering getting an attaché case. There'd be plenty of room in one of those."

"You are inspired by Professor LaFleur perhaps?" Kaarina asked as she sat back down.

"No. I've always thought attaché cases were kind of cool. It's like a spy thing or something."

"Ah."

"Speaking of spy things," Cynthia said, "I guess we should start figuring out our next move, eh?"

"Yeah." Calvin settled back in his chair and sipped his

beer as he pondered the matter. "Our only real suspects at this point are Byrne and Kranhauser, so we should operate on the assumption that one of them has the card. I'm just not sure how to figure out which one it is."

"Simple," Kaarina said. "We follow them. If one has card, sooner or later he leads us to it."

"Easier said than done. I mean, they're in classes and their offices most of the day. It would look really obvious and suspicious if we just sit around Chandler Hall waiting for them to leave. And if, say, Kranhauser has the card in his house, how would we ever know just by following him home?"

"We break into house again."

Calvin shook his head. "After that little incident in his driveway, he's gonna be more security-conscious than ever. And probably really, really trigger-happy. I'm not sure I'm ready to risk that."

"So what do we do then?" Cynthia said.

"I don't know."

"I do," Kaarina said. She took a big swallow of beer, then sat forward. "We must become close to professors. It is only way."

"What?" Cynthia said. "What do you mean?"

"We must get close to them. Gain their trust. Put ourselves in their confidence. Best way is to offer something that makes them want to get closer to us. Like worms for fish."

"Bait, you mean," Calvin said. "Do you have anything specific in mind?"

"Yes. We know Professor Kranhauser likes his young pretty girl students." She waved a hand at Cynthia. "And here is very pretty girl student."

Despite her immense pleasure at once again hearing

Kaarina call her pretty, Cynthia spread her hands palms out in a stop gesture and exclaimed, "Whoa whoa whoa. What exactly are you suggesting here?"

Kaarina smiled and rolled her eyes. "I do not say make sex with him. But make him think you will. Visit him in office and play silly, sexy girl with crush on clever older man. Let him invite you to house."

"And then, what, exactly? Play hard to get till he falls asleep?"

"No. Give him roofie."

Calvin and Cynthia looked at each other, both of them wondering if they had understood her correctly.

"Like, the date rape drug?" Cynthia said.

"Yes, yes. Rape drug. But you do not rape him. Only make him sleep. Probably he will offer drinks. Wine or something. You wait until he looks away, then you put roofie in his drink. He drinks. He sleeps. Then you call us and let us inside, and we search house as threesome."

"Yeah, but when he wakes up he'll know I drugged him."

"He will not be sure. Roofies do not leave aftereffect. And you will leave note, explaining that he drinks too much and falls asleep and you are hurt and insulted, so you call friend to pick you up. He will be too embarrassed to even talk to you after that."

"Wow, that's—that's pretty good," Cynthia said.

"Yeah," Calvin said. "It's brilliant and dastardly. You've got a great future as a criminal mastermind if you ever turn to the Dark Side."

Kaarina laughed. "Thank you."

"Except, where exactly are we going to get a roofie?"

"I have roofies."

"You what?"

"Yes. One time in Italy, boy try to use roofie on me, but I catch him and rough him up and take whole bottle. I think maybe I will find use for them someday, and now I have."

Calvin and Cynthia looked at each other again.

"Works for me," Calvin said. "You willing to risk getting close enough to Kranhauser to pull this off?"

Cynthia heaved a sigh. "I guess. I mean, I won't like it. The guy's a skeevy creep. But it does seem like a valid plan." She drained the last of her beer. "What about Professor Byrne, though?"

"He is trickier," Kaarina said. "He does not lust for pretty girl students. But there must be something that will be good bait for him."

"Like what?" Calvin asked. "He doesn't exactly seem to have a lot of extracurricular interests."

"Tell you what," Cynthia said, standing up. She tossed her empty beer can into the plastic bag Calvin used for recyclables. "Nature's calling. Why don't we all give the matter some thought while I hit the ladies' room?"

Calvin's floor was male-only, which meant she had to head one floor up to use the bathroom on her own floor. As she stepped out of Calvin's room, she glanced back and saw that he and Kaarina had already fallen to chatting in voices too low for Cynthia to decipher. Seeing their smiles, Cynthia recalled how excited Kaarina had been when she saw Calvin's house yesterday, and how she had practically draped herself all over him in the tower room.

Cynthia's stomach knotted with jealousy and dread. She suddenly feared what might happen between Kaarina and Calvin while she was gone. Sure, they weren't exactly sitting side by side the way she and Kaarina had been, but they were alone and they'd been drinking and she felt sure there was at least as much of an attraction between them as there was between herself and Kaarina. *Let the cards fall where they may,* Calvin had said. But Cynthia had never been very lucky at cards.

She speed-walked down the hall to the stairwell, then bounded up the stairs three steps at a time. She burst through the door that led onto her own floor, dashed a short ways down the hall, and then shouldered into the ladies room.

Two girls were already in there—a plump, doughy blonde in a very tight and very unflattering gold lamé dress and a cute petite black girl with a midnight-blue velour dress and piercings in her ears, nose, lips, eyebrows, and who knew where else. Both of them were leaning over adjoining sinks and inspecting themselves in the mirrors. They gave Cynthia a brief, disinterested glance as she passed behind them and entered a stall, and then they resumed their conversation.

"She sucked his fucking dick while Waverly was right in the next room," the blonde said.

"Holy fucking shit," the black girl said. "Didn't she, like, hear anything?"

"She was too busy playing *Mario Kart.*"

"Oh, that figures."

The clink of Cynthia's belt buckle as she unfastened her pants and yanked them down obscured the next few words, but as she settled onto the toilet seat, she heard the blonde girl say, "—spat his semen right into the trashcan."

The black girl gasped. "Did Waverly see it?"

"I don't think so. Todd made sure to cover it over with Kleenex and stuff. But I was wondering more if she could smell it, you know? That shit gets rank pretty fast."

"I know. God, Amanda is such a fucking slut. And

men are such fucking cheating assholes."

"Tell me about it. I mean, letting her suck him off like that, with Waverly, like, right there. God."

Cynthia cupped her forehead in her hands and shook her head. This talk of surreptitious blow jobs couldn't help but fill her head with all sorts of horrible visions about what might be happening in Calvin's room right now.

Then again, knowing him, he could very well be too enthralled by the problems posed by the hunt for the card to give much thought to sex. Sometimes he—

She sat bolt upright with a grin.

That was it! That was the answer!

Chapter 20

"So how will you redecorate big old house of yours when you move in?" Kaarina asked Calvin after Cynthia was gone.

"I don't know," he said. "I haven't really thought about it all that much. I'll definitely have to replace all those boring country pictures in the front hallway. And I'll want to install wifi, and a better sound system. And a new computer. The one Mr. May had is so antiquated by now it's not even funny. Beyond that, though, I have no idea. To be honest, there's a lot of stuff I haven't even gotten around to sorting through yet—stuff in the basement, stuff in the office. Tons of stuff."

"I see." Kaarina finished her beer. She tossed the can into Calvin's recyclables bag, then headed over to the mini-fridge. She squatted down and opened it. "You should think about security system, too."

"Yeah. I really should." He frowned. "Now that I think about it, it's kinda weird that Mr. May never had anything installed. I guess he thought secrecy was the best security of all."

"You cannot keep secret forever, though," Kaarina said, taking a fresh can of beer from the fridge. "You need better protection. Especially with amazing and unique things that you have."

"Very true."

She held up the can she had taken out of the fridge. "Do you need new beer?"

"Um…" He regarded the nearly empty can in his hand. "Yeah, sure. Although I probably shouldn't. I'm not really a big drinker. If I have too much more, I'll probably wind up doing something embarrassing."

"Oh?" Kaarina took out another beer, then closed the fridge door and stood up. She cocked an eyebrow at him, smiling. "Like what? Confess secret desire for someone?"

He laughed. "You can't keep secrets forever, remember."

"No," she said. "No, you cannot."

She stopped beside his chair and handed him his beer. As he took the cold can, his fingertips touched hers, making his heart jump and his penis stir. He realized with a thrill that she was standing unnecessarily close to his chair, her belly level with his face. She was so close he could see the fine, downy hairs on her stomach. He could see the smooth convolutions of skin in the hollow of her navel. He could read the Levi's logo embossed on the buttonfly of her jeans. The scent of vanilla surrounded him. His thoughts reeled.

Even though he had taken the beer from her, she remained there, unmoving. He looked up into her face. She was smiling down at him.

"You should never keep desire secret," she told him. "It is bad for mental health."

"I, uh, I'll take that under advisement."

She nodded, then turned and headed back to the futon, much to Calvin's disappointment.

"I do not understand why you do not have girlfriend," she said as she sat back down. She pulled the tab on her beer can. The can hissed sharply. "Handsome rich young man like you should be having pick of women." She gave him a playful grin and flicked her eyebrows. "You should

171

be waking up with much tiredness every morning."

He laughed. "I don't know. I'm guess I'm just kind of too caught up with work and classes and stuff."

She tutted and shook her head. "That is important, yes, but you must find time for fun, too."

Calvin was considering saying something like, "Maybe you could help me with that," when the door opened and Cynthia came back in. He cursed her timing but hid his irritation behind a smile.

It did the job. Cynthia didn't notice a thing. She had felt a vague greasy certainty in the pit of her stomach that she would return to find Kaarina dabbing her lips with a Kleenex while Calvin reclined in his chair with a dopey grin. Instead the two of them looked much the same as when she had left.

Relieved, she hurried across the room to the fridge.

"I've got it!" she told them. She opened the fridge and grabbed a beer.

"Got what?" Calvin asked.

"The Ur-Tarot!" She flung herself onto the futon next to Kaarina, then cracked open the beer. "Byrne might not lust after girls like Kranhauser, but we know he at least lusted after one of the Ur-Tarot cards, and you've got three of them. We can use those as bait, the same way we'll be using me as bait."

"Oh, no." Calvin shook his head. "I'm not risking the cards."

"You don't actually have to use the cards themselves. You still have those pictures you took of them, right?"

"Yeah…"

"So show him those. Tell him you got the pictures off a website."

"But then he'll want to see the website, won't he?"

Calvin said. "I don't have any experience setting up websites, and we don't really have a lot of time anyway."

"It doesn't matter. Just tell him the site's been taken down already. Tell him the owner of the site was receiving threatening emails from weirdoes and crazies, and he decided to just shut the whole thing down. But before that happened, you got in touch with the site owner and now you're corresponding with him, only he made you swear not to reveal his personal info to anyone else, so you can't tell Byrne. But tell Byrne that neither you nor the owner of the cards knows a whole lot about them, so you were hoping that a specialist in medieval history might know more. See, this way, you're setting yourself up as a link to more cards, something he wants. He'll want to keep you real close after that."

"Yes!" Kaarina said. "That is good plan."

"No, no, no," Calvin said, shaking his head. "This isn't gonna work. It'll look too suspicious. I mean, what, I just happen to stumble across an Ur-Tarot website and come to him for help right after he stole one from somebody else? He'll smell a rat for sure."

Cynthia's shoulders slumped. She sat back in her seat and took a big swig of beer.

"There must be a way to make this work," she said.

"Yes," Kaarina said. "Idea is too good to let go so quickly."

After a moment's thought, Cynthia shot bolt upright again.

"I've got it!" she said. "It's simple! Just tell him the truth. Or at least part of the truth. Tell him you were in the Student Center the day Skerrit's body was found, and you saw them carrying the body out. You spotted the piece of parchment in his hand and got curious about it, so you searched online, and you came across the website." She spread her arms with a smile. "Sweet and simple. What do you think?"

Calvin nodded slowly. "I think that might work."

"Very smart idea!" Kaarina told Cynthia. "I am impressed."

Cynthia grinned, delighted that she had both solved the problem and earned Kaarina's praise.

"You know, we make a damn good team," Calvin said.

"Hear, hear," Cynthia said, raising her beer.

"To great team, and great friends," Kaarina said, raising hers too.

Smiling and glad, they clinked their cans together and drank, then settled back to iron out the details of their scheme.

Chapter 21

When Calvin, Cynthia, and Kaarina met for lunch in the Food Court the next day, their expressions were grim. The big news on campus that morning was that maintenance supervisor Lou Guglio had been murdered. His body had been found in some bushes near the Heating Plant at around one a.m. last night by a passing student. Guglio appeared to have been beaten to death with a blunt instrument. The lack of blood at the crime scene suggested he had been murdered elsewhere, then dumped in the bushes. When asked if this murder was connected to that of Guglio's fellow Maintenance Department employee Judd Skerrit, Detective Lee Anderson had said only, "It does seem like a plausible hypothesis."

"I can't help but think that we had a hand in this," Cynthia said.

"What?" Kaarina said, her eyes wide with alarm. "What do you mean?"

"Well, remember how Guglio acted when Calvin asked him if Judd Skerrit had any dealings with the faculty? He acted like he suddenly remembered something."

"You think maybe he was following up on that and got killed for it?" Calvin said.

"Something like that, yeah. I mean, maybe he put the pieces together and figured out who killed Skerrit, then went and confronted the guy."

"Why would he confront a murderer, though? Why wouldn't he just go to the police?"

"I don't know. Maybe he only suspected the truth and was snooping around in search of confirmation when the killer caught him."

"Or maybe he makes blackmail," Kaarina said. "And murderer is not happy to be blackmailed."

"Is anyone else having second thoughts about our plans for today?" Cynthia said. "Cozying up to possible murderers suddenly doesn't seem like the wisest idea."

Calvin nodded. "Yeah. I know what you mean. But what else can we do? This is what we signed on for. It's not all gonna be wacky fun. In this line of work, we're gonna have to take some big risks sometimes."

"And I think plan is very sound," Kaarina said. "We use professors' own desires against them. I think all will be well."

Cynthia gave her a weak smile. "I hope you're right."

Chapter 22

If Professor Kranhauser had murdered Lou Guglio, he gave no sign of it during Intro to Philosophy that afternoon. Nor did he seem to recognize Calvin and Cynthia as being the ones who had forced him off his driveway over the weekend. Nor, in fact, did he display the slightest trace of paranoia or anger or any other emotion that would indicate his home had been invaded. He was his usual snarky and provocative self. The curly-headed brunette in the front row laughed and nodded thoughtfully at all the appropriate places in his lecture along with everyone else. If Calvin and Cynthia hadn't seen the truth with their own eyes, they wouldn't have guessed she had spent Saturday night (at least) in Kranhauser's bed.

When class ended and Kranhauser began to gather up his papers and stuff them into his black briefcase, Calvin and Cynthia hurried out of the room and down the hallway. It would have been a simple matter for Cynthia to approach Kranhauser and deliver her spiel right there after class, but they had decided during their discussions last night that it would be best to talk with the professors somewhere where there was little risk of interruption. Like their offices.

Kaarina was waiting for them next to the drinking fountain. There, the three of them pretended to chat while they surreptitiously watched the doors to both Kranhauser's and Byrne's classrooms. Byrne's latest class ended at the same time as Kranhauser's, and neither professor had another class that afternoon.

After about thirty seconds, Kranhauser emerged from his classroom. He ambled down the hall, occasionally greeting passing students and faculty as he went, then crossed the lobby and headed up the stairs. He didn't appear to have spotted the trio next to the drinking fountain.

Shortly after Kranhauser vanished around the bend in the stairs, Byrne emerged from his classroom. He strode quickly down the hall, glancing this way and that as if he expected to be accosted at any moment.

"Wow, he's tense," Cynthia said.

"Maybe because he commits murder last night?" Kaarina said.

"Maybe," Calvin said.

Byrne headed up the stairs.

They waited one more minute, then Calvin said, "Okay. Let's go."

"Good luck," Kaarina told him and Cynthia. "I wish I could help. Instead, I sit down here and wait for you. If there is trouble, shout for me. I will come."

"We will," Cynthia said.

Calvin and Cynthia made their way through the slowly thinning traffic in the hallway, then ascended the stairs. When they reached the top, they saw that Byrne's office door was shut. Through the frosted glass window they could see that a light was on inside.

"Here's my stop," Calvin whispered. "Good luck."

"Good luck," Cynthia said.

She headed down the hall toward Kranhauser's office. Behind her she heard Calvin knock on Byrne's door. A few seconds later she heard low voices, and then a door opening. She looked back just in time to see Calvin disappear through the doorway. The door closed behind him.

She took a deep breath and continued down the hallway. The noise from the first floor diminished the farther she went, and by the time she had reached the dead-end where Kranhauser's office was, she was immersed in near silence, which only heightened her nervousness.

Kranhauser's door was shut like Byrne's. But also like Byrne's, a light shone inside.

Cynthia knocked.

"Yes?" came the immediately reply. "Who is it?"

"Hi, Professor," Cynthia said. "My name's Cynthia Crow. I'm one of your students. I was just in Intro to Philosophy."

The door opened a crack. Kranhauser peered out, his face drawn and suspicious. For a moment Cynthia feared that he had indeed recognized her as one of the housebreakers from Saturday night, but then his expression softened, and a smile crinkled his droopy face.

"Ah, yes!" he exclaimed. "Come in, come in."

He opened the door wider and waved her in. As she entered, he leaned out the doorway and took a quick glance down the corridor as if to make sure no one else was around. He shut the door behind her, then motioned at an empty chair in front of his desk. She sat.

Instead of circling around the desk to his own chair as Cynthia had expected, Kranhauser sat on the right front corner of the desk barely two feet away from her, close enough to reach out and touch her if he wanted. She had to tilt her head back a little to look him in the eye. The scent of Old Spice filled her nostrils.

"And what can I do for you, Miss, ah...Crow, you said?"

"That's right."

He spread his hands. Cynthia couldn't help but notice that he held them exactly parallel to her breasts. "I apologize. I am bad with names. So many classes. So many students. You understand."

"Oh, I totally understand," Cynthia said with vigorous nod, playing up the role of the witless coed starstruck by her distinguished professor. She hated acting this way, especially when the professor in question was a) male, b) old, and c) creepy. It was dishonest and demeaning. But she couldn't deny that it worked like a charm: As Kranhauser took in her exuberant tone and her infatuated expression, his smile widened and a lecherous light sparked in his eyes. "I mean, a busy guy like you. You have way more important things on your mind. I totally get it."

"So how can I help you today, my dear?"

My dear? Oh, God. She hoped he couldn't see her skin crawling. "Well, I'm planning to switch my major to Philosophy, and I wanted to know if you'd be willing to be my faculty advisor. I mean, after all, you're the reason I decided to switch."

His eyebrows flew up. "Am I?" he said.

"Yeah! I mean, you make the subject so...so *exciting,* you know? Your lectures are so incisive and witty and...and *penetrating.* I mean, your class is literally the high point of my day. I can't wait to see you." She put a hand over her mouth and giggled with feigned nervousness and embarrassment. "I mean, you know, I can't wait to come here." She rolled her eyes and laughed at her own faux awkwardness. She bit her lower lip for good measure.

Somehow Professor Kranhauser's smile managed to become even bigger and sleazier.

"Ah, another philosopher in the making," he said. "It

is such a pleasure to know that I have made a convert."

"Yeah, I mean, my previous major—Environmental Studies—it was nice and all, but it was just somehow...*unsatisfying*. I needed something more fulfilling, you know?"

"Jah, jah," Kranhauser said. "I understand." His accent was becoming more pronounced, a sure sign that he was getting excited. Cynthia hated to think what was going on in his brain right now. "Environmental Studies—that is very noble and good, but some of us need to, ah, probe deeper into things, jah? And to be honest, I vas hoping this vould happen. It might surprise you to know that I noticed you right at de start of de semester. I could tell you vere a very smart young lady. Gifted, even."

She pshawed with false false modesty. "Oh, please. I'm not all that."

"Oh, but you are. I have had my eye on you all along."

"Gosh," she breathed. "I had no idea."

"Jah. I vill alvays help de best und de brightest."

"So, you'll, like, be my advisor, then?" Cynthia said with an excited bounce.

"Jah, jah. I vill be more than happy to have you. Ehm, so to speak." He chuckled with mock embarrassment at his "unintentional" double entendre.

She giggled. "Oh, professor. You've gotta watch that mouth of yours."

"Maybe you should vatch it for me, eh?"

She giggled again and rolled her eyes. "See, that's one of the things I love...er, I mean, that I *like* so much about you: You have such a great sense of humor. There's an openness to you that I just don't find with other members of the faculty."

"Jah." He nodded. "It is important to me to try to cul-

181

tivate a special *closeness* vit my better students." He gestured at the backpack she wore. "Did you bring de advisor form for me to sign?"

"No. Actually, I haven't gotten it yet. I kinda wanted to make sure I had your approval first."

Smile widening, he leaned forward a little and gazed into her eyes. "Vell, you definitely have my approval."

She met his gaze. "I'm so glad." Good Lord, if she had to maintain this idiotic charade much longer she was afraid she would be physically sick. "I'll probably get it tomorrow. Then maybe I could bring it to you after class on Wednesday, if it's okay with you."

He started to nod, then stiffened and raised a finger as if a brilliant notion had suddenly struck him.

"You know," he said. "Instead of vaiting that long, you could stop by my house tomorrow evening, if you have de time. It vould help speed along de process."

She gasped with delight, then reined in her fake glee with a display of fake token hesitance. "Oh, I don't want to impose or anything…"

"Nein, nein. You vould not be imposing at all. I vould be more than happy to have you at my house. There is little I vill not do for my favorite students."

"Well, if you're sure I wouldn't be in the way or anything." She bit her lower lip again and let her gaze drop to his ringless ring finger. "I mean, if your wife, or, y'know, whatever…"

"Oh, I am not married. I am a free man."

"A bachelor, huh? That's…interesting."

"Jah." He stiffened again as he pretended to have another brilliant idea. "You know, like many bachelors, I have taught myself how to cook, und I have gotten quite good at it. Since you are planning to come by, vhy don't I cook dinner for you?"

"Oh, I couldn't!" She was appalled at how easy this was. Were all men this manipulable?

"Nein, nein. It vould be my pleasure. I so rarely get the chance to share my culinary skills vit others."

She gave him a coy, sidelong look, biting her lip again for good measure. "Are you sure?"

"Jah! I am certain." He tore a sheet from a pad of paper on the desk and plucked a pen from the desk set. He scribbled something down on the paper, then handed it to her. "This is my address, vit easy directions on how to get there from campus."

"Gosh. Thanks." She stared in awe at the paper as if it were a million dollar bill.

"Try to be there at, say, seven o'clock?"

She beamed at him. "No problem! Do you want me to bring anything? Some wine, perhaps?"

"Bah," he flapped a hand at her dismissively. "I have vine. I trust red is good?"

"Oh, I love red!"

"Excellent."

"Wow. I can't tell you how much this means, Professor."

"Perhaps you vill find a vay to tell me tomorrow night."

She dropped her gaze and bit her lip again. She'd better wrap this up fast; her lip was starting to hurt. She stood up.

"Well, I don't want to keep you from your work any longer…"

He stood too. He placed a hand on her bare arm and escorted her toward the door. His hand was cool and dry. She resisted the urge to wrench her arm away.

"I look forward to seeing you tomorrow night," he said.

"I look forward to it, too," she enthused.

They paused beside the door. His hand remained on her arm.

"You know," he said, suddenly looking more serious. "It is perhaps best if you do not tell anyone about our plans. Some people might not understand."

She nodded. "Yeah. I totally get it. Some people have small minds. Limited viewpoints."

"Precisely," he said. "They are not like us. They do not see things the way we do. As philosophers, we refuse to blindly accept the standard views of reality. We transcend the artificial boundaries of society and popular opinion. We roam the fields of life, free to experience whatever we desire."

"Yeah!"

He grinned. She was suddenly reminded of the stuffed and mounted animals in his house, of the poor dead bear being used as a coat rack.

He opened the door. She stepped outside.

"Till tomorrow," he said with a small bow.

She gave him a small curtsey in return. "Tomorrow."

He shut the door. Her smile immediately winked out. She strode down the hall, putting as much distance between herself and Kranhauser's office as she could as quickly as she could.

How, she wondered, was she ever going to make it through tomorrow night?

Chapter 23

After wishing Cynthia good luck, Calvin rapped on Professor Byrne's office door.

From inside came the creak of a chair. A few seconds later a man-shaped shadow appeared on the other side of the frosted glass window.

"Who is it?" Byrne said through the door.

"Um, it's Calvin. Calvin Beckerman? One of your students?"

The door popped open just enough for Byrne to peek out. At first his expression was tense and wary, but as soon as he saw who it was, he relaxed.

"Ah," he said, opening the door wider. "Come in."

Calvin stepped inside. Byrne shut the door. He motioned for Calvin to take a seat on the chair in front of the desk, then headed around the desk and sat down in his own chair.

"What can I do for you?" Byrne asked.

"I don't know if you remember me, but I'm in your World History class. The one on Tuesdays and Thursdays at ten forty-five?"

"Yes, of course I remember," he said with a smile full of amused hauteur. "How could I forget? You were the one who was asking about advanced prehistoric civilizations."

"Um, yeah." Calvin had forgotten about that. Maybe he wasn't the best choice to deal with Professor Byrne. Then again, the incident no doubt established Calvin as a kook in Byrne's eyes and would make his curiosity about ancient Tarot cards seem perfectly natural and totally harmless.

"So have you found proof of Atlantis yet?" Byrne asked.

Calvin started to rise to the bait and protest that he hadn't been talking about Atlantis at all, but he restrained himself. That wasn't why he was here.

"Actually I had a question about something from old European history. That's your specialty, right?"

"Yes. The Early Medieval period, primarily."

"Yeah, that's the period. See, I'm trying to find out information about something called the Ur-Tarot."

Byrne went rigid, his eyes full of surprise. He quickly got himself under control and said, "What makes you so interested in such an obscure topic?"

"Do you remember that murder last week? The maintenance guy who got killed in the Moma?"

Byrne eyed him closely, his expression guarded. "Of course."

"Well, I was in the Student Center that day. I was there in the crowd, watching the cops do their thing. And as they were carrying out the body, the dead guy's hand flopped out from under the sheet and this piece of old parchment fluttered down from his fingers. It was a little triangle, like a corner broken off a bigger piece."

Byrne nodded almost imperceptibly to himself, as if receiving confirmation of something he had long suspected. Calvin pretended not to have noticed and went on with his story.

"It landed right in front of me, so I got a really good look at it before one of the cops snatched it up. It had this kind of viny design on it. Well, I got curious, so I looked it up online. It took a lot of searching, but I finally found a site that told me what it was. Like I said, it turns out it was from the Ur-Tarot. The website had only some scanty information about their history, but it claimed they were made sometime way back around 900 A.D., and they contain vast occult powers." He saw Byrne start to roll his eyes then catch himself. "The site even had pictures of a few of them."

Byrne gawped at him. "It did?"

"Yeah. In fact, I brought a printout to show you, in case you didn't know what I was talking about." Calvin dug into his pocket and pulled out a trio of folded sheets of paper that bore copies of the photos he had taken of the cards in the Collection. He unfolded the sheets and handed them to Byrne.

Byrne looked at the papers, his eyes growing bigger with each one. He laid out the sheets in a line on his desk and stared at them for a minute, every now and then shaking his head, as if he were having trouble believing what he was seeing.

"So I take it you've heard of these before," Calvin said.

"Yes. Yes, I've, uh, I've run across reference to these." He licked his lips. "They're quite rare, though. It's surprising to find pictures of them online. What's the name of this website?"

"Actually, the site's not even there anymore. The guy who ran it had to take it down because he was getting all these weird, threatening emails. I guess lots of crazies are really obsessed with these cards."

"Did you happen to find out where these pictures came from, and who owns the cards?"

"Yeah. The guy who ran the website owns the cards. I got in touch with him shortly before he shut the site down, and I'm corresponding with him now."

"Who is he? Is he a medievalist or something?"

Calvin shifted in his seat with feigned uneasiness. "Uh, actually, to be honest he kind of made me promise not to share his personal info with anyone under any circumstances. You know, because of all the threats and stuff."

"Oh. I see."

"I mean, it's nothing personal," Calvin hastened to add. "I'm sure you're trustworthy and everything. But I made a promise, so I feel duty-bound to honor it."

"Understood. And respected. Integrity like that is rare these days." In truth, Byrne looked a bit miffed.

Calvin had a sudden burst of inspiration. He wasn't sure it would pay off—in fact, if he miscalculated it might blow up in his face—but it was worth a shot.

"You'd understand his feelings even better if you saw the emails he was getting," he told Byrne. "He showed me some of them, and they were really disturbing. One guy kept sending these creepy, manipulative messages. It was obvious he wanted to get the site-owner to reveal exactly where the cards were, probably so he could steal them or something. He used a really weird pseudonym, too." Calvin frowned and pretended to think hard. "What was it? Professor Strange or something like that."

Byrne stiffened. "It wasn't Doctor Enigma, by any chance, was it?"

"Yeah!" Calvin cried with mock surprise. "How did you know that?"

"Son of a bitch," Byrne muttered. He shook his head, his lips pressed into a thin, angry line.

"What's going on?" Calvin said. "You know something about this, don't you?"

Byrne regarded Calvin in silence for a moment, his

eyes narrow and thoughtful. Finally he nodded slowly and said, "Yes. Yes, I do. For I, too, have had a run-in with Doctor Enigma."

"What do you mean?"

"I..." Byrne licked his lips, then leaned forward, his elbows on the desktop. "If I tell you something, it has to be strictly confidential, you understand? It doesn't leave this office. Do I have your solemn promise on that?"

"Sure."

"Not too long ago I managed to come into possession of one of these cards. Normally I'd never be able to afford something like that, but I, uh, I lucked out. I got a remarkable deal."

Yeah, a veritable steal, Calvin thought.

"The deal had been brought to my attention by this Doctor Enigma character," Byrne went on. "I ran into him in a medieval studies chatroom. I didn't suspect anything amiss. I thought he was only some eccentric but helpful fellow scholar. Turns out the whole thing was a set-up. No sooner had I brought the card home than someone broke into my house while I was at work and stole it."

"And you think it was Doctor Enigma?" Calvin asked.

"Actually I know who the burglar was. It was Judd Skerrit, the murdered maintenance man."

"How do you know it was Skerrit?"

"Because after I found out that my house had been broken into, I asked a few of my neighbors if they had noticed anyone or anything unusual that day. And one of them told me she saw a man hurrying away from my house that morning and getting into a car parked at the curb. She remembered him primarily because of the brown cowboy boots he was wearing, the exact style and color of boots that Skerrit always wore. The man's general description and the make of his car matched Skerrit's, too. And to top things off, Skerrit was murdered later that very same day."

"And, what, you think he was Doctor Enigma?"

Byrne shook his head. "I think it was Doctor Enigma who murdered him. I think the whole thing was orchestrated by Doctor Enigma. I think he tricked me into getting the card, then hired Skerrit to steal it. Then I think he murdered Skerrit to cover his tracks."

"Geez."

"What's more, I'm fairly sure I know Doctor Enigma's real identity."

"Really?"

"Yes." Byrne leaned even farther forward, a bitter glint in his eyes. "I believe that Doctor Enigma is none other than Professor Hans Kranhauser."

"No way!" Calvin exclaimed, masking his complete lack of surprise by widening his eyes and dropping his jaw. "He's my Intro to Philosophy professor!"

Byrne raised an eyebrow. "Is he, now?"

"Yeah, and boy, is he a weirdo! But how can you be sure it was him?"

"Several reasons. For one thing, early last week I had to come back to my office one night after hours. When I got up here, I saw Kranhauser and Skerrit talking quietly right outside his office. The moment they saw me, they darted into the office quicker than cockroaches. Admittedly, it's not unheard of for Kranhauser to be working that late, but Skerrit had no reason to be here. It was after hours. He was off shift. And their behavior was nothing if not suspicious. Honestly, I didn't attach too much importance to the incident at the time, but after I discovered that Skerrit was the burglar, it of course took on a whole new significance. What's more, Doctor Enigma had sent me a few emails in the course of our correspondence. In the wake of the theft and the murder, I tracerouted those emails and discovered they had come from somewhere in this building. And the times they were sent coincided with times that Kranhauser spent alone in his office. Putting the pieces together, I realized that Kranhauser was almost certainly the mastermind behind this whole thing. He's always been a crank, raving about power and strength and nonsense like that. He's exactly the type of person who would be drawn to the cards."

"Totally," Calvin agreed.

"After that, I started following him when I could. I didn't learn much, though he was behaving very oddly. For instance, he disappeared into Chandler's basement for over an hour on Friday night. I don't know what that was all about. I thought maybe he had hidden the card down there, but later on I spent two hours searching the place and didn't find anything."

"Huh. That's weird." Calvin had to struggle with every fiber of his being to hide his excitement. Now he knew who they had seen in the steam tunnels. It was Kranhauser!

"And on Saturday night," Byrne went on, "someone called me up and lured me onto campus. They were masking their voice electronically, so I couldn't tell for sure who it was. But while I was gone, my house was broken into yet again."

Calvin's heart skipped a beat. His excitement was now a distant memory. "Oh, uh, really? How do you know?"

Byrne gave a grim smile. "Oh, I learned from past mistakes. I haven't had the time to have a security system installed, but after the first robbery, I had newer, better locks put on the doors. I figured that might not be enough, though, so I set up measures to alert me if anyone broke in while I was out."

"What, like hairs strategically placed in drawers, or something like that?"

"Something like that."

But Calvin knew it wasn't hairs. It was the queen of spades. Byrne must have propped it against the door or slid it into the gap along the top of the door, and then when Calvin, Cynthia, and Kaarina opened the door, the card had fallen onto the mat.

"Kranhauser already had the card," Byrne went on, "so I don't know why he would need to break in again. Maybe he wanted to make sure I didn't have any other cards. Then again, it looked like someone was in my home office, so maybe he was hoping to get on my computer and delete the Doctor Enigma emails."

"That would make a lot of sense," Calvin said, eager to keep the suspicion on Kranhauser. It occurred to him that at this point it would be logical to ask why Byrne didn't just go to the police. But Calvin knew the answer to that, and rather than put Byrne on the spot, he decided to avoid the topic entirely. Best to just keep playing the uncritical esoterica geek. "This whole thing is crazy. It's like some-thing out of a movie. Conspiracies and murders and an-cient artifacts." Calvin shook his head with affected awe.

Byrne sat back with a crafty smile.

"You know," he said, "I think maybe it's fate that brought you here. I think maybe we can help each other out."

"Really? How?"

"I want my card back. I went through too much to get

it to let it go so easily. But I need help to do it. I can't do it myself. If you help me, there's a lot I could do for you in return, even apart from giving you a chance to see and handle a genuine piece of occult history up close. I can guarantee you'll get an A-plus not only in World History, but also in any other classes of mine you might take. And there are all kinds of other ways I can help you out in your college career. It can't hurt to have a friend on the faculty to pull some strings for you when you need it. How would you like that?"

"Sure," Calvin said. Actually, none of this was anything Calvin thought he needed. His grades were excellent, and he wasn't obsessive enough about school to care about getting an A-plus in anything. Having a friend on the faculty wasn't so bad, but having a paranoid, thieving so-called friend on the faculty who would probably wind up worrying that you would steal his precious card *would* be bad. But Calvin played along anyway. "That's very generous of you. But how exactly can I help?"

"We need to fight fire with fire. He broke into my house. It's only fair we do the same to him. But not just his house. I was thinking we could start with his office. Like I said, he's been spending a lot of time after hours here in Chandler, so he may well be hiding the card here."

"But doesn't he keep his office locked? How are we gonna get in?"

With a smirk, Byrne reached into his pocket and pulled out a key. It was shiny and new, with not a scratch or smudge on it anywhere.

"With this," Byrne said. He handed it to Calvin.

"Is this for his office?"

"It is indeed. I'm thinking it would be best if you performed the search yourself. After all, it would be awkward for me to get caught down there. I have no reason to be in that area. But since you're a student of his, you have the perfect alibi. The best time for you to go would be during World History tomorrow. Kranhauser teaches a class at the exact same time, and the halls are usually pretty empty then. If need be, I can cover for you and say you were in my class. And in the unlikely event you get caught, just claim that you stopped by to ask Kranhauser a question about something from class and you found the door open and the light on. You assumed he was in the bathroom or something, so you were waiting for him to come back. No one'll be able to prove differently."

"Why don't I just go after he's left for the day?"

Byrne shook his head. "Not a good idea. To search the office, you'll need to turn the lights on. Kranhauser or someone else might see it from outside. It's actually safer during the day, when we'll know exactly where he is."

"Makes sense." Actually, he wasn't sure it did, but he didn't want to tell Byrne that. "So, um, where did you get a key to his office, if you don't mind my asking?"

Byrne suddenly looked cagey.

"Oh, I have my sources," he said. His mouth twitched, as if he were reining in a grimace, or perhaps a smile.

Calvin felt a chill race down his spine. Although he accepted Byrne's theory that Skerrit had been murdered by Kranhauser, that still left Lou Guglio's recent death unexplained. Could Guglio have been Byrne's source for the key? Till now Calvin had been coming to the conclusion that Kranhauser was the only homicidal party in all of this and that aside from stealing the card at the history symposium, Byrne was innocent. But now he wasn't so sure.

"So do we have a deal?" Byrne asked.

Calvin nodded.

"Absolutely," he said. "I mean, how can I pass this up? Not only do I get to help see justice done, but I'll have a chance to see an actual artifact of great mystical power." He grinned excitedly for added effect.

Byrne grinned, too. But his was a smug grin, a predator's grin, the grin of the cat who knows the canary is his.

"Excellent," he said.

Chapter 24

After her meeting with Kranhauser, Cynthia headed back downstairs. As she passed Byrne's closed office door, she thought she heard Calvin's voice inside saying something about hairs and drawers. She hoped that Calvin's meeting didn't turn out as weird and creepy as hers had been.

Kaarina sat waiting on the bottom step of the stairs.

"How was meeting?" Kaarina asked as Cynthia sat down next to her.

"Technically it did what it was supposed to do," Cynthia said. "I've got a dinner date at Kranhauser's house tomorrow evening. But personally, I'm gonna need an all-night shower before I feel clean again." She stuck out her tongue and made a retching sound. "That guy is a total sleazoid."

Kaarina laid a hand on her upper back and gave her a sympathetic smile. "I am sorry you must do these things."

"Uh, yeah." The truth was, Cynthia's feelings of griminess were already gone, blotted out by Kaarina's soft, warm touch. Kaarina was keeping her hand there an awfully long time, wasn't she? Cynthia glanced at Kaarina and saw that Kaarina was staring fixedly at something on her back. But what?

Even as she wondered this, Kaarina lifted a lock of Cynthia's hair.

"You have such beautiful hair," Kaarina said as she watched Cynthia's red tresses glide through her fingers.

"I do?" Cynthia said. She stared at Kaarina's face. It

was so close. So beautiful. So kissable. Her heart was beating very hard.

"Oh, yes." Kaarina's gaze shifted from Cynthia's hair to Cynthia's eyes. She smiled. "When I was girl, I wanted red hair like yours."

"Really? I thought everyone wanted blonde hair. I know I did."

Kaarina smiled. "And blondes want other things. What is expression? Bushes next door are greener? Or something like that, yes?"

"Yeah, something like that." She was barely aware of what she was saying at this point. All she could think about was how badly she wanted to kiss Kaarina. She wasn't sure if she should, though. This probably wasn't the best time. But then again, when was?

Kaarina stared at Cynthia a moment longer, then let go of Cynthia's hair and leaned back with her elbows on the step behind her. She gazed off across the lobby, her eyes distant and musing.

"Perhaps I should dye hair," she said.

"Um, yeah," Cynthia muttered, annoyed with herself for letting the moment pass unseized. But then she glanced down, and her eyes widened. Kaarina was wearing her Black Lodge cropped baby doll tee, and the way she was leaning back made her breasts jut out until they looked as if they would rip right through the light-blue fabric. Below the shirt's bottom edge was a mouth-watering swath of naked skin in the center of which was Kaarina's belly button with its gold ring. Cynthia imagined herself sliding her tongue into Kaarina's navel, feeling the warm skin and the cold golden metal on her tongue at the same time.

Cynthia realized that Kaarina had gone abnormally

still. She glanced up at Kaarina's face, and a jolt ran through her when she saw that although Kaarina's head was still facing the far side of the lobby, her eyes had swiveled around and were looking right at Cynthia. Kaarina smiled slyly, knowingly, and raised one blonde eyebrow.

"Looking for something?" she asked.

"Oh, I, um—I—I was just looking at your navel ring."

"Ah." Kaarina stuck her belly out and wiggled the ring back and forth with a fingertip. "My ring. I get it in Tokyo. Do you like it?"

"Yeah. It's…it's nice. Do you have any other piercings?"

"Not yet. But I am thinking of one in lip."

"Oh?" Cynthia lifted her gaze to Kaarina's mouth.

The mouth smiled.

"Not that lip," Kaarina said. "Lip down here." She spread her legs and patted her crotch.

"Oh!" Cynthia stared at Kaarina's crotch for a moment, then realized she probably shouldn't gawp at it for too long. She swiftly shifted her gaze back to Kaarina's face. "Uh, that would hurt, wouldn't it?"

"Probably at first. But I hear that after you are used to it, it feels very good when making sex."

"Re—" Cynthia's throat had gone dry as a bone, choking off her words. She cleared it. "Really?"

Kaarina grinned. "That is what I hear, yes. I want to find out if it is true. It will be nice if it is. But of course, I need to find just the right person to help me find out."

"Um, yeah." Was that a come-on? Had the unseized moment returned? Did she have a second chance?

A door opened and closed near the top of the stairs. Cynthia and Kaarina looked up. A moment later Calvin came into view and began to hurry down the stairs. Cynthia cursed his timing. But then she saw the huge, triumphant grin stretched across his face. Kaarina saw it, too. The two girls sprang to their feet.

"I've got it," he whispered when he reached them. Or at least it was an attempt at a whisper. He was so excited that he was having trouble keeping his voice at an even level.

"Got what?" Cynthia asked.

Calvin glanced up at the top of the stairs, then headed toward the exit and motioned for them to follow. "Come on."

They went outside and strode quickly down the path toward the Student Center. Once they had put a good amount of distance between themselves and Chandler Hall, Calvin slowed his pace and said, "It's Kranhauser. Kranhauser has the card."

"Are you certain?" Kaarina asked.

Calvin related his conversation with Professor Byrne.

"And you believe him?" Cynthia said.

He nodded. "Well, except for the bit about how Byrne himself got the card. It's clear he was trying to paint himself in the best light possible, as a poor wounded innocent. But the rest of it, yeah. Everything fits the facts perfectly."

"Wow," Cynthia said. "Real progress at last. That makes my unpleasant interlude with Kranhauser actually kind of worth it."

"Unpleasant? Why? What happened?"

She filled him in on the details of her meeting with Professor Kranhauser.

"What a creep," Calvin said. "Sorry you had to endure all that. Unfortunately, your little dinner with him tomorrow is more critical than ever now. It'll be our big chance to find the card."

"I'm not so sure," Cynthia said. "I mean, judging by what Byrne told you about Kranhauser disappearing into the basement, Kranhauser might have hidden the card in the steam tunnels somewhere. Or somewhere that's accessible via the tunnels. Maybe we should be focusing our efforts down there."

"Yeah, but it sounds like Kranhauser was only down there the one time. For all we know, he might have gone down there just to dispose of evidence or something. Or he might have hidden the card down there right after Skerrit's death, then went down there Friday night to get it and move it somewhere else. And in any case, I'd rather not undertake an extensive search of a sprawling underground tunnel system unless we're damn sure that what we're looking for is actually down there."

Cynthia sighed. "All right, all right. I guess I have to venture into the lion's den, after all. It was just the most pitiful sort of wishful thinking to believe otherwise."

"Don't worry," Calvin said, clapping a hand on her shoulder. "We'll be right behind you."

"Yes," Kaarina said with a crisp nod. She clapped a hand on Cynthia's other shoulder. "And once lion has roofie, he will be sleepy little pussy cat."

Chapter 25

Calvin was in the middle of brushing his teeth when there was a knock on the door. He rolled his eyes, sure he knew who it was. Indeed, he had been more or less expecting it, though not quite this late. It was nearly ten-thirty p.m.

After a quick dinner in the Food Court, Calvin, Cynthia, and Kaarina had spent nearly two hours going over their plan. In theory it shouldn't have taken that long, since it was a fairly simple plan: Cynthia would go into Kranhauser's house looking delectable, drop the powdered roofie into Kranhauser's wine at the earliest available opportunity, wait till he passed out, then let in Calvin and Kaarina, and the three of them would search the place from top to bottom.

But Cynthia couldn't stop worrying about possible hitches. Calvin appreciated foresight and contingency planning as much as the next guy, and he did understand Cynthia's concerns. After all, she was the one braving the wrinkled hands of a septuagenarian lecher. But still...

"What if he doesn't drink the wine?" Cynthia had asked.

"Then you make a toast," Kaarina said. "Make him drink."

"Well, what if he doesn't leave his glass unattended, and I can't put the powder in?"

"Then you will use bathroom. While there, you send us text message, and one of us will call him on his home phone and distract him. Then you put powder in."

"What if he turns the phone off?"

"Then you'll spill your wine," Calvin said, trying hard to keep the exasperation from his voice. "Like any guy, he'll insist on cleaning it up himself and then getting you another glass. He wants to get you drunk, after all. While he's doing that, then you drug his own glass."

"What if the powder doesn't dissolve fast enough? What if he sees it in his wine?"

"He will not," Kaarina said, likewise sounding on the thin edge of exasperation. "Roofie dissolves very fast."

Eventually Cynthia ran out of questions, though she didn't really look any less worried. Calvin knew her well enough to know that it was only a matter of time before she raised a new crop of highly unlikely worst-case scenarios.

Which meant that maybe it was best that their evening together ended earlier than expected. It wasn't even nine o'clock when Kaarina shot to her feet with a gasp.

"I must go!" she exclaimed, pulling on her backpack. "I forget: I have test tomorrow. I have been spending so much time with two of you lately, I forget all about it. I have not studied. I must go."

"We could help you study, or something," Cynthia said.

"No, no. Thank you, but I will be okay."

Kaarina left. Without her, some spark had gone out of the evening. Calvin and Cynthia hadn't felt much like drinking any more beer (there was still nearly half the case left), and there wasn't much left to discuss vis-à-vis tomorrow's plan. Unless, of course, Cynthia came up with more questions, which Calvin felt sure she would do at any moment. But she didn't, and twenty minutes after Kaarina left, Cynthia announced she was heading up to her room.

"I want to make sure I'm rested up for tomorrow," she told him. "I have a feeling it'll wind up being a very wearying day, one way or another."

Alone for the evening for the first time in days, Calvin hadn't known what to do with himself. He read several pages of William Corliss's *Neglected Geological Anomalies* and then watched an old episode of *Buffy the Vampire Slayer* on Hulu before deciding he might as well go to bed early himself for a change. Cynthia had been right: Tomorrow could well be a busy and trying day.

But now it seemed that Cynthia hadn't gone to bed quite so early after all. No doubt she had been what-iffing instead and wanted to share her new worries with Calvin.

Another knock sounded. Calvin spat the blue-white toothpaste foam into the sink, set the toothbrush into its holder, and hurried to the door.

He opened the door.

It was Kaarina.

"Uh, hi," Calvin said.

She gave him a small, tight smile. "May I come in?"

"Of course." He stepped aside and waved her in, then shut the door behind her.

She walked to the center of the room, then stopped, her back to him.

He came up behind her and looked at her long, straight blonde hair and the tight blue shirt below it. He had turned off all the lights except his desk lamp in preparation for bed, and the dim light made the room seem small and intimate, yet also unreal, dream-like.

"So what's up?" he asked.

She didn't move or respond for a moment. He was about to repeat the question when she suddenly turned to face him. Her eyes were large and worried.

"I am sorry to bother you," she said. "But I…I just need to talk to someone."

"Why?" he said. "What's up?"

She shook her head. "I do not understand what is wrong with me. I become scared out of nowhere. I sit and read notes for class, and suddenly I am struck by fact that two people are dead. *Dead.* I realize we could become dead too. This is not just fun adventure. This is not just games. Tomorrow we go into house of man who is probably murderer. I think of his guns and his dead animals and…" She looked down at the floor. "You probably think I am silly girl to be so scared."

"No," he said. "Just the opposite. I'm scared, too. It's normal to feel that way in a situation like this. You'd be a fool if you weren't at least a little scared."

"I suppose so," she mumbled. She heaved a sigh that hitched halfway through as if she were fighting back tears. She didn't look up from the floor.

Seeing that his words hadn't comforted her as much as he had hoped, Calvin stepped forward and gently put his arms around her. She made a soft, contented sound and nestled against him. Her arms closed around his back. The delicious scent of vanilla filled his nostrils.

"Thank you," she murmured against his neck. Her warm breath fluttered against his skin. She lifted her head and looked him in the eye. "You make me feel…better. Safer."

"I'm glad," he said.

They stared at each other a moment. Her gaze flicked down to his lips, then rose back up to his eyes. Her lips parted slightly.

"Calvin…" she whispered.

Feeling as if he were caught in the grip of forces bigger

than himself, as if he were following a script that was encoded in every atom of his masculine being, he leaned in and kissed her. With a small sigh of satisfaction, she kissed back.

They kissed gently at first. But their kisses swiftly grew harder and more passionate. Her fingers curled into claws and clutched at his back. Her tongue darted into his mouth. His own tongue met it and slid wetly against it. His cock was an iron rod in his jeans. She ground her pelvis against it. He stiffened with a gasp.

Growing bolder, he moved his hands down from the small of her back to her ass and squeezed. In response she growled and lightly nipped his lower lip. He squeezed her ass harder, kneading it. One of her hands slid down to his crotch. It settled on the hard bulge in the front of his jeans and began to stroke it. He sucked in a sharp breath.

Kaarina dropped to her knees and fumbled at the snap of his jeans. Before he knew what was happening, his pants were halfway down and she was delicately biting his penis through his boxers.

"Oh, God," he muttered.

She hooked her fingers under the waistband of his boxers and yanked them down. His cock sprang free. He wiggled his feet out of his jeans and underwear, leaving him clad in nothing but his socks and his T-shirt.

Grinning up at him, Kaarina gripped the base of his cock with one hand and gently rolled his balls with the other. Then she extended her tongue and swiped it across the tip of his penis. His cock twitched in response. She gave a low, lusty laugh, then leaned forward and engulfed his penis in her warm, wet mouth. She moved her head back and forth with smooth, practiced ease.

"Oh, God," he said again. He closed his eyes and let

his head drop back. His fingers burrowed into her golden hair.

Her head moved faster. Her hand continued fondling his balls. The other hand let go of the base of his cock. He kept expecting it to reappear somewhere else—his butt or his chest or something—but it remained MIA.

He opened his eyes and looked down. The hand, he saw, was now stuffed down the front of her jeans. The bulge under the denim moved back and forth across her crotch with a slow, regular rhythm.

Her eyes met his as she continued sucking his dick. The shaft of his cock glistened with her spit. Her cheeks were sunken as she sucked.

Calvin almost laughed out loud with delight. He couldn't believe this was happening. He was finally getting it on with a girl. And not just any girl. He was getting his cherry popped by a beautiful, intelligent Nordic goddess. This was much better than giving up his virginity too early to some pimply girl behind the high school bleachers. He was making up for lost time and then some. He was living out every young man's fantasy on his first go.

Her movements grew faster and faster until her head was bobbing like a metalhead in a mosh pit. Her blonde hair was swishing back and forth. A series of rhythmic grunts were rising from her throat.

Calvin's breath grew faster. His body tensed. He wasn't going to last much longer. Should he break this off before he came so they could do some actual fucking?

Before his thoughts could proceed any further, his arousal hit critical mass, and his mind went white with an orgasm. His hands clutched her hair as if he meant to tear it out of her head, and his cock spasmed and jetted blast after blast of semen into her mouth. She swallowed every drop, her throat visibly expanding and contracting, then kept his cock in her mouth, still sucking gently, until it was limp and drained.

She pulled away, licking her lips, and stood up.

"Did you like that?" she asked, grinning.

"I loved it." He pulled her close and kissed her. He could taste the salty tang of his semen on her lips. He didn't care. "But you didn't get much out of that."

"I get enjoyment from giving you enjoyment. Besides, you are young and healthy. You will be ready again in no time. In the meanwhile, you can give favor back to me, if you are understanding what I mean."

He understood perfectly. He cupped her face and kissed her on her lips, her cheeks, her neck. He pulled her Black Lodge shirt up and off and cast it aside. Her breasts were perfect: full and round, with small, tight nipples. He took a nipple in his mouth and sucked it while lightly tweaking the other with one hand. His other hand snaked down to her denim-covered crotch and started rubbing.

She groaned and ground her pelvis against his hand. He kissed and licked his way down her taut belly, unable to resist giving her navel ring a quick flick with his tongue as he passed it, until he was on his knees before her. He tugged her jeans down over her hips, revealing a pink thong beneath. A faint line of dampness ran along the thong's crotch. Kaarina kicked off her shoes, then stepped out of the jeans.

Calvin ran the back of his finger down the front of her thong. He felt the tiny bump of her clitoris through the fabric and felt the moistness and warmth below it. Then he peeled off the thong, revealing the treasures beneath. Her pubic hair was shaved to form an inverted blonde triangle, like an arrow pointing to her pussy. Calvin stared in awe at the smooth, rosy folds of her labia, atop which her clitoris sat like a crown jewel. The slit of her vagina glistened. He could smell the musky scent of her arousal mixed with vanilla.

He leaned forward, stuck out his tongue, and flicked its tip across her clit.

"Nn," she grunted. She grabbed his head and pulled it toward her while thrusting her hips out to meet it, with the result that his face was nearly squashed against her crotch. Her pubic hair tickled his nostrils.

He started licking her clit. At first he worried that he wasn't doing it very well. This was his first time, after all. But any doubts were soon dispelled by Kaarina's obvious enjoyment of the tonguing. Her breath quickened. Her legs began to tremble, the muscles of her inner thighs quivering like the flanks of a skittish horse. Her pussy grew even slicker and wetter. When he thrust two fingers inside her, the walls of her vagina felt as if they had been slathered with Astroglide.

"Faster," she hissed through gritted teeth. "Lick me faster. Don't stop."

He complied, and less than ten seconds later her vaginal muscles clenched around his fingers. Her whole body shuddered, and she let out a long, low moan.

He stood up and wiped his mouth with the back of his hand. He realized that she had been right about him being ready again soon; his cock was hard and yearning for more. Pleasuring her had turned him on.

She noticed this, too.

"Ah, you are back into action, I am seeing," she said. "Good. I am not done with you yet."

"Glad to hear it."

She kissed him, then pulled off his T-shirt. He then

removed his socks. Now both of them were completely naked.

She surveyed his nude body for a moment, then gave him a playfully lewd smile. "I think we must make sex now."

"Why, I think you're right."

They lay down side by side on the bed and kissed for a little while. Then she rolled over onto her back and pulled him atop her. They stared into each other's eyes, their warm breaths commingling. She spread her legs wider. His body settled into the space between her legs. The head of his penis poked the moist slit of her pussy.

"Um, you are on the Pill, aren't you?" he asked.

"Of course. Is not everybody these days?"

"Well, I'm not."

She smiled. "You are silly." Then she craned her head up and kissed him. With one hand she grabbed his cock and held it in line with her pussy while with the other she pressed down on his butt, driving him forward, into her.

He gasped. Her vagina was smooth and wet and fit his penis like a sheath. This felt better than he had ever imagined.

He propped himself up on his arms because he had some vague concerns about crushing her, and started thrusting in and out. His rhythm was halting and awkward at first, but he soon found a good pace. If he hadn't already come, he probably would have shot his wad in about twenty seconds. Maybe that had been Kaarina's intention in sucking him off.

Before long, she wrapped her arms around him and pulled him down on top of her. He let her. Obviously she wasn't worried about him crushing her, so he wouldn't worry about it either. He found that in this position he was able to fuck her even harder and faster.

After several minutes, when the sweat was starting to drip off him and his rhythm was slowing down from exhaustion, Kaarina pushed him up a little.

"Turn over," she said. "Onto back."

They managed to reverse positions without Calvin pulling out. Now she was on top, and she started fucking him with as much vigor as he had fucked her. She didn't piston herself straight up and down, as Calvin had expected from seeing lots of porn, but instead moved her hips forward-backward, as if she were trying to scratch an itch on her crotch. After watching her for a minute he realized that she was moving in a manner that ground her clit against his pubic bone. That was fine. When they had been going at it missionary-style, he had been a little concerned because she didn't seem to be having any orgasms. Now, though, she was working to rectify that.

She rode him hard and fast. The bed rattled and the headboard banged against the wall with every thrust. Calvin remembered the countless times he had been forced to listen to his dorm-mates' sexual antics. Now, finally, he was the one making the sounds.

Kaarina's movements suddenly became even faster. She shut her eyes, bared her teeth, and let out a long, low growl as another orgasm seized her. Her hands curled into talons on his chest, and he felt pokes of pain where her fingernails dug into his skin. Her vagina squeezed his cock in quick, hard pulses. The sensation pushed him over the edge, too, and with a groan he came.

She collapsed on top of him and kissed him, her blonde hair hanging down and hiding their conjoined faces in a golden tent. Their sweat-slick bodies slid against each other as their heart-rates and body temperatures slowly returned to normal.

"That was much fun," she said.

"I'll say. We'll have to do that again sometime."

"Hmm. There are many sometimes during night."

She kissed him again, then snuggled closer, her eyes closed, her cheek pressed tight to his. He smiled up at the ceiling through a gap in her hair. Life was good.

Chapter 26

Calvin might have dozed for a while. He wasn't sure. He was floating in a dreamy, sated post-coital haze. If he slept, it hadn't been for long, because when he finally lifted his head and checked the clock, it was only eleven-thirty.

He looked at Kaarina, who had slid off him and now lay beside him, one arm on his chest, one leg draped over his, her pubic hair a soft tangle against his thigh. At first he thought she was asleep, but then she cracked her eyelids and regarded him with sleepy eyes.

"Mm." She smiled and snuggled closer. "Do you have food? Making sex gives me hunger."

"Yeah, I think I've got something. Let me check."

"Oh, yes," she said, rolling onto her back as he got out of bed. "That is right. Your little refrigerator is nearly empty."

"There was something in there, though, wasn't there?"

"Webs of spiders."

"Har har har." He opened the mini-fridge. The cold air that poured out made his nipples harden. "There's still about half that case of beer."

"Ugh. No beer on empty stomach."

He moved a couple of bottles and found the cheddar cheese. He checked the expiration date on the wrapper. Last week. He sniffed it. It still smelled fine. He hunted around amid the heaps of books and papers atop the fridge and found a dented box of Saltines.

"We could have cheese and crackers," he said.

"That is good."

He laid some Saltines on a plate, then started cutting slices of cheese and placing them atop the crackers.

"Oh, hey," he said. "I've got a question for you. It's kind of a philosophical thing."

She groaned. "Oh, no. Philosophy."

"Is that bad?"

"Philosophy is wonderful if you do not have to be in real world. But what is question?"

"Okay, if you had to choose between being in love for the rest of your life—perfectly in love—with someone who loves you back, but never, ever having sex again, or being able to have sex as often as you like with whoever you like, but never being in love again, which would you choose?"

She frowned. "That is long question."

"Do you need me to run through it again?"

"No. I understand it, I think. And answer is easy: I choose sex."

"You do?"

"Yes. Because sex is healthy and is good for you, and it always feels good. It is, um..." She waved her hand about as if trying to conjure the word she wanted out of thin air. "Tangible?" She flashed him a wince, as if she were sure she had messed up. "That is word that makes sense, yes?"

"It makes perfect sense."

"Yes. Good. On other hand, love is emotion, and emotions are up and down. They do not last long. Love is not always good. It can be bad and black. It can make you crazy. Are you understanding what I say?"

"I understand perfectly. I said it once, and I'll say it again: You're a girl after my own heart."

213

He brought the cheese and crackers over to her, and they sat side by side on the bed and ate. While he watched her brush a few stray cracker crumbs off her bare belly, he reflected how nice it was to be sitting here all cozy and together and unselfconsciously naked with a girl he had just fucked. He felt peaceful, contented. In some ways, this was better than the sex itself.

When they were done eating (and brushing crumbs off the sheets and various body parts), Calvin set the empty plate on the bedside table and snuggled close to Kaarina again. They kissed. Their tongues grappled. Their hands moved slowly across each other's naked skin. Calvin's cock began to swell and harden.

Kaarina smiled. "Are you ready for more?"

"Oh, yeah."

She scooted down on the bed and tongued his nipple. Her fingers closed on his cock.

There was a knock on the door.

"Shit," Calvin muttered. He felt certain it was Cynthia. The worried and almost guilty look in Kaarina's eyes showed that she felt the same certainty.

What should he do? He didn't want Cynthia to know Kaarina was here. Sure, now that he and Kaarina had hooked up, Cynthia was going to have to be told, but not right now. Not like this. He had to find a way to get rid of Cynthia quickly.

"Stay right where you are," he whispered to Kaarina. "As long as I don't open the door too far, you won't be seen."

Kaarina nodded.

He didn't have a robe, so he grabbed his T-shirt and jeans off the floor and put them on. He checked the floor to make sure the rest of his and Kaarina's doffed clothes wouldn't be visible from the doorway. Everything looked fine. He opened the door a crack and peeked out.

As expected, it was Cynthia.

"Hi," she said. "I didn't wake you up, did I?"

"Uh, no. No, I was, um, just going to bed, though."

"Oh. Sorry. I guess I should have called. But I was just thinking about tomorrow, and..." She shook her head. "You know what? Never mind. We can talk about it in the morning."

"Yeah. That's, uh, that's a good idea."

She gave him a smiling, questioning look. "You seem edgy. Are you okay?" She peered over the top of his head. "Do you have a girl in there or something?" She meant it as a joke.

"No! I mean, um..."

She froze, still peering over his head, her eyes fixed on something. He looked behind him and saw that although he had checked the floor for clothes, he should have checked elsewhere: Kaarina's Black Lodge baby doll tee was draped over the back of his desk chair in full view of the doorway.

He turned back to Cynthia. She was still staring at Kaarina's shirt. Her face was blank. Too blank. It was the mask-like blankness of someone who is too stunned to feel anything. Then her lips pressed together into a thin bloodless line, and she looked at Calvin.

"It's, uh, it's not what you think," he said.

"Oh?" she said.

She thrust out a hand and pushed the door hard, forcing it out of his grasp. The door swung open far enough to reveal Kaarina sitting at the head of the bed with the sheet pulled up to her chin.

"Um, hello," Kaarina said.

Cynthia just stared at Kaarina for a moment, her lower lip and chin trembling slightly. Then she looked at Calvin. Her mouthed twisted about in what appeared to be an attempt at a smile.

"Sorry I interrupted," she said, her voice cracking. Then she turned and strode down the hall fast enough to make her long red hair billow out behind her.

"Cyn, wait," Calvin called.

She didn't. She just shouldered through the door to the stairwell without breaking stride, and was gone.

Calvin shut the door and walked slowly to the center of the room. He stood there staring at the blue shirt on the chair. He didn't look at Kaarina.

He felt like a shit. But why should he? He and Cynthia had essentially been in competition for Kaarina. Both of them had known it. And now he had won. He should be happy. Instead he felt low and slimy, as if he had betrayed his best friend. He hadn't, though. They were all adults. No one owned anyone else. No one had a right to anyone or anything. The cards had fallen where they had, and that was that.

But he still felt like a shit.

"Maybe I should go after her," he said, looking at the door. "Or maybe I should call her. If I talk to her—"

Kaarina shook her head. "I do not think she will want to talk right now. I think it would be best to wait until tomorrow."

Calvin wasn't sure he liked the idea of waiting that long. He feared that Cynthia would do something drastic. Something crazy. He had visions of her cutting her wrists in the ladies' room sink. But in the end, he decided to accept Kaarina's advice. After all, a girl would understand the intricate workings of the female brain better than he ever could.

"I suppose you're right," he said with a sigh.

Kaarina got out of bed and started pulling on her clothes.

"I should go," she said quietly, not looking at him. "I am sorry, but…my test…I…"

"It's okay. I get it. Frankly, I'm not really in the mood for company anymore anyway. I think I just want to be alone for a while. No offense."

"I understand. We can talk more tomorrow."

"Yeah. Tomorrow."

Fully dressed now, she came up to him and kissed him on the lips. Nothing passionate or sexy. Just a quick, simple kiss.

"Whatever else has happened or will happen, I had good time tonight. Very good time."

He smiled sadly. "Me too."

She left.

He sat on the edge of the bed and stared at the crumb-littered plate on the table beside it. Kaarina had been right: Love wasn't always good. It could be bad and black indeed.

Chapter 27

Cynthia managed to make it all the way back to her dorm room without shedding a single tear. But, oh, how she wanted to. How every fiber of her being howled to unleash all her rage and despair in one great and terrible outpouring.

But she refused. She didn't want to parade her misery about for all the world to see. Not that there was actually anyone around right now. The hallways on her floor were empty, and the only signs of life were the muffled strains of music coming from a few rooms, and a burst of collective laughter from RA Cindy's room.

When Cynthia got back to her room, she slammed the door so hard the pens and pencils in the coffee mug on her desk resettled themselves with faint clinks. Down the hall a girl cried, "Quiet!"

"Fuck you," Cynthia muttered, her lips contorted into a sneer. "Just fuck you. Just—just—"

She shut her eyes, balled her hands into fists, and scrunched up her face as if she were about to scream or punch the wall.

Instead she burst into tears. She flung herself face down across her bed and sobbed until her throat was raw and her eyes were red and there were two wet spots the size of silver dollars on the sheet.

"Why?" she moaned. "God damn it, why?"

She had known this might happen, but that didn't make it hurt any less. Part of her wanted to hate Calvin and Kaarina, but she couldn't. Well, okay, maybe a little bit. In fact, maybe even more than a little. But she knew she shouldn't. It wasn't anyone's fault. It was just fate, chance, her perpetually shitty luck with girls, the random falling of the cards.

She really thought she had found the right girl this time, finally had a chance for something real. She thought she might even have been starting to fall in love with Kaarina. Beautiful, clever, sexy Kaarina. And Cynthia had felt sure she had seen definite interest on Kaarina's part. Had she been wrong? Had she been misinterpreting Kaarina's feelings so completely?

She wasn't sure how long she lay there, trying not to cry but crying anyway, trying not to wallow in misery but wallowing anyway, trying not to envision what Calvin and Kaarina had done and were maybe still doing even now but envisioning every awful detail anyway. Her blubbery interlude was probably only about twenty minutes, but it felt like hours, like a little eternity of agony.

However long it was, it was ended by a knock on the door.

"Cynthia?"

It was Kaarina. Cynthia's heart leaped. Then she hated herself for responding so eagerly to that voice that had no doubt been moaning Calvin's name not long ago. But she couldn't help it. Something about Kaarina—about her feelings for Kaarina—made it impossible for Cynthia not to respond. Like Pavlov's stupid dog salivating at the sound of the bell.

"Hold on," Cynthia said, wincing at the shaky, stressed-out sound of her voice. She got up, wiped her eyes, and checked herself in the mirror. Her eyes were red-rimmed and bloodshot. Not much she could do about that.

She opened the door. There stood Kaarina, fully clothed now, looking perfectly normal. If Cynthia hadn't seen otherwise, she never would have known that the clothes now draping Kaarina had been strewn about Calvin's room half an hour ago, that Kaarina's body had been in his bed.

Then again, the nervous smile Kaarina was giving her would have provided ample evidence that something was definitely wrong.

"Can I come in?" Kaarina said. "Please?"

Cynthia considered saying no and slamming the door in her face. But she couldn't. She just couldn't. The bell rang. The drooling doggie scampered forward.

Cynthia stepped aside and Kaarina entered. Cynthia shut the door.

Kaarina walked to the center of the room, then turned and faced Cynthia.

"I am sorry," she said.

Cynthia dismissively waved a hand, trying to show that she was as blasé and mature about these matters as experienced, globe-trotting Kaarina. The trembling of her lower lip rather spoiled the attempt.

"Don't be," Cynthia said. "I don't blame you for anything. You didn't do anything wrong."

Except lead me on, she added mentally. But she didn't know if that were really true. Perhaps her own stupid eager hopefulness had led her on.

"Do not blame Calvin either," Kaarina said. "He did not—"

Cynthia sighed. "I don't blame him either. It's just…just one of those things, I guess. You two hit it off better than you and I hit it off. That happens, right? That's life."

She felt fresh tears building up inside her. She didn't want to start crying in front of Kaarina, but she wasn't sure if she could hold them back.

Kaarina looked down at the floor for a moment, frowning slightly. When she looked up at Cynthia again, her eyes were sad and troubled.

"I do not know if I agree with that, exactly. I...I did not intend for that to happen with Calvin. It just happened."

"Well, maybe that just means it was meant to be."

Kaarina firmly shook her head. "No. It was not. I enjoyed it, yes. But only on physical level. I..." She faltered, looked down again. Then she took a deep breath and looked back up at Cynthia. "Until now, my relationships have been physical things only. There has never been anything else. But now, with you, something is different. With you, there are feelings. Deep feelings. I did not realize this until I see hurt on your face earlier and I feel that hurt as if it is my own. It is as if my heart is now linked to you. When you hurt, it hurts. When you smile, it is happy. I have never felt such a thing before. The feelings are so strong they frighten me."

Cynthia's breath caught in her throat. Her tears receded unshed. She blinked at Kaarina with amazement and hope. "What?"

Kaarina took a step forward, bringing her within an arm's length of Cynthia.

"Please forgive me," Kaarina said. "I know now what you are to me. I am sorry I did not understand before."

Cynthia stared at her, spellbound, wanting her so badly her whole body ached with desire. She flashed back to the sight of Kaarina in Calvin's bed, but the memory was already hazy, distant, increasingly irrelevant, overwritten by this new revelation. All sins could be forgiven now that love was again in reach.

Kaarina took one more step forward, bringing her within Cynthia's personal space, close enough that her blonde-framed face blotted out everything else. Kaarina's eyes were heavy-lidded with desire.

"I want you, Cynthia," Kaarina said in a soft voice. "I want you as I have not wanted anything else in my life." She reached up and ran the backs of her fingers down Cynthia's cheek. The touch sent shivers throughout Cynthia's body.

"Oh, Kaarina…" Cynthia croaked.

Kaarina leaned forward, cupped Cynthia's face in her hands, and kissed her. Cynthia embraced Kaarina and pulled her close, pulled her tight, as if she meant to never let her go again.

They stood there kissing in silence for over a minute. Then one of Kaarina's hands closed on Cynthia's right breast. Cynthia wasn't wearing a bra, so Kaarina easily found her nipple through the thin cotton fabric of her T-shirt and lightly pinched it and rolled it between her thumb and forefinger.

"Ah," Cynthia gasped. Her tongue darted into Kaarina's mouth. Kaarina's tongue thrust into Cynthia's. Cynthia's hands found Kaarina's full, heavy breasts and squeezed them.

Kaarina wrapped her arms tightly around Cynthia and began to walk backward, pulling Cynthia after her while never breaking their kiss. Cynthia realized that Kaarina was navigating them toward the bed.

When they reached the edge of the bed, Kaarina maneuvered Cynthia around until Cynthia's back was to the bed. Then, still kissing, their lips and tongues still working feverishly, Kaarina pressed forward. Cynthia staggered backward until her calves hit the edge of the mattress. Kaarina continued pressing forward, forcing Cynthia to lean back farther and farther until she lost her balance and fell backward, with Kaarina falling atop her. They remained enwrapped in each other's arms the whole time, and their lips never parted. Cynthia squirmed, enjoying the feel of Kaarina's warm wonderful weight pinning her to the mattress. Cynthia's lips curved into a delirious smile beneath Kaarina's incessant kisses.

Kaarina kissed and licked her way down Cynthia's cheek and jaw and neck. She stopped at Cynthia's breasts and spent a while caressing them and nipping at the hard bumps of Cynthia's nipples through the T-shirt. Then she drew back a little and yanked up Cynthia's shirt, exposing her pale breasts and belly.

"You are so beautiful," Kaarina murmured. She took one hard red nipple in her mouth and sucked. She tweezed the other between two fingers and twisted it just hard enough to sting.

Cynthia flinched and sucked in a sharp breath between her teeth, both aroused and alarmed at the pain.

Kaarina's other hand glided down Cynthia's belly to the top of her jeans and unbuttoned the fly and unzipped the zipper. Fingers slid under the elastic waistband of Cynthia's underwear and snaked their way through the thatch of red pubic hair until they found the engorged and throbbing pink nub that till now no hand but Cynthia's had touched.

Still sucking and tweaking Cynthia's nipples, Kaarina began to rub Cynthia's clitoris, at first slowly and gently, but gradually picking up the pace, going faster, faster.

Kaarina beat her tongue across Cynthia's nipple in syncopation with her racing hand.

"Oh, God, Kaarina," Cynthia said, writhing in pleasure. She grabbed up fistfuls of sheet and raised her hips as Kaarina's hand worked at a frenzied pace. Exquisite tension built all throughout her body. Her back arched. Her teeth clenched. Kaarina's fingers kept strumming faster, faster.

The most intense orgasm of her life exploded through her. For a moment she couldn't even breathe. From the depths of her pleasure she heard a shrill sound and realized a moment later that it was herself, crying out in ecstasy.

Kaarina's fingers slowed. Cynthia rode the tail end of her pleasure back to reality, a few last twitches and shivers periodically shaking her body.

While Cynthia lay gasping, her sweat-shiny chest rising and falling, Kaarina pulled her hand from Cynthia's pants, let go of Cynthia breasts, and climbed off the bed. She knelt on the floor at the edge of the bed between Cynthia's legs.

Cynthia looked at her down the length of her body. Kaarina grinned impishly at her.

"You are wearing too many clothes," Kaarina said. "You must get naked for me now."

With that, Kaarina tugged off Cynthia's shoes and socks. Cynthia removed her T-shirt, then lay back and raised her hips to allow Kaarina to pull off her jeans.

After casting the jeans aside, Kaarina regarded Cynthia's panty-clad crotch. The plain white cotton panties were a bit askew from Kaarina's masturbatory ministrations.

Kaarina pushed Cynthia's legs apart, then leaned in

and nuzzled Cynthia's clitoris and labia through the fabric. As Kaarina's nose bumped back and forth across her clit, Cynthia felt her arousal swiftly growing again.

Kaarina looked up into Cynthia's eyes and smiled as she hooked her fingers under the waistband of Cynthia's underwear and slowly, teasingly, peeled them off. Cynthia moaned softly as she felt cool air wash over her warm, drenched pussy. She realized she was now completely naked before the still fully clothed Kaarina. She felt bare, exposed. And also hornier than she had ever felt in her life. Her pussy throbbed for Kaarina's touch.

It got it. Kaarina leaned in and lapped at Cynthia's clit with animalistic vigor. Three fingers slid into Cynthia's vagina and began to fuck her hard. In no time Cynthia was groaning and arching her back with her second orgasm. It was just as incredible as the first.

When it was over, Kaarina kissed and licked her way back up Cynthia's naked body, tonguing the salty sweat from her skin. Then they kissed long and passionately. The cotton of Kaarina's shirt and the denim of her jeans were pleasantly coarse against Cynthia's body.

"Your turn," Cynthia said. She rolled over on top of Kaarina, then imitated much of what Kaarina had done to her: first peeling off her clothes, then sucking and biting her nipples, and finally giving Kaarina's pussy a vigorous tongue-lashing.

Kaarina took longer to come than Cynthia had, perhaps because she had already come with Calvin (though Cynthia tried not to think about that too much). When an orgasm finally seized her, she gasped and muttered a few words in Finnish and drove her sopping pussy into Cynthia's face, smearing Cynthia's nose and lips and cheeks with her slick, glassy juices.

Afterward they lay together on the bed for a long while, kissing and caressing and leisurely exploring each other's body.

There was a knock on the door.

Cynthia and Kaarina stiffened and then looked at each other. Cynthia had a sinking suspicion she knew who it was.

"Who is it?" she called.

"It's me," Calvin said.

She rolled her eyes, then climbed off the bed and padded to the door.

"What do you want?" she called through the door.

"Um, I just thought we should talk," he said. "About, you know, what happened."

Part of her wanted to be mad and tell him to go to hell, but she was too sex-sated to be mad, and he sounded genuinely contrite and unhappy. Besides, she had won. At least according to her own criteria. Calvin had briefly claimed Kaarina's body, but Cynthia had claimed Kaarina herself. Her heart. Her soul. And that was what really mattered.

"I was in bed, actually," Cynthia said. "I was...sleeping. Can we just talk about it tomorrow?"

"Are you sure?" Calvin said. He sounded dubious. Not just about postponing the discussion, but about her having been sleeping. She should have feigned a drowsy voice. Shit. "I mean—"

"Calvin, I'm fine, okay? This'll keep till tomorrow."

"I don't want you to be mad."

"I'm not mad."

There was a long silence on the other side of the door. She stared down at the shadows of his feet breaking the bar of light at the bottom of the door. The feet didn't move.

"We shouldn't let this, you know, fester or anything," he said.

She rolled her eyes again. He wasn't going to go away until they had spoken face-to-face. He must be feeling pretty guilty. Maybe he was worried she was going to jump out the window or something.

She glanced back at the bed. The bed was visible from the doorway even with the door only cracked. Kaarina sat watching amid the rumpled sheets, her expression unreadable. Kaarina had made no attempt to cover herself, and Cynthia briefly let her eyes savor that exquisite body.

Cynthia hurried over to the bed, grabbing up Kaarina's clothes off the floor as she went.

"Get behind the door," she whispered to Kaarina, handing her the clothes. Kaarina nodded and scurried off into the corner.

Cynthia grabbed her bathrobe off the hook in the closet and put it on, then returned to the door just as Calvin called, "Are you still there?"

"Yeah, hold on."

She cracked the door and peered out at him. She squinted a little to make it look as if she had just woken up. Her messy hair no doubt added to the effect.

"Um, hi," Calvin said, giving her a wincing, guilty smile. "I'm sorry if I, uh, if I woke you up or something."

"I was only half asleep, actually."

He squirmed, his guilt increasing. She felt weirdly glad to see it. Then she felt a little guilty herself for feeling glad.

"I just..." Calvin grimaced and ran a palm over his hair. "I just feel like we should talk."

"Calvin, I'm tired, okay?" she said, filling her voice with every ounce of conviction she could muster. "Let's just do this tomorrow."

"Are you sure?"

"Yes, I'm sure." This time she couldn't keep an edge of annoyance out of her voice.

He grimaced again and dropped his gaze. Then he blinked, and the guilty expression vanished. His eyes widened.

She glanced down to see what he was looking at and realized that the top of her hastily tied robe had fallen open enough to expose the inner curves of her breasts and below that, a tall, narrow triangle of her pale abdomen, extending to just below her navel. It wasn't much, admittedly, especially not compared with what some girls wore these days. But she wasn't one of those girls, and this was the most that Calvin, or anyone (well, except Kaarina) had ever seen.

Flushing, frowning, she grabbed the sides of her robe and drew them together.

Calvin's eyes bounced back up to her face. When he saw the anger in her eyes, his own face reddened.

"Um…" He licked his lips. His face burned brighter. "I just…I just…I don't want you to be mad."

Again, she felt that cruel, petty satisfaction at seeing him squirm. What was wrong with her?

"I'm not mad," she said.

"You're really not?" He gave her a sidelong look, his expression puzzled and a little relieved.

"No." She thought that would be the end of it. But then to her surprise as much as Calvin's she found herself blurting out, "In fact, Kaarina's staying the night with me."

Calvin's face went slack with surprise.

Then he smirked and snorted out a laugh. He seemed

to think she was lying. He probably thought she was just trying to get even with him.

"Oh, really?" he said.

"Yes, really," she said coldly. His smug certitude infuriated her.

His smirk faltered. He glanced over her shoulder at the room behind her, but there wasn't much to see.

"Kaarina?" he called. "Are you there?"

For a moment there was no answer, and Calvin's smirk started to return.

But then Kaarina's voice, small and nervous, came from behind the door: "I am sorry, Calvin. Please do not be mad with me. Or with Cynthia."

He maintained a great poker face. Only a slight stiffening of his back and a brief flash of hurt and shock in his eyes betrayed his true emotions.

His eyes met Cynthia's. They stared at each other for a few seconds.

"Yeah, well, have fun," he said. He was trying to sound cool and casual but sounded merely terse and bitter instead. "Maybe I'll see you tomorrow." He shrugged. "Or maybe I won't."

He turned and walked away without a backward glance.

Cynthia shut the door and shook her head at herself. Why had she done that? Was she really that petty and spiteful?

She looked up at Kaarina, who had stepped out from the corner.

"I don't know," Cynthia said. "Maybe I should've—"

Kaarina stopped her words with a kiss. She opened the front of Cynthia's robe, baring Cynthia's body. Kaarina pulled at the sides of the robe, forcing Cynthia forward, into her. Their bare torsos smacked together.

"Shush," Kaarina whispered. "Worry about it later. Right now, there is only us."

"But—"

But Kaarina was leading her back to the bed. When they got there, Kaarina tugged the robe off Cynthia's shoulders and let it drop to the floor. Then she wrapped her arms around Cynthia's body and pulled Cynthia down onto the bed with her. For a moment, Cynthia was bothered by Kaarina's apparent lack of concern over what had just happened, but then all thought dissolved when she felt Kaarina's tongue on her neck, Kaarina's teeth on her nipples, Kaarina's fingers on her clit…

Chapter 28

After an hour-long blur of skin and tongues and what seemed like a hundred orgasms apiece, Cynthia and Kaarina lay in bed, snuggling and giggling and chatting about whatever topics their sleepy, contented brains happened to stumble across.

"Oh, hey," Cynthia said. "I've got a question. More of a personality test, really." She was about to add that Calvin had come up with it, but decided not to bring him up right now.

"Mm?" Kaarina cocked an eyebrow. "What is it?"

"If you had to make a choice between either having all the sex you could possibly want for the rest of your life but never being in love, or being in love with someone who loves you back for the rest of your life but never having sex ever again, what would you choose?"

"Oh, that is easy. I choose love, of course."

Cynthia beamed at her. "I knew it!"

"How could anyone choose anything else? Sex is fun, yes." She patted Cynthia's bare thigh in demonstration. "But it is brief and only of body. People are more than body. They have higher needs. Love is more...fulfilling? Is that correct word?"

"Yeah. Exactly."

Kaarina snuggled closer to Cynthia. "Of course, I would prefer to have love *and* sex."

"Mm. Me too." Cynthia's hand slid down Kaarina's belly, angling for the nest of golden hair and the pink folds below it that she had grown so intimately familiar with over the last hour and a half.

Kaarina grinned, then glanced at the clock and shot up into a sitting position. She gave Cynthia a wincing, apologetic smile. "It is already after one o'clock."

"So? What's wrong?" Cynthia could already tell she wouldn't like the answer.

"Do you remember what you tell Calvin? That I spend night? I...I cannot. I am sorry."

"What? But..."

"I have test tomorrow, remember? I have not studied, and I must pass test. It is of great importance."

"Oh. Well, you could always get your books and study here."

Kaarina shook her head. "No, I am sorry, but I must study alone." She smiled and swept her eyes over Cynthia's nude body. "If I were here, I could not concentrate on studying."

Cynthia smiled back, unable to help feeling pleased and flattered despite her disappointment.

Kaarina gave Cynthia a long, lingering kiss, then got out of bed and started putting on her clothes. Cynthia watched regretfully as Kaarina's gorgeous body vanished behind fabric.

When she was dressed, Kaarina leaned over the bed and gave Cynthia another kiss. "Maybe tomorrow night, after successful mission, I stay and we celebrate."

Cynthia brightened. "That would be nice."

Kaarina headed to the door. She laid a hand on the knob, then looked over her shoulder at Cynthia. She smiled.

"I see you tomorrow, then," she said.

Cynthia opened her mouth, then shut it. She wanted to

say, "I love you," but realized it would be sappy and fool-ish and grotesquely premature.

Instead she said, "Good luck with your test."

Kaarina looked down at the doorknob. Her smile seemed to widen.

"Thank you," she said.

And then she left.

Chapter 29

Cynthia couldn't sleep. She lay in bed for over an hour, still naked, staring at the ceiling, at the wall, and finally at the clock, which plodded through the seconds and the minutes with glacial slowness.

At 2:15 a.m., with sleep as far away as ever, she sighed, got out of bed, and pulled on her clothes.

She had to talk to Calvin. Much as she hated to admit it, he had been right when he came up to visit her earlier: They couldn't let things fester between them. But she had been too pissed at him and too Kaarina-happy to grasp it then. She had acted like a total cunt. Which was only fair, since he had acted like a total prick. But now they needed to straighten this out. Which meant she was going to go down to his room right now and talk to him. She didn't think she had to worry about waking him up; she suspected he was having as much trouble sleeping as she was. She was more concerned that he wouldn't be there, that he would have decided to burn off his anger and heartbreak with a midnight stroll around campus or something.

No, wait. This was Calvin. If anything, he would disappear into his work. He would immerse himself in books or websites about strange phenomena, or he would drive to May and while away the lonely hours of the night reading through the files.

She took the stairs down to his floor. Aside from the sounds of computer-game gunfire coming from one of the rooms, the floor was quiet.

She stopped in front of his door. Light shone under it. She stood there a few seconds, trying to work up the nerve to knock and also to figure out what she wanted to say. As she raised a fist to rap on the wood, there was a thump from inside, and she faintly heard Calvin mutter, "Shit."

She knocked.

"Calvin?" she said. She kept her voice low. After midnight the floors were supposed to be male or female only. The rule was violated all the time, and the RAs ignored any infractions as long as the violators weren't too egregious about it. Cynthia had not yet gotten in trouble for anything in college and didn't want to start now.

There was another, louder thump, followed by a hollow metallic clatter that she realized was Calvin's metal wastebasket falling over.

"Are you okay?" she said.

There was no answer.

Her mind filling with all kinds of awful scenarios—that he had had an accident, or that in a fit of grief he had tried to kill himself—she tried the knob. It was unlocked. She opened the door. She looked inside.

Her jaw dropped.

Calvin lay supine on the floor, his feet toward her, his raised head wobbling unsteadily as he looked at her down the length of his body. His eyes were blurred. His mouth gaped slackly. His desk chair lay on its back in front of his desk. His wastebasket lay on its side, and crumpled fast food wrappers and wadded tissues spilled out across the carpet. The Starbucks cup had rolled under his desk, trailing drops of cold coffee behind it. A stack of papers had cascaded off the desk and onto the floor. Some of the papers bore numerous shoeprints, as if he had been pacing back and forth across them without realizing it. Or maybe just without caring. In his left hand was one of the cans of Molson's. Strewn around him were the rest of the cans, all empty. He had drunk the rest of the case from the look of it. Seven cans.

"Whaddafuggeryudooinere?" he said. His head fell back and struck the floor with an audible smack. "Ow."

"Oh, God," she muttered, not sure whether to be amused or disgusted. She stepped into the room and shut the door behind her.

Calvin mumbled something too low for her to hear, though she thought she caught the word "cheese" in the middle of it.

She knelt beside him. His eyes were closed now. The stink of alcohol rose off him like heat from a furnace.

"Calvin," she said.

He grunted but didn't open his eyes.

"Calvin, come on. Let's get you to bed."

He cracked his eyes. "Fugyoo. Idoneedagodabed."

"Yes, you do. At least, if you said what I think you said."

She grabbed his arm and pulled. After resisting with a childish pout for a moment, he let out a frothy belch and then helped her help him to his feet. He wobbled for a moment and seemed about to fall over, but Cynthia wrapped an arm around his shoulders.

"God, you smell like Ernest Hemingway," she said.

"Whadayoocare?"

"I care. You're my friend. And as for what happened earlier…well, we both said and did some things we maybe shouldn't have. Or at least not in the ways we did them."

"Wudever."

"Calvin, we can't let this stuff come between us. We're a team. We have to be adults about this." She frowned.

"Though in your current state, that might be too much to expect.

"Hardeefugginhar." He belched again, then held his stomach and frowned. "Idonfeelgud."

"You're not gonna throw up, are you?"

"Uh-uh. Nodagain."

"'Again'? Okay, come on. Let's get you to bed."

He made a noise that might have been assent.

She led him to the bed and let him drop onto it on his back. He didn't move once he was on it, didn't try to arrange himself into a more comfortable position. He just lay there and groaned again.

She leaned over him. "Are you gonna be okay?"

He mumbled something she couldn't decipher. It was more like a rhythmic exhalation rather than actual words. Then his head fell to one side and he slept.

She took off his shoes and set them on the floor next to the bed. The beer can, fortunately empty, was still in his hand, so she wiggled it free and put it on the dresser. Then she spent a few minutes straightening up the room. She gathered up the papers and put them back on the desk. She righted the chair and the wastebasket. She sopped up the spilled coffee with some paper towels. She collected the beer cans and stuffed them into the recyclables bag.

She returned to the bed. Calvin hadn't moved. He seemed almost comatose. She had to watch his chest to make sure he was breathing. A line of saliva had run from his open mouth to puddle on the pillow.

She had never seen him this drunk. She didn't think he had ever had more than three or four beers in one night before. She couldn't leave him alone like this. What if he got alcohol poisoning? What if he choked on his own vomit in the middle of the night like some skuzzy heavy metal drummer?

"Thanks a lot, dickweed," she muttered. She sat down on his futon, arms folded, to begin her lonely vigil.

Five minutes later Calvin started snoring.

Thirteen minutes after that Cynthia started snoring, too.

Chapter 30

"What happened?" Calvin said.

Cynthia jerked awake. She looked around. Bright yellow early-morning sunlight shone around the edges of the curtains. The clock on the dresser read 9:05 a.m. She had slept on the damn futon all night.

"What happened?" Calvin repeated. He sat on the edge of the bed, his eyes puffy and bloodshot, his clothing rumpled, his face slightly green.

"You don't remember?" she asked.

He thought about it. His expression clouded over. Then he shrugged. "Some of it. How did you get in here?"

"Your door was unlocked. I came up here to talk. To make peace. But you weren't in any state to make anything except puke and piss."

"Oh." He started to stand up, then turned a deeper shade of green and sank back onto the bed with a groan. He massaged his forehead. "How many beers did I have?"

"All of them."

He groaned again.

"Come on," she said, getting up. "We have a big day ahead of us, remember?"

"Great."

"We both need to take showers and get changed, and you probably need about twenty gallons of coffee." She stood next to where he sat on the bed and held out her hand.

He reached out to take it, then hesitated and eyed her

with a closed, icy expression, obviously recalling the low points of last night. She was afraid he might swat her hand away, but after a pause, he sighed and took it, and she helped him up.

He looked around the room, then at Cynthia.

"Where's Kaarina anyway?" he said. "I thought you said she was staying the night with you."

"She…I was wrong. She couldn't stay overnight. She had to go. She had that test, remember? She had to study."

"Ah." He looked slightly pleased.

She resisted the urge to roll her eyes. "Are you going to Social Psychology?"

"Screw that. All I can think about right now is coffee."

"Okay. I'm gonna go wash up and everything. You should too. We can meet for breakfast once we're done. I know you probably don't want to talk about all this. And frankly, neither do I. But we should. Right?"

He looked weary at the thought.

"I guess," he said with a sigh.

"See you soon," she said.

"Right."

Chapter 31

When Cynthia arrived in the Duffy Hall cafeteria half an hour later, Calvin was already there. He sat in a shady corner, well away from the headache-exacerbating sunlight that streamed in through the windows, and was listlessly poking at some barely touched scrambled eggs with his fork. Cynthia sat down across from him with her own tray, which contained a cup of coffee and a dish of vegetarian casserole. Both she and Calvin had showered and changed into fresh clothes that didn't stink of beer and/or sex, but they still looked tired, and Calvin still looked slightly green.

"God, I'm famished," Cynthia said. She began to tear into her casserole.

Calvin watched her eat with his upper lip drawn back in revulsion. His green tint darkened slightly.

"What?" she said, a forkful of cheese-slathered chunks of noodles and eggplant poised halfway to her lips.

He shook his head and laid a hand on his belly. "That looks exactly like what I feel like heaving up right now."

"Do you have to say that while I'm eating?"

"Sorry." He took a tiny bite off a strip of bacon and washed it down with a sip of coffee. Then he resumed prodding his eggs with the tines of his fork. He didn't want to bring up what had happened last night and all the pain associated with it, but it had to be done. "So, um…about last night…"

"Yeah, look, I'm sorry I was such a bitch. I was hurt and mad and, you know…"

"Yeah, and I'm sorry I was…well, whatever I was. Especially anything I don't remember. Um…" He frowned down at his steadily cooling eggs. "So, Kaarina…I mean, what happened there? She told me she was going home. How'd she wind up in your room?"

Cynthia was reluctant to tell him the truth, since she feared it would sour his mood and shatter the truce between them. But she couldn't think of any way to prevaricate or dodge the issue without falsely getting his hopes up. It was best to be honest and upfront. Calvin appreciated truth.

"She, um, she told me that after what happened, after I stopped by your room and saw her there and everything, she realized she had, you know, feelings. For me."

She felt like a shit when she saw how he shrank down in his chair.

"I don't understand," he said. His voice wobbled with emotion. "I mean, she had a good time last night. She said so."

"Yeah, but…"

"But what?"

"I hate to be blunt, but I think with you and her—it was just sex. Just a casual hookup. But with me, it's something more. And ultimately she wants something more than just sex."

He looked at her like she was crazy. "No, she doesn't."

"Yes, she does."

"She does not! She told me so last night. I asked her my question. My sex-versus-love question, and she made it abundantly clear she's far more interested in sex. In fact, she was very critical of love since it's just a fleeting, inconstant emotion, and…" He finally noticed Cynthia shaking her head. "What?"

"That was before. I asked her the same question later on, and she told me she would choose love over sex. She was very adamant about it.

"I don't understand. Why would she lie like that?"

"She wasn't lying. She just changed her mind. It's like I said, when she saw how much I was hurting, she realized she had feelings for me, and I guess that sort of changed things for her. She came to see that sex without love is empty and meaningless."

He snorted.

Cynthia frowned. "Why is that funny?"

"What, she has a sudden epiphany and does a complete one-eighty on the subject just because she realizes she likes you? That's absurd."

She glared at him. "What, she can't have strong feelings for me?"

"No, she can. It's just, even if she does, she's not going to change her whole outlook in the blink of an eye like that. It's ridiculous. It's like something out of a crappy romance novel."

Her face reddened.

"Like you'd even know anything about romance," she snapped.

His eyes narrowed, and he regarded her in silence for a moment.

"I know enough," he said. "I know enough to tell when someone's tailoring their responses to suit our personalities and beliefs."

She rolled her eyes. "Oh, please! You know what I think? I think you're just fishing around for some way to deal with the pain of losing her."

"Yeah? Well, you're fishing around for some way to deny the obvious because you want to preserve your warm, fuzzy romantic illusions."

"Illusions? I don't think so."

"I do. It seems pretty clear to me she was telling us what we wanted to hear. I'm just not sure why."

He forked up a wad of eggs and popped them into his mouth. He didn't look green anymore. In fact, he looked pretty good. Energized, even. Cynthia realized he was turning this into work, framing Kaarina's behavior as a mystery to be solved. But was there really a mystery? She wasn't sure. She wanted to say no, but much as she hated to admit it, Calvin did have a point. Still, she wasn't ready to cast aside her faith in Kaarina, in love, and in her own instincts simply because of a single seeming inconsistency.

"I'm sure there's a perfectly logical explanation," she said.

"Like what?"

"I don't know!"

He took another bite of his eggs, then said, "Where is she anyway? What time was her class? The one with the test."

"I don't know. She never said exactly."

"Hm."

"What?"

He got out his phone.

"What are you doing?" Cynthia said.

"I'm gonna call her."

"What?"

"What's wrong with that?"

"She could be taking her test right now!"

He shrugged. "Then she probably has her phone turned off, so I'll leave a message." He started pressing buttons.

She gasped in exasperation, then laid a hand over the

phone.

"I'll call her," she said.

He raised an eyebrow. "What, are you afraid of me talking to her? Are you jealous?"

"Don't be ridiculous. It's just…"

"Just what?"

"It's just…I have more of a reason to be calling her at this point."

He grimaced.

"Okay, fine," he snapped, putting the phone away. "You call her."

"Sorry, but it's true."

"Yeah, yeah. Just call her already."

She got out her phone and dialed Kaarina's number. The phone was answered halfway through the first ring.

"Hei? Isi?"

"Kaarina?"

There was a moment of silence, except for a faint repetitive clicking sound in the background.

Then: "Cynthia. Hello. What's, um…what is up?"

"I was just wondering how you are. I was thinking maybe we could talk."

"Oh. I, um, I cannot talk right now. I am busy." The clicking noise ended with a loud, sharp clack. There was a muffled roar like a car accelerating, then some whooshes. "I have to, um—there is problem with my father. I must stay off phone in case he calls. I am sorry, but I will have to call you back later. Goodbye." She hung up.

"Well?" Calvin said.

She told him what Kaarina had said.

"Where was she?" Calvin asked.

"I don't know. She didn't say. It sounded like she was in a car, though. I heard blinkers in the background, and noises like other cars passing her."

"Interesting," Calvin muttered, his eyes narrow. He looked like a detective digesting new clues.

"What? How is that interesting? So she was driving somewhere. So what? I just hope her dad's okay."

"Oh, come on, Cyn. You really believe what she said?"

"Why shouldn't I believe it?" She shook her head. "God, you're getting paranoid."

"Well, her behavior has been inconsistent, at best. And, hell, she never even mentioned she had a car."

"She did say she had a driver's license."

"True..."

"And besides, if she was inconsistent, so what? That isn't necessarily evidence of malicious intent. I think you're expecting people to make too much sense. Maybe she had never really sat down and thought about her feelings on the subject of love and sex before last night. Maybe she thought she thought one thing, but then realized she didn't. I mean, people aren't machines. They can be messy and confusing and sometimes completely nonsensical, even to themselves."

He thought about this for a moment, then gave a grudging nod.

"Yeah. That's...that's true. Maybe you're right."

They ate in silence for a while. Despite having had his argument rebutted, Calvin's appetite remained hearty; he wolfed down his breakfast as if he hadn't eaten in weeks. Cynthia, however, was now only picking at her own food.

She wasn't happy. She should have been, of course. She had won Kaarina. She had defended Kaarina against Calvin's suspicions. She and Calvin had avoided a poten-tially friendship-destroying conflict. All, it seemed, was right with the world.

Except it wasn't. Something was nagging at the back of her mind. Something about Kaarina. It was as if Calvin's doubts about Kaarina's honesty had awakened some niggling, semiconscious doubt of her own. The problem was, she wasn't sure of the source of this doubt.

She shook her head. This was ridiculous. Aside from a single, trivial inconsistency, Kaarina had been nothing short of perfect. She had been a good friend and an amazing lover, and she had been a huge help with the investigation: Her lock-picking skills had proven indispensible; she had offered spot-on advice and brilliant insights; she was even the one who had noted the possible connection between the mysterious foreigner linked to the Kidwell brothers' deaths and—

She gasped.

Calvin glanced up at her, a forkful of scrambled eggs halfway to his open mouth.

"What?" he said.

"Remember when we were in Professor Kranhauser's office, and Kaarina pointed out that the man with the foreign accent could be Kranhauser?"

"Yeah."

"I don't recall ever telling her that Kranhauser had an accent. Do you?"

"No." He shrugged. "Maybe she heard about him from someone else. I'm sure we're not the only people she's talked to since she moved here."

"Yeah, but remember: She acted like she'd never even heard of Kranhauser before that night."

"Oh. Yeah. That's right." He frowned and sat forward. "What's up with you? Just a minute ago, you were all, 'Oh, Kaarina's a saint; you're just paranoid.' Now you're getting all Torquemada on her."

"I'm not. It's just…I don't know. It just occurred to me."

"Hm." He finished off the last few bites of his food, then pushed his tray away. Cynthia took a few more picks at her own food, but her appetite was long gone. She pushed her tray away, too.

"So what are you saying here?" Calvin said. "That she was deceiving us for some unknown reason?"

She winced. Yes, that had been more or less what she had been suggesting, but to hear it stated so baldly made her squirm with guilt, as if they were maligning Kaarina unjustly. What if Cynthia was wrong? What if one of them *had* mentioned Kranhauser's accent to Kaarina?

But she was sure they hadn't.

"She must have known more about Kranhauser than she was letting on," she said.

He sat back, frowning thoughtfully. "You know, when you start thinking like that—that she might not be entirely on the level—all kinds of other things suddenly take on new significance. Just little things, true, but…"

"Like what?"

"For one thing, remember how nervous she got around Detective Anderson? It seems kind of excessive in retrospect, especially given her supposed interest in criminal justice. You'd think a prospective investigator would be a little more at ease around the law. And then there's her lock-picking skills. I mean, she owns her own lock-picking set and obviously has had a lot of practice with them. Plus, she just happens to own date-rape drugs, too."

"She explained that, though. She told us she got them off some kid in Italy."

"That's what she told us, sure. But all we know about her is what she told us. If it turns out we can't trust what she says, then maybe we don't know anything about her at all. We don't even know exactly where she lives. She only mentioned some vague apartment on the edge of campus that was conveniently too unfurnished to meet in."

Cynthia opened her mouth to object, to insist that he was taking things too far, that he was just being excessively paranoid. But then she shut it, unsure. They really *didn't* know anything about Kaarina that hadn't come solely from Kaarina's lips.

But no. Kaarina was one of the good guys. There was ample proof of that. Cynthia reminded herself of her thoughts a minute ago, of how Kaarina had helped them out with the investigation in all kinds of ways. Kaarina was on their side. She had to be.

Except the more Cynthia thought about it, the more she realized that Kaarina hadn't simply helped the investigation, she had been quietly directing it every step of the way, no matter the illegalities involved—and practically every step they had taken had involved some kind of criminal activity. It was Kaarina who gained them entry into the locked Moma and the steam tunnels. It was Kaarina who suggested breaking into the professors' offices and homes. It was Kaarina who devised the plot to drug Kranhauser. It was Kaarina who came up with the idea to...

"Put ourselves into their confidence," Cynthia muttered. "Like worms for fish."

"What?"

"That was her plan. With the professors. She said we should insinuate ourselves into their confidence by figuring out what they most desired and dangling it in front of them."

"And, what, you think she's been doing the same thing

with us?"

"I…" She wasn't ready to say that out loud yet. "I don't know. It was just a thought."

"That makes perfect sense, though. I mean, think about when we first met her. She introduced herself to us in Byrne's class right after we had been talking about the Ur-Tarot and our investigation. She might have overheard us. She might have just been using us all along to—"

He stiffened, his eyes as big as planets.

"What!" Cynthia said.

"The cards! My cards! We showed her the cards. She knows where they are. She might take them. She might have taken them already."

Cynthia shook her head. She was ready to concede that Kaarina may have been dishonest in some ways. But she was not yet ready to accuse Kaarina of betrayal and thievery.

"Calvin, I don't know. You might be overreacting…"

"Yeah, I might be. But I think we ought to head down to May and find out for sure."

He started to stand up. Cynthia sighed and waved him back down. She held up her phone.

"Let me call Donovan," she said. "He can check. It'll be faster. The spare key's still in the fake rock next to the front steps, right?"

"Yeah. But isn't Donovan in school right now?"

"He's supposed to be, but this is Donovan we're talking about, remember? There's a good chance he won't be. And even if he is, Violet probably won't be. Actually, wait a minute…" She checked the time. "Yeah, it's between classes at the high school right now. If I hurry, I can catch him."

She dialed Donovan's number. The phone rang, then

rang again, and again, and she was beginning to fear that it would go to voice mail, but then Donovan answered.

"Cyn?" he said. She could hear the noisy high school hallway in the background. "Is that you?"

"Yeah, it's me. I take it you're in school?"

"Yeah."

"Damn. The one time I was hoping you'd have skipped it."

"Why? What's up?"

She quickly explained that someone needed to stop by Calvin's house to see if anyone was there and if the Ur-Tarot cards were still there. She told him where the hidden key was and that they needed this done as fast as possible.

"I don't want you to miss any school, though," she said. "What about Violet? Maybe she can—"

"I can do it. Really. My next class is a study hall. They never take attendance in there. I can get out and back, and no one'll even know I was gone."

"Donovan—"

"Besides, I honestly have no way to get in touch with Violet. She's not in school today."

"Doesn't she have a phone?"

"Not presently. She broke it. Again."

She sighed. "All right. You're sure you won't get caught?"

"Hell, yeah. I've done it before. Sometimes me and Violet skip out of study hall and, you know, have some fun in the woods behind the school."

"Okay, okay. I don't need the details. Just be quick, and don't get caught."

She hung up. As she set her phone on the tabletop, she noticed that Calvin was smirking at her.

"What?" she said.

"See, I was right. You were pooh-poohing the whole *Global Frequency* thing. Well, aren't you glad we had an agent in place to call into action?"

"He's not an agent. He's my brother. And he wasn't in place; he was in school."

"Yeah, but you see the validity of the idea."

She rolled her eyes. "Okay, fine, whatever. I think we have more important things to worry about right now. Like Kaarina, and what's really going on."

"Well, I think that's pretty obvious: She wants the cards. She was using us to get them."

"Maybe. We don't have any actual proof of that, Calvin."

"Not yet," he said, with a meaningful nod at the phone.

"And even if she is up to something, she might not be the evil mastermind you're trying to paint her as. She might actually have a good reason for this."

"Like what?"

"I don't know. Maybe...maybe she's being coerced into doing it."

"Or maybe you're just coming up with lame explanations to excuse her behavior."

She glared at him.

"Look, Cyn, she was totally playing us," Calvin said. "Once we clear the hormones from our brains, I think we can see that." He frowned. "In fact, maybe last night was part of it, too." His voice was soft, almost inaudible, as if he didn't want to hear himself say what he was saying.

"What do you mean?"

"I mean, after my meeting with Byrne yesterday, we now know who has the card. Which means that if she *was* simply using us to help her track down the card, we're of no further use to her. So what if what happened last night—what we did—what *she* did—what if all of that was just a way to try to divide us? To keep us at each other's throats long enough for her to swoop in and get Kranhauser's card and my cards and be long gone before we could figure out what was really going on?"

Cynthia just gawped at him a moment, stunned by the idea. Then she shook her head as if to dislodge the notion from her mind.

"I'm not ready to go that far based on what scanty evidence we have," she said. "I mean, we don't even know that your cards have been gotten. Why don't we wait for Donovan to call back before we start building a stake to burn Kaarina on?"

He started to protest, but then sighed. "No, you're right. We need confirmation."

They waited. Time ticked past. Around them students chattered and ate and strode by with food on plastic trays, but Calvin and Cynthia didn't notice any of it. They kept staring at the cell phone on the table as if it were a bomb about to go off.

Then it did. It rang and vibrated, rumbling faintly on the tabletop.

Cynthia snatched it up and checked the display to see who it was. Part of her was hoping that it was Kaarina calling to apologize for her brusqueness on the phone earlier and to make plans for later.

But it was Donovan.

"Yeah?" she said into the phone.

"They're gone," he said.

For a moment she couldn't breathe. She felt a huge fist squeezing her chest, her heart.

"Are you sure?" she asked.

"Yeah. There's just an empty space between that *Little Mermaid* video and the melted trophy."

She put a hand over the receiver and lowered the phone to tell Calvin, but she saw from the look in his eyes that she didn't need to; her distressed expression had already told him all he needed to know.

"Shit!" he cried. Nearby diners twisted around in their seats to look at him. "Shit shit shit!"

"Thanks," she said into the phone. She was amazed that her voice wasn't shaking. Instead it was flat and dead. "We owe you one. Now get back to school."

"Do I have to? I'm already out."

"Yes. Go."

She hung up. Calvin rose.

"Come on," he said.

She rose, too. "Where?"

"To find Kranhauser. He has the other card. She'll go after him, too."

"She's had a full night's head start. She probably found him already."

"Yeah. But what else can we do?"

"So, what, we head out to his house?"

"Not yet," he said, heading for the exit. "Let's check Chandler Hall first."

Chapter 32

Calvin and Cynthia pushed through Chandler Hall's main entrance, then paused. The building's lobby and the main hallway were empty, the current classes being in mid-session. Through closed classroom doors came the muffled drones of lecturing professors.

"Does Kranhauser have classes right now?" Cynthia asked.

"I don't know," Calvin said. "Let's see if he's in his office."

They hurried up the steps, then screeched to a halt when they reached the top. Professor Byrne's office door stood open, and a man was hunched over behind the desk, his black-suited back all that was visible as he rummaged through the desk's bottom drawer.

Assuming that the figure was Byrne, and not wanting Byrne to see them right now since it would only complicate things, Calvin and Cynthia started to slink out of sight of the open doorway. Before they could get far, the figure sat up.

It was Detective Anderson. When he saw the duo in the hallway, he cocked an eyebrow.

"What are you doing here?" he said.

Calvin and Cynthia looked at each other in confusion, then walked over to the open doorway.

"What's going on?" Calvin asked, glancing around the office. No one else was in there. "Why are you in Professor Byrne's office?"

Anderson leaned back in the desk chair as if it were his own. "You haven't heard?"

"Heard what?"

"Professor Byrne is dead."

"What?" Cynthia said. "What happened?"

"He was murdered in his home sometime overnight, shot once in the head, apparently as he slept. I was given the case on the assumption it's tied in with the other campus murders. Where were the two of you between ten o'clock last night and now?"

Calvin and Cynthia answered more or less in unison:

"Sleeping," Calvin said.

"With a friend," Cynthia said.

Anderson's mouth curled up in a faint smile. "You were sleeping with a friend?"

"No," Cynthia said, her face flushing so hard it looked like she'd been bitch-slapped by an octopus. "*First* we were with a friend, *then* we were sleeping,"

"Ah. I see. Who is this friend? I'd like to speak to them."

"What, you think *we* killed Professor Byrne?" Calvin said.

"At this point I'm not ruling it out."

"That's ridiculous!" Cynthia said.

Anderson cocked an eyebrow. "On the contrary, the two of you keep inserting yourselves into this case."

"We were just passing by on our way somewhere else!" Calvin protested. "We saw you in here and stopped to find out what was going on. How is that inserting ourselves into the case?"

"Where were you going, then?"

"To talk to Professor Kranhauser, one of our other professors. His office is down the hall."

"What were you going to talk to him about?"

"Well, actually, I'm the one who was going to talk to him," Cynthia said. "See, I'm changing majors, and I want him to be my new faculty advisor." She jerked a thumb at Calvin. "He's just along for the ride."

"Mm-hmm," Anderson said, obviously not sure if he should believe it. He eyed them in silence for a moment, his chilly blue eyes flicking back and forth between them. Then he heaved a sigh and swept his hand at them in a backhanded shooing gesture. "Go on, then. Get out of here. I have work to do."

They got out of there and hurried down the hall toward Kranhauser's office. When they were safely out of earshot of Byrne's office, Cynthia whispered, "Do you think..." She paused, swallowed. "Do you think Kaarina was the one who...who..." She couldn't finish.

"Not necessarily," Calvin whispered. "I mean, it seems pretty certain that it was Kranhauser who killed Judd Skerrit. Maybe he killed Byrne, too."

Cynthia nodded. "That seems more likely. I mean, whatever else she might have done, I just can't see Kaarina as a murderer."

He shot her an almost pitying look. "At this point, I'm fairly certain that the Kaarina you think you know is not the real Kaarina."

She frowned, wanting to deny what he was saying. But she knew she couldn't.

Kranhauser's office door was closed, but through the frosted glass window they saw the hazy globe of light from Kranhauser's desk lamp.

Cynthia knocked.

Silence.

She knocked again, harder, louder. "Professor Kranhauser?"

Silence.

"He must not be in," she whispered to Calvin.

"Maybe," he whispered back. "But his light's on."

"Maybe he left it on. He might have class right now. Or he might have gone to the bathroom or something."

"Or he might be dead like Byrne."

Cynthia stared at the closed door, reflecting that there might be a corpse on the other side. And not just a corpse: the murderer—whoever it was—might still be there, too.

She glanced at Calvin and saw him eyeing the door with a worried expression similar to her own.

He looked at her, then inclined his head toward the door and mimed twisting a doorknob.

She nodded reluctantly.

"Careful," she said, lowering her voice even further. "Quiet."

He nodded. He looked down the hall to ensure that no one was in sight, then grasped the cold brass doorknob and turned it slowly, so as to make as little noise as possible. There was a rasp, a muffled rattle, and then the knob would turn no further. He turned it the other way. Same result.

"Locked," he said, speaking so low now that he was practically only mouthing the words.

"What now?" she said, speaking just as low.

He dug into his pocket and pulled out the shiny new key Professor Byrne had given him yesterday. He held it up for her to see. She nodded. He slid the key into the keyhole and unlocked the door as quietly as he could. Which wasn't very quietly at all: In the silence of the corridor, every little rumble of the tumblers sounded as loud as a dresser being dragged across a bumpy hardwood floor.

The door unlocked with a sharp click that made both Calvin and Cynthia wince. After waiting a moment to make sure the sound didn't rouse a response from either within the office or down the hall, Calvin slid the key out, put a hand on the knob again, and looked at Cynthia with his eyebrows raised, as if to ask "You ready?"

Cynthia took a long, slow, silent breath, then nodded.

Calvin turned the knob and opened the door.

Both of them stiffened with surprise to find Professor Kranhauser sitting at his desk, staring right at them. He sat with his back rigid and his hands splayed out on the desktop. His white hair was tousled, tufts of it sticking up in little horns, as if he had been wearing a hat and someone had yanked it off. His lips were pressed together into a thin line. His wide eyes looked almost frightened as he regarded them in silence. Then his gaze settled on Cynthia. His eyes sparked with recognition.

"You!" he said. "Vhat do you vant? Vhat are you doing here?" His eyes darted left, toward the door.

Calvin and Cynthia stepped into the office.

"We, uh…" Cynthia wasn't sure how to proceed. Should she continue with the faculty advisor bullshit? Should they tell him the truth and warn him that his life was in danger? Then again, he probably already knew that. Wait, had Kranhauser been sitting here the whole time, listening to them break into his office? Maybe he had been asleep at his desk. That would explain why his hair looked like that. "I, um…about that faculty advisor form…."

Kranhauser opened his mouth to say something, then glanced at the door again. Or was it *behind* the door?

Cynthia started to turn her head to look. "Is something—"

The door banged shut behind them and a voice said,

"Good morning."

They whirled around. In the corner behind the door stood a man neither of them had ever seen before. He was about six-foot-one, with blond hair and a short blond beard that was going gray at the corners of his mouth. His eyes were gray like smoke from an electrical fire. He wore a charcoal-gray suit and black Oxfords. He was pointing a semiautomatic pistol at Calvin and Cynthia.

The man smiled. In an accent similar to Kaarina's, he said, "You must be the ones my daughter has been telling me about."

Chapter 33

Calvin and Cynthia were so busy goggling at the gun that it took a few seconds for the man's words to sink in. When the words finally registered, their eyes rose from the gun to his face.

"You—you're Kaarina's father?" Cynthia said.

The man smiled and gave a small bow.

"Pekka Nurmi," he said. "A pleasure to make your acquaintance, short though it will be. You've caught me at a rather awkward moment." He nodded at Kranhauser, who was glowering at him with undisguised hatred. "I've been trying to persuade my old 'friend' the professor here to reveal the whereabouts of the card he recently came into possession of. I know it's not at his house. I searched that quite thoroughly last night. When I couldn't find it, I remained there most of the night, waiting for him to come home, but he never did. I had to come to campus this morning and catch him here in his office. Upon questioning, it turns out he spent the night at a motel with one of his students. Suffice it to say, he has been far less forthcoming about where he hid the card. I had been about to resort to less pleasant but more certain methods of extracting information when you two showed up."

"I vill never tell you a thing!" Kranhauser snarled. Spit sprayed from his mouth as he spoke and dotted the blotter between his spread hands.

"Oh, you will," Nurmi said. "No question about that. Just wait and see. All I need is five minutes and a pair of pliers, and I'll have you telling me things you didn't even know you knew. But first I must decide what to do with our young friends here."

Cynthia glared at him. "Where's Kaarina?"

"I sent her to gather up the cards you so witlessly showed her. I must confess, I was most pleasantly surprised when she told me that she had located the three Ur-Tarot cards that eluded my grasp all those years ago. I had often wondered where they ended up."

"You!" Calvin said. "You're the one who killed the Kidwell brothers."

"Indeed. Moronic little men, their heads awash with New Age drivel. They are better off gone."

"And I take it you killed Byrne and the two maintenance workers."

"No no no." Nurmi waved a hand back and forth, palm out, as if modestly refusing a compliment he had not earned. "Byrne yes, but not those unfortunate maintenance men. I believe that accolade falls to Kranhauser here."

Kranhauser frowned down at his desk. "I vill say nothing," he muttered.

"But why kill Byrne?" Calvin said. "He didn't even have the card anymore. He was no threat to you."

Nurmi grunted.

"It was repayment for the inconvenience he put me through," he said. "Kaarina told me about the email you found on his computer. The truth is, I was the one to whom Professor LaFleur was delivering The Lovers at the history symposium in Italy."

"Delivering the what?" Cynthia said.

"The card." He shrugged. "The Ur-Tarot have no names, of course, but the card in question is clearly the one that became The Lovers in the modern deck. I had spent a whole year and a small fortune tracking it down. I had traveled to half a dozen cities on three continents. I had wormed my way into the confidence of important scholars. I had even broken into a renowned architect's home to learn the floor plan of a certain building in Paris. And then, of course, I had to convince Professor LaFleur to turn the card over to me lest various unsavory consequences ensue. You can therefore imagine my chagrin when the prize I had worked so long and hard to acquire was snatched from my grasp at the last moment by an insignificant history professor from Ohio. But then I remembered who else taught in Ohio." He looked pointedly at Kranhauser. "And I realized that Byrne either had an accomplice, or, more likely, he had a puppet-master secretly pulling his strings. Is that not right, Herr Professor?"

Kranhauser didn't respond. He just continued frowning down at his desk.

"Anyway," Nurmi went on, "while I took care of a few, ah, loose ends in Europe—"

"What, like LaFleur?" Calvin said.

Nurmi adopted an exaggerated expression of sorrow. It reminded Calvin of the tragedy mask that had hung on the wall during The Black Lodge concert.

"Ah, yes," Nurmi said. "The poor man met with an unfortunate auto accident on his way home from the symposium. A real tragedy." He chuckled. "At any rate, while I cleaned up in Europe, I sent Kaarina on ahead of me to do a little reconnaissance here in Ames. I couldn't risk doing it myself, for Kranhauser knows me and would have recognized me immediately. But I have made sure to keep my daughter out of the spotlight, which makes her extremely useful in situations like this."

"She's nothing but a tool to you, isn't she?" Cynthia

said coldly.

Nurmi snorted. "Don't be absurd. You know nothing about us or our relationship. Whatever you think you know is simply what we wanted you to know. Anyhow, it was quite a surprise when, in the course of shadowing Byrne, Kaarina overheard the two of you discussing not only the murder, which was clearly linked to the card, but a trio of other Ur-Tarot cards, as well. After she gained your confidence and learned that you were investigating the murder on your own, we naturally decided to let you do most of the work and then reap the rewards ourselves."

"And then make sure we had a little accident, too, I take it," Calvin said.

"Actually, no. Kaarina had persuaded me not to. She assured me that she would be able to keep you distracted long enough for us to get what we wanted and depart your wretched country. Normally I prefer more...*final* solutions. But I chose to go along with her plan, for I didn't wish to upset her unduly. Now, though, you have guaranteed her distress. She will be most unhappy to learn of your deaths. She was so sure her ploy was sound, but it seems she misjudged the strength of the bond between you."

"She wanted you to spare us?" Cynthia said. Hope swelled in her breast. Maybe she hadn't been completely wrong about Kaarina and what she thought she had felt between them.

Nurmi shrugged. "I wouldn't read too much into it. Like most girls her age, she can get carried away by her emotions. Thankfully for her, she has me around to help her keep her head on straight."

"It sounds like you're just twisting it up even more," Cynthia said. She hated to imagine Kaarina's life with this murderous, manipulative asshole. He had turned her into a little blonde extension of his own greed and lunacy. She had probably been that way for so long she didn't know anything better existed.

Nurmi smiled at her. She didn't like the smile. It was too knowing and mocking, as if he could read her thoughts.

"You wish to rescue her from what you see as a life of crime and dissolution, is that it?" he said. "You wish to be the crusading lover coming to the rescue of the beautiful damsel in distress."

Cynthia flushed and said nothing.

"Let me assure you," Nurmi went on, "she neither needs nor desires rescuing. I provide her with a life that most would envy. She wants for nothing. We have traveled the globe, dined in the finest restaurants, slept in the finest hotels, seen all the wonders of the world."

"Yeah, when you're not busy murdering people and generally being a greedy, power-hungry lunatic."

He chuckled. "How naïve you are. To desire power is not mad. All great men and nations aspire to power. And often other men and nations must be trampled to achieve that power. It is the way the world works. Only hopeless idealists like you believe otherwise."

Kranhauser grunted and mumbled something.

Nurmi turned to him. "Have you something to add?"

"Jah!" Kranhauser snapped, his droopy jowls wobbling. "You are a child! A child grasping at de tools of your betters, you *scheisskopf.* You know nothing of true power."

"You think not?" He pointed the pistol at Kranhauser, who shrank back with a whimper. "Who has the power here? Certainly not you, you pathetic old man."

There was a knock on the door, and Kaarina's voice, low and urgent, said, *"Isi? Olen palannut."*

"Ah." Nurmi shot an annoyed glance at Calvin and Cynthia. Keeping the gun trained on them, he opened the door just wide enough for Kaarina to slip inside.

When Kaarina saw Calvin and Cynthia, she stopped as if she had run up against an invisible wall, and the broad, happy smile on her face collapsed into a gape of shock.

An instant later her face went blank as she drew a shade across her feelings. She opened the folder she was carrying and pulled out the three Ur-Tarot cards from Calvin's house, still sealed in their plastic sleeves. She held them up for her father to see.

"I got them," she said.

"Perfect," he said. He turned to Kranhauser and motioned at the cards. "You see? Who has the power here?"

Kranhauser eyed the three cards with a pained, yearning look, like a desperate junkie watching a five-pound bag of heroin being dangled just out of reach. Nurmi laughed at the sight.

Cynthia barely noticed any of this. All her attention was on Kaarina, who was studiously keeping her own attention on her father and not even glancing at Calvin and Cynthia.

"Why?" Cynthia asked her. "Why are you doing this? I know you're a better person than this. I know—"

Kaarina whirled toward her. "Shut up! You think you know me? You think you understand me? Think again! You don't know shit!"

"Wow," Calvin said. "Your English has certainly improved."

"My English is excellent. I told you that. I told you that Finnish schools were excellent, and you still didn't question my awkward syntax. Morons. You Americans are so fucking predictable. You turn all gushy and patronizing the moment you meet an attractive foreigner speaking broken English."

Cynthia winced as if stung. Calvin's face reddened, and he looked down at his shoes.

"You're twisting everything all up," Cynthia protested. "It wasn't like that at all. We were nothing but nice to you."

"I was nothing but a piece of meat to you. A prize to be won to help puff up your little egos."

"You know that's not true," Cynthia said, her voice low. She was getting angry. She was *letting* herself get angry so she wouldn't feel so helpless and lost. "We were your friends, damn it. And don't tell me that our—that what we did—that that meant nothing."

Kaarina squared her shoulders and cocked an eyebrow at Cynthia. "Our brief interlude last night was very pleasant, I admit. But if you think there was something more on my end, then you are sadly mistaken. You are undoubtedly projecting your own thoughts and feelings onto me."

Cynthia's face contorted with a host of emotions—rage and anguish and despair and hate.

"You fucking cunt," she said, her voice husky and quavering.

Kaarina flinched as if Cynthia had slapped her. Then she frowned and turned away.

"I wouldn't let it bother you too much," Calvin said to Cynthia, his own voice wavering slightly. He was managing to keep his emotions under control better than Cynthia was, but not by much. "She's obviously not worth the trouble. She's just a liar and a crook and a daddy's girl."

That got a response. Kaarina whirled on him.

"Fuck you!" she said. "What do you know about me? What do you know about why I do what I do? Nothing!"

"A liar's a liar. The reasons—or excuses—don't change that."

Nurmi cleared his throat. "I think this has gone on long enough. Now I must decide what I'm going to do with you." He smiled grimly and gestured with his pistol to call attention to it. "Or, more accurately, *where* I am going to do it."

Chapter 34

At Pekka Nurmi's pronouncement, Calvin and Cynthia saw Kaarina close her eyes for a second and draw in a sharp, silent breath. Despite her nastiness toward Calvin and Cynthia a minute ago, she clearly wasn't happy with this outcome. But it was equally clear that she wasn't going to defy her father. Their relationship, however strange and misguided it might be, was based on blood and a lifetime of togetherness, and was thus far stronger than whatever feelings a week of fake flirting and a couple of hours of casual sex may have roused in her.

"You can't shoot us," Calvin told Nurmi. "It would make too much noise and attract too much attention."

"Yes," Nurmi said. "I have considered that and—"

Kaarina gasped as if suddenly remembering something, then spoke rapidly to her father in Finnish. Calvin and Cynthia understood virtually none of it, but both of them caught the word *poliisi,* which sounded an awful lot like "police." Kaarina must have noticed Detective Anderson in Byrne's office on her way here and was telling her father about it. It was heartening to know that Anderson was just down the hall. Unless, that is, the detective had left since Kaarina passed by.

When Kaarina finished speaking, Nurmi regarded Calvin and Cynthia with a narrow, calculating gaze for a moment. Then he said, "A trip to the steam tunnels is in order, I think. A one-way trip for the two of you."

Calvin felt his stomach turn to concrete. How the hell

were they going to get out of this? He glanced at Kranhauser, who was glowering petulantly at the cards as Kaarina tucked them into the folder once more. Kranhauser wasn't going to be of much help. All he cared about was the cards. Even if Calvin and Cynthia could persuade him to help out in exchange for the cards, he would just betray them the first chance he got.

Maybe Anderson. Their route to the stairs went past Byrne's office; maybe they could somehow alert Anderson as they passed. But what if Anderson had already left?

Calvin glanced at the clock on Kranhauser's wall. It was ten-forty. Classes let out in only five minutes. If Calvin could stall Nurmi for a few minutes, he could time it so that they would arrive on the first floor just as classes let out. Nurmi wouldn't dare enter the basement with so many people around; it would attract too much attention. And maybe Calvin and Cynthia would be able to slip away in the swarm of students. It was, he had to admit, a pretty weak plan, but it was the only one he could think of.

Now all he needed was a way to stall Nurmi...

"Why do you hate Kranhauser so much anyway?" Calvin asked.

Nurmi frowned, looking slightly offended.

"Hate him?" he said. "I hate him no more than I would hate a fly that keeps landing on my food. He is an irritant, at best. Hardly worthy of any intense emotion." He paused, then fixed Kranhauser with a dark, appraisive look. "Then again, there was that time you informed the Finnish authorities that I was in Germany. That cost me quite a bit of trouble. I still owe you a great deal of pain for that."

"The Finnish authorities are after you?" Calvin said. "You must have done something really bad. I mean, I've always heard the Finns were really nice, tolerant people."

Nurmi snorted with derision. "The Finns. Ridiculous little nobodies. If I hadn't been forced to flee the country, I would have left anyway."

"You had to flee?"

"It was a…misunderstanding. They believed I had murdered my wife."

"What, with ovarian cancer?" Cynthia said.

"What do you mean?"

"That was me," Kaarina said quietly. "I told them mamma died of cancer."

Father and daughter stared at each other, their expressions dark and unreadable. Then Nurmi turned back to Calvin and Cynthia.

"No," he said. "It wasn't cancer. It was an accident. She fell off a roof."

"Yeah, right," Calvin said. "I bet there was more to it than that. I bet you gave her a nice big push."

Nurmi's eyes narrowed. The ends of his jaw bulged as he gritted his teeth.

"That's it, isn't it?" Cynthia said. "That's what happened. You're nothing but a—"

"Shut up!" Kaarina yelled. She stepped forward as if she were about to attack Cynthia. Her hands were balled into fists at her sides. Calvin and Cynthia were shocked to see pure, unadulterated hate in her eyes. "You aren't fit to speak of my mother, so shut your fucking mouths!"

"I think we've dawdled far too long as it is," Nurmi said coldly. He gestured at Calvin and Cynthia with the pistol. "Both of you turn around."

"Why?" Calvin said. "If you shoot us now, you'll just attract attention."

"Whose? That policeman down the hall? He's alone. If

he interferes, I'll shoot him, too, and then Kaarina and I will make our escape before any other police can arrive. I would prefer to kill you without attracting attention, of course, but if you force my hand, I'll do it right here, right now. Do you think I've never been in a situation like this before?"

Calvin said nothing.

"Now turn around," Nurmi repeated. "Both of you."

They did.

"When we exit the room," Nurmi went on, "I will be holding my gun in my jacket pocket. It will be pointed at one of you. You will not know which one. If either of you does anything foolish—if you try to flee, or if you talk to anyone, including each other, or if you look at each other or perform any other action that could be interpreted as a signal—I will shoot whichever one of you the gun is trained on. In other words, if one of you does something stupid, you might be killing yourself...or you might be killing your friend. Do you understand?"

"Yes," Calvin and Cynthia said in unison.

Nurmi spoke to Kaarina in Finnish. Again, Calvin and Cynthia understood very little of it. They guessed, though, that he had told her to stay behind and keep an eye on Kranhauser, for when he was done speaking, she grunted with what sounded like assent, and then there was a rustle of movement and the creak of a chair as she sat down.

"Now then," Nurmi said, "open the door and step out into the hall."

They complied. Despite their hopes and prayers, Detective Anderson was not crouched beside the door with his pistol in his hand and a finger to his lips. A SWAT team armored up like black beetles was not creeping stealthily toward them. There was just the silent, empty hallway stretching away like the barrel of a gun.

Nurmi stepped out behind them and shut the door.

"Now walk toward the stairs," he said quietly.

They obeyed, their sneakers squeaking softly on the floor tiles. Nurmi followed slightly less than an arm's length behind them. His dress shoes clicked and clacked.

Calvin wondered what time it was. Had he delayed Nurmi long enough? Had he delayed him too long? He couldn't check his watch since Nurmi might consider it a signal and pull the trigger. Calvin wished he had thought to take one last look at the clock in Kranhauser's office before they left. But then, he had had other things on his mind.

As they neared Byrne's office, Calvin felt a surge of hope to see that the office door was still open and the light was still on inside.

They drew parallel to the office door. Calvin strained his eyes as far to the right as he could without turning his head. He caught a quick glimpse of Detective Anderson sitting at Byrne's desk and flipping through the contents of a manila folder. Anderson started to raise his head, but just then Calvin was forced to look away so as not to walk past the stairs.

As the trio headed down the stairs, there was a creak from Byrne's office. It was the creak of a chair from which a weight has just been lifted. Nurmi drew in a sharp breath.

They rounded the half landing and began to descend the lower flight of steps. They were now facing the direction they had come, which gave Calvin and Cynthia the chance to look up at the top of the stairs without moving their heads in a suspicious way.

Detective Anderson ambled out of Byrne's office, his

hands in his pockets, a small frown creasing his forehead. He stopped at the top of the stairs and openly watched them descend.

Cynthia met Anderson's gaze, then widened her eyes and raised her eyebrows. She was about to roll her eyes to the side as a lame way of indicating Nurmi, but before she could do so, they descended far enough that she couldn't maintain eye contact with Anderson without tilting her head back and thereby giving Nurmi cause to pull the trigger.

They had nearly reached the first floor when a susurrus rose up from the classrooms. Doors opened all along the corridor, and the susurrus swelled into a cacophony of voices. Students poured out of the rooms and filled the hallway.

Nurmi grumbled something to himself. Calvin smiled with triumph. His plan had worked even better than he had hoped. Nurmi didn't dare go into the basement with so many people around, but he couldn't order Calvin and Cynthia to head back upstairs either since Anderson was there.

Calvin's joy died when Nurmi leaned in and whispered, "When you reach the corridor, turn right. Walk to the end of the hallway, then turn around and head back."

Crap. It was a good plan. Too good. It would get them out of sight of Anderson, who, since there was nothing obviously illegal going on, might simply shrug his shoulders and return to Byrne's office. Plus, Nurmi's plan would keep them moving so they wouldn't look suspiciously immobile. By the time they went to the end of the hallway and back, most of the students would have dispersed, and hardly anyone would be around to see the three of them heading into the basement.

Calvin and Cynthia's only chance now was to try to ditch Nurmi in the crowd. But how? Nurmi was sticking close behind them, leaving no room for anyone to get between his pocketed gun and Calvin and Cynthia's un-protected backs. If they tried to dodge away, one of them would surely wind up with a bullet in their spine.

They crossed the lobby to the main corridor, then turned right and joined the stream of students. As they turned, Calvin swiveled his eyes as far to the right as he could for a look at the stairwell. It was empty. Anderson had probably returned to Byrne's office, after all. Out of sight, out of mind.

How the hell were they going to get out of this one?

They hadn't gone more than twenty feet down the hallway when a figure darted out of the river of students surging past in the opposite direction, and said, "Guys! Hey, guys!"

It was Brandon Taylor. He stopped directly in front of them, giving them no choice but to come to an abrupt halt. Behind them, Nurmi huffed with annoyance.

Calvin and Cynthia stared at Brandon in silence. They were afraid that if they spoke Nurmi would shoot them.

Brandon didn't seem to notice their uncharacteristic si-lence. He had shrugged off his backpack the moment he stopped and was now rummaging through it and talking faster than an auctioneer.

"I've got it!" he said. "That poem I told you about! You know, the one inspired by the two of you that I told you about in the Food Court the other day? I finally fin-ished it. And it turned out pretty damn good, if I do say so myself. Hold on a sec, and I'll read it to you. I've got it in here somewhere. Ah!" He pulled out a dog-eared compo-sition notebook and opened it up. "You ready?"

Nurmi loudly cleared his throat and said, "Young man, we don't have time for this. We have important business to—"

"Yeah, yeah, this'll just take a second," Brandon said without even glancing at Nurmi. Before Nurmi could say another word, Brandon launched himself into his poem:

> "O you who shine nacreously in the moonlight,
> Wonder of wonder, sport of nature,
> Black sheep of the fecund earth,
> Seek the corners, the crannies, the caverns,
> Plumb the inky depths,
> Eternity is not enough…"

Nurmi let out a long, exasperated breath and muttered, *"Huono runous. Olen helvetissä."* He leaned in close to Calvin and Cynthia and whispered, "Move around him."

Reluctantly Calvin and Cynthia tried to comply. The wall was to their right, which prevented any movement in that direction, so they tried to sidle to the left. They couldn't. The stream of students flowing past them was too swift and dense for them to penetrate. Even standing still, they kept getting jostled by passing bodies.

> "See the newborn babe,
> So pink, so normal,
> Just another face, another pair of hands,
> Another cog in the machine,
> But hidden in the blackness
> Of its Gray-alien eyes and
> In the folds of its raw palm,
> Untold universes shimmer…"

A tall guy with short curly blond hair, a ratty ASU sweatshirt, and the stink of cigarette smoke permeating his every pore shouldered past Nurmi, sending Nurmi bumping into Calvin.

"Outta the way, dude," the student snapped.

"Haista vittu," Nurmi said through gritted teeth.

> "O sail to the farthest shore,
> The spires of Atlantis, Lemuria, Mu—
> An atlas of wonder—
> Waver in the distance,
> Awaiting the intrepid explorer…"

Nurmi leaned over Cynthia's shoulder and said to Brandon, "Young man, we need to get past. We have important business to attend to. Time is of the essence."

But Brandon merely held up one finger, telling Nurmi to wait, and kept on reading:

> "And dig through the stratigraphy of awe!
> Here, on the surface, we find
> The haunted husks of ancient homes,
> But deep beneath it we discover,
> The forgotten bones of unmarked graves,
> Roman coins,
> Norse verses on shale,
> The fangs of unknown dinosaurs…"

"Young man!" Nurmi said.

> "Coal skulls, grooved spheres,
> Million-year-old mortars,
> The Permian in the Pennsylvanian

And the Pennsylvanian in the Permian,
Fronds in the Precambrian…"

"Young man, we need to get past!"

"And there at the bottom, at the base,
At the blackest depth of all,
We find the ultimate wonder:
The—"

"Your poetry is awful!" cried Nurmi. "It is not fit for old women!"

That got Brandon's attention. He blinked at Nurmi for a moment, then scowled with indignance.

"Who are you, and what the hell do you know about poetry?"

"I know yours is terrible! Now then, my young friends and I must get through, so if you will just—"

"Now hold on just a minute, my good man! What are your qualifications to judge my work? Do you even read poetry?"

Nurmi snorted. "I have published poems of my own. I have—"

"Is there a problem here?" said a voice behind Nurmi.

Calvin, Cynthia, and Nurmi all turned. It was Detective Anderson. He stood there with his hands still in his pockets and a friendly smile on his face.

"Oh, it's you two," he said to Calvin and Cynthia. To Nurmi, he said, "I hope these two little scamps aren't giving you any trouble." His tone was warm and avuncular, which was so disturbingly out of character that Calvin and Cynthia understood immediately that he suspected something was wrong.

"Oh, they're no trouble at all," Nurmi said. "They're fine young folks."

"You know them?"

"Of course. They, uh, they're students of mine. I teach European Literature."

"Ah." Anderson nodded at Brandon. "And him?"

"He, uh—"

"He's my boyfriend," Cynthia said.

"Whoa," Brandon said.

Cynthia watched Anderson closely, hoping he remembered that she was a lesbian and that her lie would confirm for him that things were not what they seemed. He appeared to get the hint: His eyes narrowed slightly and his spine straightened a fraction more. Otherwise, though, he displayed no outward sign that he suspected a problem. The friendly, unassuming smile remained fixed on his face.

Nurmi, of course, also knew that Cynthia was gay and he, too, seemed to notice Anderson's subtle response. His hand dug a little deeper into his jacket pocket.

Everyone just stood there a moment, smiling fake smiles at each other. Except Brandon, who was staring at Cynthia with his mouth agape. He was clearly entertaining ideas.

Around them the crowd began to thin out as students filed into classrooms or disappeared out the exits.

"So how's the investigation going, Detective?" Calvin asked. After making sure that Nurmi's attention was fixed on Anderson, he added, "Any luck finding the killer?" As he spoke the last two words he quickly pointed a finger at Nurmi, then just as quickly let his hand drop back to his side.

Anderson couldn't have missed the gesture, but he gave no outward sign that anything had changed. Still smiling, he shrugged and said, "Oh, you know, it's coming along. I'm sure we'll get the parties responsible eventually. Justice always wins out in the end."

"I hope it wins out soon," Nurmi said. "I know I for one will sleep sounder once that lunatic is no longer on the loose."

"We're working on it." Anderson cocked his head. "You know, you have quite an interesting accent. Whereabouts are you from?"

"Norway," Nurmi said.

"Ah." Anderson nodded. Then his smile faded and he looked around as if only now noticing that the hallway had nearly emptied. "Oh, geez, I'm sorry. I must be keeping you guys from class or something."

"It's quite all right," Nurmi said. "It's always a pleasure to meet the local police. But we do need to get going."

"Of course," Anderson said.

"But I haven't finished my poem," Brandon said.

"Oh, I think you have," Nurmi said. He turned to Calvin and Cynthia and nodded at the far end of the hallway. "Let's go, you two."

Calvin and Cynthia turned, putting their backs to Nurmi's gun once again. Their hearts were hammering. They were suddenly afraid that Anderson was just going to let them stroll away. Maybe he hadn't seen or understood Calvin's gesture after all.

"Oh, one other thing," Anderson said.

They turned back around. Anderson had a pistol pointed at Nurmi. His chummy smile had been replaced by his normal icy expression. Calvin, Cynthia, and Brandon edged away from Nurmi and out of Anderson's line of fire.

"Take your hands out of your pockets," Anderson told

Nurmi. "Slowly."

Nurmi feigned a look of surprise. "Whatever you say, Detective. But I don't see why—"

He lunged to his right, and the right front pocket of his jacket dissolved in flame as he fired three shots.

The moment Nurmi had started moving, Anderson had hunched down and dodged to his right, narrowly avoiding Nurmi's first two shots. The third grazed his left shoulder. He didn't even seem to realize he had been hit, and he fired off two rounds of his own. Both of them struck Nurmi square in the chest, and Nurmi's lunge became a drop. He hit the floor with a heavy, sickening thud and didn't move again.

Cynthia gaped at Nurmi's body, amazed at how fast it had all happened. One second Nurmi was talking and smiling, the next he was a lifeless heap on the floor.

Doors opened all along the hallway. Frightened faces peeped out.

"Everybody remain in your classrooms," Anderson called out. "Do not leave until I say so."

The faces withdrew. The doors banged shut. From one room a girl cried, "Oh, my God!"

Cynthia gasped and looked at Calvin.

"Kaarina!" she said. She whirled and raced for the stairs.

Calvin's eyes widened.

"My cards!" he cried. He raced after her.

"Hey!" Anderson said. "Where the hell do you think you're going?"

Brandon just stared at Nurmi's corpse, which now lay in the center of a steadily widening pool of blood.

"Damn!" he said. "This is hardcore."

Chapter 35

Calvin caught up with Cynthia halfway up the stairs, and they entered the second floor hallway more or less simultaneously. They ran about ten paces down the hall, then stopped.

Kaarina was sprinting toward them, her eyes big with panic.

"What happened?" she cried. "Where is my father?"

Cynthia held up her hands, palms out in a placating gesture. "Kaarina, please, we—"

Kaarina reached behind her and pulled a pistol from the waistband of her jeans. She pointed it at them.

"Where is he?" she shouted. "What happened?"

Calvin and Cynthia gaped at the gun, too startled to speak. The gun looked exactly like the picture on the Luger box they had found in Kranhauser's house. Kranhauser must have had it on him when he arrived at his office this morning. Nurmi had then no doubt frisked him and found it, then given it to Kaarina when he set her to guard Kranhauser. After all, he wouldn't have left her alone with a known killer without a weapon.

Hands still held out, Cynthia took a step toward Kaarina, who was slowing her pace as she neared them. "Kaarina, listen, just put down the gun. Nobody wants to hurt you."

Footsteps came pounding up the stairs behind them. Cynthia had time to whisper, "Oh, no," before Anderson appeared, his own pistol raised.

"Get down!" he shouted.

Calvin obeyed, flattening himself against the floor. Cynthia remained where she was.

"Don't!" she said.

But no one heard her over the simultaneous booms of the two pistols. Anderson's luck held; Kaarina's shot went wide, and a hole appeared in the wall a foot to his right. Anderson's shot hit home. Kaarina made a whoofing sound and stumbled backward, a small round hole in her shirt about an inch to the left of her navel. She crashed to her back on the floor. The gun fell from her hand and clattered away.

Ignoring Anderson's cries to stay back, Cynthia ran over to her. She knew she shouldn't, but she couldn't help herself. Despite everything logic told her, her heart still hoped for a happy ending.

She knelt down next to Kaarina. Kaarina was clutching the gunshot wound with both hands. Her eyes were squeezed shut, and her whole body was trembling. Her breath hissed through her clenched teeth.

"Kaarina?" Cynthia said. "You're gonna be okay, okay?"

Kaarina opened her eyes and stared at Cynthia. Her breath continued hissing. Her nostrils flared with the pain.

"Do you understand?" Cynthia said. "Everything's gonna be okay."

Kaarina raised her head a little as if she wished to say something. Cynthia leaned forward until her hanging hair brushed Kaarina's forehead.

"What is it?" Cynthia said.

Kaarina's lips puckered, and for a moment Cynthia felt sure that Kaarina wanted to kiss her.

Instead Kaarina spat in her face.

Cynthia stood up, the viscous, bubble-filled spit ooz-ing down her left cheek. She stared expressionlessly at Kaarina for a moment, then turned and walked away.

Anderson brushed past her and trained his gun on Kaarina.

"Don't move," he told her.

She sneered at him, then lowered her head and closed her eyes again.

Calvin came up beside Cynthia, who stood with her back to Anderson and Kaarina, her eyes on the floor.

"You okay?" he asked softly.

She didn't answer. He realized she didn't want to talk right now, so he headed over to watch Anderson pat down Kaarina.

Cynthia ignored Kaarina's muttered curses and grunts of pain as Anderson rolled her this way and that. She simply continued staring down at the floor. She made no move to wipe off Kaarina's spit. She didn't need to. Her tears were already washing it away.

Chapter 36

While Anderson called for backup and an ambulance, Calvin stared down at Kaarina. Her hands were cuffed now. Her eyes were closed, and she had stopped trembling, which almost made it look as if she had fallen unconscious. Only the way she kept grimacing with pain made it clear that she was still awake and alert.

A flash of movement off to Calvin's left caught his eye. He looked up. Professor Kranhauser was striding briskly past, his hat and coat on, his black leather briefcase in hand. He looked as if he were on his way to an important appointment.

No one else noticed him: Cynthia was still gazing at the floor, and Anderson was arguing with someone named Captain Thomas about how many officers should be sent out to secure the scene. When Kranhauser saw that Calvin had seen him, he flashed a big, friendly smile and tipped his hat.

Still dazed by everything that had happened, Calvin robotically smiled and nodded in return. He started to turn back to Kaarina, then stopped.

"Hey!"

Everyone looked at him. He pointed at Kranhauser, who had frozen in place with his head down and his shoulders up as if he were bracing himself for a blow.

"That's the guy who killed Guglio and Skerrit," Calvin said.

Anderson hung up and strode over to Kranhauser.

"Is that right?" he said.

"I vill say nothing," Kranhauser muttered.

Anderson ordered him to set his briefcase on the floor and face the wall with his arms and legs spread. While Anderson frisked him, Calvin snatched up the briefcase. Ignoring Kranhauser's outraged protests, Calvin popped the latches and opened it. As he had suspected, the three cards from the Collection were inside. He took them out, then shut the briefcase and set it back on the floor next to Kranhauser.

"What exactly do you think you're doing?" Anderson said.

"These are mine," Calvin said.

Anderson laughed derisively. "Not at the moment. They are now part of a crime scene, and you can't touch them."

"Sure we can," said Cynthia, who had just joined them. Her cheeks were dry now, and her expression was sober and humorless and in no mood for bullshit. "Especially since we—that is, Calvin and I—solved this case. Not you."

Anderson stared at her, his smile slowly fading.

"Sit on the floor and don't move," he told Kranhauser. Kranhauser glowered at him and mumbled something in German, but did as he was told. Then Anderson took Calvin and Cynthia by the arm and led them a short distance down the hall from Kranhauser.

"Okay," Anderson said in a voice too low for Kranhauser to hear. "What's your game here?"

"No game," Cynthia said. "Just cold, hard facts. We solved the case, right? We figured out who done it, and how, and when, and blah blah blah, while you were still scrounging for clues down in Byrne's office. So much for you perfect record."

"Yeah," Calvin said, trying hard not to grin now that he understood what Cynthia was up to. "I mean, you can try to take credit for it, and sure, you shot the bad guy and saved the day, but if you try to claim you actually put the pieces together, then we'll have no choice but to go right to the press and set the story straight. Geez, it'll look kind of embarrassing when people find out that a couple of skinny little college kids outthought the great detective."

"I wonder if they'll take away that award he won," Cynthia mused.

"Oh, I don't know. I doubt it. His previous record still stands. Of course, any future accolades of that kind are pretty much kaput now."

Anderson smiled again. It was the iciest, most humorless smile Calvin and Cynthia had ever seen.

"What do you want?" he said.

"To take Calvin's cards," Cynthia said. "They're only incidental to this case anyway."

"If they're your cards, how did the old guy get them?"

"Kaarina, the blonde girl, stole them from my house this morning," Calvin said. "And Kranhauser—the old guy—he must have grabbed them after she ran out here to find out what was happening."

Anderson shook his head. "But if you want her tried for robbing your house, you'll have to—"

"I don't care if she's tried for that," Calvin said. He glanced at Cynthia. "I think she's in more than enough trouble as it is."

Anderson snorted. "Trouble doesn't even begin to cover it. Attempted murder of a police officer? That girl is toast."

Cynthia swallowed and started to turn her head to look

at Kaarina. But then she stopped herself and forced her attention back on Anderson.

"Anything else?" Anderson said.

"Yeah," Cynthia said. "We don't want to be involved. Nothing about us in your report, no court appearances, nothing like that. We'll tell you whatever you want to know, and you can say you figured it out on your own."

"And we want the other card," Calvin said.

"What other card?" Anderson said.

"That's what this was all about." Calvin sketched out the situation for Anderson.

"But where *is* this other card?" Anderson asked. "How are you gonna find it?" He jerked a thumb at Kranhauser. "I have a hunch he's not gonna spill the beans."

"I don't think he'll have to," Calvin said. "I have a pretty good guess where the card is hidden. But we want it for ourselves. And if Kranhauser does spill the beans, you can just say you looked for the card but didn't find it and have no idea where it might be."

"And if I do this—let you have the cards and keep you out of the limelight—you'll stay out of my hair from now on, right? No more mucking about in my cases?"

"Scout's honor."

"And you'll get to keep your perfect record," Cynthia said.

Sirens rose in the distance. Anderson turned and looked out the window at the far end of the hallway even though he couldn't see anything through it from here except a rectangle of blue sky.

After a long pause he said, "I would have solved it eventually, you know."

"I'm sure you would have," Calvin said.

"We never said differently," Cynthia said.

Anderson nodded. "Just as long as we're clear on that."

And then the cops and the ambulance arrived. The cops led Kranhauser away in handcuffs. A few minutes later some paramedics, with a police escort, took Kaarina away on a gurney. Calvin and Cynthia cringed when they heard her shrieks upon seeing her father's corpse on the first floor.

And that was that.

Chapter 37

The next day, when Calvin met Cynthia for lunch in the Food Court, he had some news.

"Anderson called me last night," he said as he squeezed copious amounts of ketchup all over his double cheeseburger and fries. "We sort of compared notes and worked out most of what happened."

"Oh?" Cynthia said, sprinkling soy sauce over her tofu lo mein. "Do share."

"Well, Kranhauser's been trying to say as little as possible, but Anderson managed to draw enough out of him to be able to fill in most of the gaps himself with some forensic evidence and educated guesswork. Apparently Kranhauser somehow found out that this Professor LaFleur guy was going to hand over the card to Nurmi at the medieval history symposium in Italy. Kranhauser didn't dare go himself, since Nurmi knew him and would recognize him, but he knew that Byrne was going, so he concocted the Doctor Enigma identity and started hanging out in chatrooms and message boards that Byrne frequented, and very carefully he lured Byrne into a plot to get the card.

"The cops are still working their way through the contents of Byrne's and Kranhauser's computers, so it's not really clear yet what kind of deal Byrne had with Kranhauser's alter ego. Maybe Kranhauser told Byrne he'd buy the card off him, or something like that. I don't know. But whatever the deal might have been, Kranhauser had no intention of honoring it. After Byrne stole the card and brought it back to Ames, Kranhauser bribed Judd Skerrit to break into Byrne's house and steal the card while Byrne was at work. Later that day Kranhauser met with Skerrit in the Moma, ostensibly to pay him off and get the card. Since Kranhauser had no business being in the Moma and didn't want anyone to see him coming or going, he'd had Skerrit supply him with a key to the steam tunnels. I guess Skerrit never stopped to wonder why they couldn't just meet in Kranhauser's office. The truth was, Kranhauser wanted to meet in the sound-proofed auditorium so he could shoot Skerrit without anyone hearing it."

"What about Lou Guglio? How does he fit in?"

"That's a bit sketchier. Like I said, Kranhauser isn't saying much. But the coroner made an interesting discovery: In amidst all the bludgeoning trauma on Guglio's head, there were imprints that resembled a small, mustached face. Sound familiar?"

Cynthia frowned in bafflement. Then the light-bulb went on, and she stiffened with realization.

"The Nietzsche bust! That's right! Why didn't I realize that earlier? The bust had been sitting on the front right-hand corner of his desk when we searched his office. But when I went to visit him alone, he sat down on that corner. The bust wasn't there anymore."

Calvin nodded. "He had disposed of his murder weapon. This morning, the cops found bloodstains on the carpet in Kranhauser's office. They haven't had time to test them yet, but it seems all but certain they're Guglio's. Kranhauser must have caught Guglio snooping around in his office and killed him with the nearest blunt instrument at hand. Of course, *why* Guglio was there is another question entirely. It seems likely that Guglio was the one who supplied Byrne with the key to Kranhauser's office. Perhaps that fact was also connected somehow with whatever it was that Guglio remembered or realized when I asked him about Skerrit's contacts with the faculty. Maybe Skerrit had told Guglio something, or Guglio overheard a phone conversation, or maybe like Byrne, he saw Skerrit and Kranhauser together. Whatever the case, Guglio connected enough dots to compel him to sneak into Kranhauser's office and…" He shrugged. "Well, we don't know exactly what he was up to. Maybe he was playing amateur sleuth himself, or maybe he was hoping to set up a blackmail scheme. Whatever he was doing, Kranhauser caught him and killed him, then lugged the body through the steam tunnels and dumped it near the Heating Plant."

"Did Kranhauser say where the card is?"

"No. He refuses to admit he even knows anything about any card."

"He's probably hoping it'll remain where he hid it until he gets out of prison."

"Yeah, well, he's gonna have a long wait. He murdered two men in cold blood. He's going away for a long, long time. Given his age, there's a very good chance he'll die in prison."

"So where *is* the card, then? You said you thought you knew."

"I think I do, but to find out we'll need to get into the steam tunnels. I special ordered a lock-picking kit online this morning. It should get here tomorrow. My lips are sealed until then."

She rolled her eyes. "Of course."

They ate in silence for a minute. Then Cynthia cleared her throat and said, "So, um, any news on Kaarina?" She was trying to sound casual, as if Kaarina were only a trivial addendum to the case, but she couldn't fully hide the tightness in her voice.

"Still in the hospital," Calvin said. "The bullet didn't hit anything vital, but it was still, you know, a bullet in her gut. She should be okay, though."

Cynthia sighed and pushed her plate away even though half her tofu lo mein was still uneaten. Calvin eyed her with concern as he took another bite of his double cheeseburger.

"How can someone do that?" Cynthia said.

"Do what?"

"Lie like that."

"People lie all the time." He shrugged. "Just usually not so much all at once."

"Yeah, but..."

"It just seems worse because you trusted her. Because you, you know, *liked* her. I did, too."

She shook her head. "It's not the same. I..." She rolled her eyes and gave an embarrassed laugh. "I mean, I think I was actually starting to fall in love with her, you know? But now...I mean, I wonder how *could* I have been? What was I falling in love *with*? How can you love a mask? You know what I'm saying?"

"I think so."

"I mean, how can you feel something so good and pure and true for something that's not good and pure? That's not even real? It means love isn't always real. It means love can be a complete lie. It means you can't trust your own feelings."

"See? It's like I'm always saying: It makes more sense if you leave out all the abstract stuff about love and souls and whatnot, and accept that it's all just neurochemicals sloshing around in your brain."

"But I don't believe that. I'm not that cynical."

"I'm not cynical! I'm a realist."

"You? A realist? Mr. *Global Frequency?*"

Calvin started to say something, but then thought the better of it and took another bite of his cheeseburger instead.

She watched him eat for a moment, then grabbed her plate, pulled it back toward her, and stuffed a heaping forkful of tofu lo mein into her mouth.

"At any rate," she said around her food, "that's why I'm switching majors to Philosophy."

"You are? I thought that was just something you made up to worm your way into Kranhauser's confidence."

"It was. Then. But after everything that's happened, I keep thinking about that kind of thing. I find I'm really interested in pursuing questions like that."

"Yep, that sounds like you: Asking questions no one can possibly hope to answer."

"The mysteries of the unexplained!" a familiar voice intoned melodramatically.

They looked up. It was Brandon.

"Hey, Brandon," Calvin said.

"Hey, guys," Brandon said. He pulled out the chair next to Calvin's and sat down. "Man, yesterday was pretty extreme, huh?"

"Yeah," Cynthia said. "Hope you weren't, like, traumatized or anything."

"Nah, I can handle extreme."

"Thanks for your help with that, by the way," Calvin said. "Unintentional though it was."

"Hey, I'm totally happy to help. And wasn't I right? Didn't I say you might need some major poetry someday?"

"Yes," Cynthia said. "You were right. Shockingly enough."

"Did you like the poem? I never did get to finish it. That old dude cut me off with only one line left to go. Wanna hear it?"

"We've already heard most of it…"

"No, no. I mean just the last line. So you'll have heard the whole thing."

"Sure. Let's have it."

Brandon sat up straight, chin held high as if he were about to recite a Shakespearean soliloquy, and said, "'The uncageable, ever-changing chaos that rages behind the face of creation.'"

Cynthia nodded. "Good."

"Yeah," said Calvin. "That's some nice assonance you got there."

"Thanks," Brandon said. "I'm rather proud of my assonance, if I do say so myself." He raised his eyebrows and grinned at them, looking as animated and eager as a puppy expecting a treat. "So am I, like, officially part of the team now?"

Calvin and Cynthia looked at each other. Both of them nodded in agreement.

"We'd be happy to have you on board," Cynthia said.

"And then there were five," Calvin said.

"Five?" Brandon said. "Who're the other two?"

"My brother Donovan and his girlfriend Violet," Cynthia said. "They might be too drunk and/or stoned to be very helpful most of the time, though."

"Yeah, but still, that's awesome," Brandon said. "We're, like, an actual team now."

"Yeah," Calvin said, grinning. "We are, aren't we?"

Brandon held up his hands like a director framing a

scene. "The Anomaly Hunters."

"The *what?*" Cynthia said.

"Well, we gotta have a name, right?"

"We do? Why?"

"It's not a bad idea," Calvin said.

"Yeah, but 'The Anomaly Hunters'? It sounds like a shitty reality show."

Brandon folded his arms across his chest with a frown.

"Well, *I* like it," he said.

Chapter 38

The following night at one a.m., Calvin and Cynthia snuck through the sleep-silenced corridors of Duffy Hall and down to the basement. There, Calvin knelt in front of the door that led to the steam tunnels, unzipped his backpack (which was serving as a stopgap container for his anomaly-hunting kit until he could settle on something better), and got out the set of lock-picking tools and the copy of *Everyman's Guide to Lock Picking* that he had ordered online the previous day. The overnight delivery fee had been astronomical, but it was money well spent.

Or so he thought until he set to work trying to pick the lock.

"Geez, Kaarina made this look so easy," he groused after five minutes of fumbling. He glared down at the book, which lay open on the floor next to him, and scanned the step-by-step instructions again just in case there was something he had missed the previous ten thousand times he read it.

"Well, she obviously had tons of practice doing illegal stuff," Cynthia said. Her voice was frosty, as it was every time she spoke of Kaarina now. Over the course of the last two days, her feelings for Kaarina had congealed into contempt. It was the only emotion the bitch deserved. Well, and maybe a little pity, too, but Cynthia needed time to work up to that.

After another few minutes, Calvin finally managed to lever one of the tools exactly the right way, and the lock clacked. He sat back with a relieved sigh and wiggled his aching fingers. Then he put away the lock-picking tools and took the Mini Maglite out of his backpack, and they headed into the tunnels.

"So are you gonna finally tell me where we're going?" Cynthia asked. "And how you figured out where the card is? Or where you *think* it is."

"I'll explain everything when we get there."

"Oh, for God's sake, you can be such a drama queen. I swear, sometimes it seems like you think you're living in a comic book or a movie or something."

"Maybe we are, in a way. After all, Brandon said he wants to be our chronicler and write thinly fictionalized accounts of our exploits. That means I have to do what I can to keep things exciting."

Cynthia pondered this in silence as they made their way through the tunnels. Calvin kept pausing at every stone stairway to check the sign that designated which mechanical room the stairs led to.

Finally she cleared her throat and said, "Do you think Brandon will write about, you know, all this? About Kaarina and the cards and everything?"

"Knowing Brandon? Probably. And I'm sure he'll crank up the porno factor for our, uh, interludes with Kaarina."

She paled. "Don't say that."

Calvin grinned at her over his shoulder. "He'll probably scour his back issues of *Penthouse Letters* for just the right similes." He made writing motions with the hand not holding the flashlight. "'Hard as a…' 'Wet as a…'"

"Okay, now you're just grossing me out."

"Sorry. I just hope he makes us a little suaver than we really are. I'd hate to see our real, gooby selves all big-as-life on the printed page."

"Speak for yourself. I'm anything but 'gooby,' as you so goobily put it." Her brow crumpled with worry. "How thorough do you think he'll be? I mean, we both said and did some things that weren't exactly flattering."

"Oh, I wouldn't worry. He'll only know what we tell him, so just tell him the stuff you want him to know."

"Yeah."

"And then when you're not around, I'll tell him all the gooby stuff you *really* did."

"Hey!"

"Just kidding."

"You better be. Telling Brandon the gooby truth works both ways, you know."

"Very true."

At the next sign they came across, Calvin smiled and said, "Here we are."

Cynthia peered at the sign. It read, "6M."

"Where does this lead?" she asked.

"Beats me."

"Then what makes you think it's the right one?"

"Remember what Nurmi said? The card was the one that later became The Lovers. And the traditional number of that card is six."

"Ah. Very logical. But don't forget, the numbers on some of the Ur-Tarot don't match their modern-day equivalents."

"Yeah, I know. But if it's not six, it'll probably be five or seven or something. At least I hope so. Otherwise we could be picking our way into mechanical rooms for hours before we find it."

"Assuming that your theory is even correct, and Kranhauser didn't hide it somewhere else entirely."

"I refuse to even consider that possibility at this juncture."

They headed up the stairs. The door to the mechanical room was locked, so Calvin got out the lock-picking kit again. The lock to this door was a different, older variety than the one in Duffy Hall's basement, and picking it proved surprisingly swift and easy.

Beyond the door was a typical mechanical room, with its assortment of machines and pipes. A quick peek out the basement door revealed that they were in Brudowsky Hall, one of the dorms on front campus.

They spent over half an hour searching the mechanical room. They looked under and behind and on top of every piece of machinery. They opened every grille and panel that was openable. They found nothing.

"Damn it!" Calvin said. "I was so sure."

Cynthia shrugged. "We'll just have to check room 7M, then. Did you notice if we passed the sign for it? I wasn't really paying attention."

"I—" He stiffened. "The sign!"

They hurried out of the room and down the stone stairs. Calvin shone his flashlight on the 6M sign.

"Aha!" he exclaimed. He pointed at the screws that held the sign in place. The screws were brown with rust, except for a few obviously recent scratches that revealed the gleaming silver beneath the rust.

Calvin pulled the screwdriver from his backpack and began to unscrew the screws.

"See?" he said over his shoulder. "Wasn't the kit a good idea?"

"Yes," she conceded with a small sigh. "I suppose I should get one, too."

"You should."

The sign was screwed onto a backing panel set half an inch into the wall, and as soon as the screws were out, Calvin carefully tilted the sign away from the panel. A manila envelope began to slide out. Cynthia caught it.

Calvin hurriedly replaced the sign. Then they opened the envelope. Inside was the card, sealed in a thick acid-free plastic bag.

The picture on the card showed a young man and a young woman in medieval garb standing in a clearing in a dark forest. A skull sat on the grass between them. The woman was skinny and had long red hair and green eyes. The man was thin and had short blond hair and blue eyes. The card was numbered VI.

Calvin and Cynthia stared at the card in silence for a moment, then looked up at each other, then looked back down at the card as if to confirm to themselves that they had seen what they thought they had seen.

"That looks like…" Cynthia couldn't finish the sentence. Despite the warmth of the steam tunnels, her skin was covered with goosebumps.

"Yeah," Calvin said in a small voice. "The file said the guy who made these was psychic, so…" He paused and cleared his throat, not because there was anything in it, but to give himself the moment necessary to work up the nerve to say what he wanted to say next. "Maybe he saw *us* for some reason."

"But we're not, y'know, lovers."

"The name came later, remember? It was just someone's misinterpretation of the picture. Or of the inaccurate copies that were made of the picture."

"Oh, yeah. That's right." She frowned. "But weren't these pictures supposed to be of things connected with the end of the world?"

"That's the story."

They looked at each other. A little ways down the tunnel a valve emitted a brief blast of steam with a hiss like a snake.

"I guess we live in interesting times," Calvin said. He slid the card back into the manila envelope, and they began the return trip to Duffy Hall.

"After we write up the file on this," Cynthia said, "I think we should just stick this creepy-ass thing into the Collection and forget we ever laid eyes on it."

"Agreed. Of course, now we've got four of the cards all in one place. The legend has it that when all the cards are reunited, the end of the world will be at hand. We're a sixth of the way there already."

"Maybe we should give them away or something. Mail them off to different people in different parts of the world."

"Maybe."

Cynthia sighed. "Then again, considering my shitty lovelife, I think Armageddon will come as something of a relief."

Calvin tutted. "Oh, please. I mean, sure, okay, she turned out to be a lying psychotic bitch in the end, but you still made it with a hot-as-hell babe. What more do you want? And look at it this way: The next girl can't be any worse."

She smiled bitterly. "With my luck, yes, she can. Besides, speak for yourself. I'm looking for something a little more substantial than just making it with a hot babe."

"And therein lies your problem. You're yearning for something that isn't really real. You'd be a lot happier if you'd just admit that it's all neurochemicals. It makes things so much easier to deal with."

She rolled her eyes. "You're not gonna give up on that, are you?"

"Nope."

"Look, does it even really matter how you choose to define it? The intensity of the feeling is the same either way. Aren't we just arguing over semantics?"

"On the contrary, I'd say we're doing just the opposite. We're trying to get at the truth behind the semantic haze. Using virtually meaningless abstract terms like 'love' just thickens the haze."

"Oh, please. It's hardly meaningless or abstract…"

And when they arrived back at their dorm ten minutes later, the debate was still going strong.